About the Author

Anthony Hobbs is a sixty-year-old father of three children and six grandchildren. Schooled in Plymouth, Devon. From a family of nine children. Left school and did numerous jobs, from driving blood banks from hospital to hospital to management in retail. With a love of writing for children, he was schooled at the IFW/ICL institutes. His first children's book, *A Rough Ride,* was published in September. But he has been working on his 'debut' novel for two years. Letting him flick between adult and child entertainment.

A Robbing Hood

Anthony Hobbs

A Robbing Hood

Vanguard Press

A CIP catalogue record for this title is
available from the British Library.

ISBN 978 1 83794 179 7

*Vanguard Press is an imprint of
Pegasus Elliot Mackenzie Publishers Ltd.*
www.pegasuspublishers.com

First Published in 2024

**Vanguard Press
Sheraton House Castle Park
Cambridge England**

Printed & Bound in Great Britain

Acknowledgement

To my family. The publishing team and illustrators at
Pegasus publishing.

Dedication

I would like to dedicate this book to my sister Bernie, for whom, without her support, this work would never have come to fruition xxx

From one day to the next, we walked on eggshells, dreading our father coming home from horse racing or dog racing tracks. This dark demon was hiding beneath the exterior of a handsome gentleman. He stood six foot three with broad shoulders, deep brown shoulder-length hair, blue eyes, and a square jaw. He spent all his youth bare-knuckle fighting against anybody who challenged his right to be the best fighter in the city. He was kind and generous to all but his family. Gambling and drinking his way through life portrays this demon's different world. A man with heavy fists that he would use with any disrespect. A chauvinist pig of a man who believed women and kids were here to serve.

It was a Saturday, and I had been at Jack's house begging for something proper to eat other than the potato dinners I was getting at home, as we had no money for healthier food. Jack was a good friend and knew the state of play at home with my father, who gambled away everything trying to better himself whilst living in the most destitute of neighbourhoods. There was a knock on the door, and Jack's mum answered. It was my younger brother, Edward, crying. I raced to the door and asked him what the matter was.

"It's Mum. Dad has beaten her again. She's bleeding on her face."

This overwhelming nausea made me wretch as I hurried out the door and went home. I opened the front door only to hear Mum sobbing in the kitchen. When I entered, Mum was sitting up against the wall, trying to wipe away the tears with a discoloured towel, her face bloodied and bruised. Struggling to get my words out, I asked Mum what had happened.

"Your father punched me in the face because I refused to give him the last shilling I had. It was for food, but he wanted it for gambling," she replied.

"I'll kill the bastard one day; I swear it." I helped Mum off the floor and sat her at the kitchen table so I could nurse her face with clean water. Whilst trying to evade the wood splinters protruding from the top of the table. "I told you, Mum, to leave him repeatedly."

"Some of it is my fault, son. I should have just given in to him."

"All he does is beat you, and us. He has no respect for anybody; I wish he were dead. He's a bully and a bastard!"

"I need to finish my chores, son. I'll be okay. You look after Edward. Take him out to the playing fields."

I hated my father more than anything in the entire world.

The following day, Mum spent all day cleaning in the scullery of our dark and damp terraced house, wearing her torn plastic apron whilst washing up in the galvanised bath my sister, brothers, and I had to bathe in. Once washed, Mum would push the washing through a mangle, a heavy machine with two rollers and a cranking handle, to extract the excess water before hanging it on the washing line in our dilapidated broken-slabbed courtyard. Our yard led out to a lane always dark and dreary from the dense bushes that had formed a canopy that blocked out the very hint of daylight trying to break through. It looked more menacing as the years passed, but it was a fast route to Nantucket's, the shop at the top of Gilmore Street. This was where I would find myself, most days, picking up potatoes and powdered milk. I would often get there at five in the morning. It enabled me to pick up the half-stale bread that had sat on the shelves for a couple of days for a few pennies. But beggars couldn't be choosers; we had extraordinarily little money to live on, so life, in general, was a huge struggle.

Mum had finished mangling the washing whilst I was sitting on the cold stone floor, watching the pool of water advancing towards my feet, forcing me to stand as it engulfed my scuffed brown shoes. A tower of damp clothes resting on the scullery sink, an off-white basin with its brown-tinged crack down the centre as if something hefty had dropped on it.

Mum was perspiring, which made her long dark and greasy brunette hair stick to her face, which covered her age that had etched her skin over the years, being dragged down by the bearing of four children and the reality of being forever poor. Her hands bore witness to caring for us all and keeping a husband fulfilled. They were wrinkled and sore with scuffed dry skin and chapped nails. But even in the darkest of life, she would somehow find the inner strength to care for us all and be the best mum she could be.

"Are you going to help me put the washing out on the line, Tony?"

"Of course, Mum." I was sixteen going on thirty; I had spent most of my school years being chased by the school's board man. He was a pleasant enough guy, stout in stature with what I thought was deep brown hair, only to find out it was a wig after he tried to chase me. He had a thick dark moustache that trailed down both sides of his mouth and dark-rimmed round glasses. He was always wearing a brown suit and a brown trilby. I tried so hard to get him to chase me, hoping his wig would fall off, so I could express much laughter. Instead, he would always go red with embarrassment, which would turn to anger. If he missed me that day, he'd have the last laugh; he'd be waiting in the headteacher's office the next day.

The principal was a knobhead who'd take me to the maths teacher, Mr Jenkins, for my corporal punishment. Mr Jenkins would stand on a chair and then jump off, using all his weight to bring down the bamboo cane, which would crash onto my hands, making them sting like a furious swarm of bees had attacked me. My fingers would redden to look like a rash; I would not cry even if I wanted to; I had a brutal father raising me; the disgrace of crying would have my father enraged, and he was adept at giving backhanders for weakness. My fingers would tingle like pins and needles for hours.

However, I finally left school thinking I knew everything. It was growing up in a tough neighbourhood where I would compete in the brutal sport of bare-knuckle fighting daily, sharpening my wits to seek a future where I would erase the deprivation forever. Even the local constabulary, coppers, or pigs, as we called them, wouldn't dare to get involved; they were paid to turn a blind eye. Only the strong survived this cesspool of a neighbourhood. And as the son of the best fighter in the city, I couldn't afford to lose. It would show frailty in the family, humiliating the family name.

Once the clothes were on the line, Mum wiped the sweat from her brow with her forearm, "Well, that's that done," she said. We sat on the small brick wall surrounding a utility hole cover. Mum sat with her head bowed, looking down at the floor and did not speak; it was like she was thinking or reflecting on something.

"Are you okay, Mum?"

She looked at me and said, "I was thinking about my dad, your grandad, and how much I still miss him."

Mum never talked about my grandad; I was not born when he died. So, I never thought about asking about him. But as Mum had captured a memory of her dad, I felt the need to enquire. "What was he like, Mum?"

"He was a lovely father, and I loved him so." Then, with tears rolling down her cheeks, she said, "Did you know he was in the Royal Navy? He was a stoker, petty officer on the aircraft carrier HMS *Courageous*. I was immensely proud of him. But war broke out, and your grandad's ship was the first British ship to go down after being torpedoed by a German U-boat. I remember crying for what seemed like an eternity. Charles Campbell was his name, and you can find him on the monument on Plymouth Hoe."

"Wow, Mum, I wish he were still alive. I would have loved to have met him. I wouldn't know what I'd do if you died, Mum?"

"There is no worry about that, son. Now, I must finish the rest of my chores; what will you do today?"

"I'm going to Colin's house; he wants to pop down to Treebanks."

"Tea will be on the table around five, in time for when your father gets home. If you see Bernie tell her, I need her home."

"Okay, Mum." I grabbed my flat grey cap and headed up the street to Colin's house. He lived on the other side of Hobart Street in the posher houses with his sister, Heather, who was insanely gorgeous, and his mum and dad.

Colin Bray was the same age as me. We both went to the same school, or prison, as I called it, St. Peter's Secondary School. He was much more intellectual than I was and was also the tallest kid in the neighbourhood, always sporting a short back and sides haircut like me. And Heather, oh, God, did I fancy her. She was sixteen and worked in a lady's fashion store. Heather was tall and had long legs going up to her bum, a body most girls would die for. She was physically perfect. Heather had long blonde hair that came down to her backside, piercing blue eyes, and a smile that had my heart pounding every time I saw her, which was coming home late from her workplace. She also had plump cherry lips that were waiting to burst. I would love to know whether Heather liked me. I didn't get much chance to see her; she was always working.

Colin and I went to Treebanks for a swim. Treebanks were where the local pools were; we would climb around the barbed wire to get in free, cool ourselves down, and compete against each other to see who did the best dive. However, a lady dressed in a yellow blouse and a green knee-length skirt must have noticed us clambering in and promptly told us to get out or she would ring the police.

"Fucking Bitch!" I shouted as she walked away from us. "What shall we do now, Colin?"

"I am going to go home, Tony. Do you fancy coming over to mine?"

"Will Heather be there?"

"A bit later, she does not finish till five-thirty. Why do you ask?"

"No reason, just asking."

"You fancy my sister, don't you?" Colin jested.

"What if I did? She's gorgeous. Come on then; I'll come back to yours." On our way back to Colin's house, we saw my sister, Bernie, Edward, and Alan, my two younger brothers coming down the street towards us.

"Hi, Sis, Mum's asked if you could go home quickly."

"Why?"

"I don't know, Sis. Mum said tell your sister if you see her to come straight home." Bernie rolled her eyes and sighed, then shook her head. I rubbed Edward's head of curly brown hair with my knuckles to wind him up; he hated it.

"Leave my hair alone. You know I don't like it."

"That's why it's great doing it," I replied. Edward was twelve years old, a real cutie, and Alan was nine and was already keen on football. I looked down at the floor. "What's happened to your shoe, Edward?" The sole had come away; it looked like he had a talking shoe. Colin laughed whilst pointing down at Edward's shoe. But it wasn't funny. We couldn't afford new shoes; it was hard enough to have food on the table, not alone having to buy more shoes we couldn't afford. "Colin? Shut up; it's not funny. Here you go, bro." I gave him an elastic band to wrap around his shoe.

"I couldn't help it. I tripped over, and it just came apart," said Edward.

"I will tell Mum, Edward, don't worry; it's not your fault," said Bernie.

My sister was twenty-two years old and stuck to Mum like glue. She worked in a factory that produced machinery. I never saw her with any boys; it was all girlfriends; but that was great, I would listen to any discussions I could. Well, they were all in their mid-twenties. I learnt a lot about sex, something my dad would have never talked to me about. Bernie always said she would never leave home and always be there for Mum. It was more likely because she didn't seem that keen on boys.

"Come on then, let us get you two home," said Bernie as she grabbed Edward and Alan's hands.

Colin and I entered his house; his parents were both out working. I'd never seen anything like it. The house was clean and warm. Not like our house which was always dirty and smelling damp. Not that Mum didn't try her best.

"Do you want some lemonade, Tony?"

"You have real lemonade?"

"Yep, Dad always brings it home after work."

Colin poured two glasses of lemonade, and we sat to drink it. "Colin, this tastes funny; I can feel the tingling of the bubbles on my tongue and the sharp taste as it goes down my throat." It was lovely. I glance around the living room. His house was so posh; even the walls had different coloured paint. It was green in the living room, and he had a Bluebell patterned couch with a cream-coloured background. An orange rectangular carpet covered the floor. It felt warm and soft to the touch. Then I noticed a brown oval-style radio sitting on the centre of the mantelpiece. It had a circular glass centre with two cream dials evenly spaced below. I could only envy him and this palace his parents raised him in. *One day I will have something like this,* I thought.

Our house had off-white 'distemper' on every wall. It was impossible to clean. We didn't have carpet; we had a floral canvas in every room, most were frayed around the edges.

Colin turned the radio on to hear an eerie crackling of interference. He messed around with the dials, and we listened to a news broadcaster talking about the Cuban Missile Crisis. People often spoke about it; we were all fated to a terrible death. There was also the Cold War between Russia and the US.

Nuclear has been a prominent word on everybody's tongue since the holocaust of Hiroshima and Nagasaki. Everyone was scared; people had nuclear bunkers built in their back gardens to keep them safe from nuclear fallout. My father put up a shed; that was all we could afford. He put grey army blankets, some food tins and plastic containers filled with water, inside. Other houses had good underground bunkers built with ample food and water contained within them. But money was the evil of all things. If you had it, you could get anything; if you didn't, you were screwed.

I left Colin's house and walked around briefly, visualising everything I'd have if I had the money. Time moved on, and unfortunately, it was teatime, so I hurried home. I had to bypass the school that still haunted me; with its barbwire fences up around the playgrounds and steel bars on the windows, we were caged in like wild animals. I was glad I was no longer there, but Edward was still there and would experience all the traumas I had to endure.

Even the cut I made in the fence in the playground was still there, right in the corner where nobody could see it. I chuckled as I recalled all the times, I played truant by climbing through that fence at every opportunity. I eventually returned home if that's what you'd call it.

"Hi, Mum, I'm home." But there was no answer. It was peculiar, as Mum was always in the kitchen.

Then my sister came out of the kitchen and said, "Tony, go upstairs with your brothers."

"No! Why should I go upstairs? What's going on?"

"Dad has beaten Mum again. She might need stitches."

I forced myself past my sister and into the kitchen, where I saw Mum trying to stem the blood from a cut underneath her eye. "I will kill that bastard!" I shouted.

"Tony, calm down; your father will be home shortly," said Mum.

I sat at our chipped brown wooden table, with its splintered shards across the top. I kept my hands away from the table, careful I didn't puncture a hole in them. Crying inside, wishing I had the bottle to kill the fucking pig. I sat opposite Edward and tried to pull a face at him. Desperate for someone to jest.

"Mum, Tony is pulling faces at me."

"Will you two stop it? I'm trying to sort tea."

"Mum, Tony is still pulling faces at me."

"Will you two stop it, now?"

"You little grass, bro." I turned to Bernie and said, "Hey, sis, seen any good-looking boys out there, not counting me, of course?" Trying to wind her up.

"Seriously, Tony, I don't need boys. And you need to grow up?"

Then we heard the front door creak as it opened; we sat there in a deathly hush.

"Your father's home," Mum whispered, raising her index finger to her closed lips, looking ashen faced. The front door then clunked as it closed. Alan looked across at me motionless as if time had stood still. *What face would my dad be wearing?* I thought, as we waited for him to walk into the kitchen.

Father was a real bastard to us all—a dictator, not like that lunatic of a dictator, Hitler. Dad didn't kill millions; he just dictated to the family and used his brutal beatings and derogatory remarks—a bully in its worst form.

Father was a gambler who spent most of his time at the racetrack, whether horse racing or greyhound racing; that's if the racing were still on; if not, he'd be in the casino gambling and drinking till the early hours of the morning.

He owned and raced greyhounds to fix races by feeding the dogs some drugs to stop them from running with their customary zest after the toy rabbit, as it went around and around the track. Dad would wait till the odds on his dogs were high, and then he'd let them go, and they would win. His pitfall was not gambling on his dogs but betting in all the other races where he would lose more often than win.

When he walked into the kitchen, he had a face like thunder. Mum ushered Edward and Alan upstairs out of the way, even though they had not finished their tea.

"Go, quickly." Her face would squint in fear as she tried to hurry them upstairs, following behind them. Bernie and I sat beside each other, fearful even of uttering a word.

"Where's my tea?" he pressed as he laid his black trilby on the table. He then sat down and swilled tea from his cup. It was so quiet you could hear him gulp the tea as it went down his throat. I was hoping he'd choke on it. He was angry once again, and we knew what that meant.

"It is coming now, dear; I am just sorting the kids," Mum shouted. I stood up and went upstairs to take care of Edward and Alan.

"Please, don't go down, Mum; I beg of you."

Mum cradled my face and said, "Look at me, Tony. It will be okay; look after your brothers, and whatever you do, you make sure none of you come down. Do you hear me?"

"Yes, Mum."

"Come on, woman! Where is my tea?" he shouted as his tone intensified.

Mum went back downstairs to give him his tea. I cuddled Edward and Alan on the bed and prayed silence would win tonight. Bernie left the house to go to a friend's house, so it was just Mum, this demon, and us boys.

About twenty minutes passed by when I heard a colossal crash! First, the pottery hit the floor, and then I listened to the raised voices as Mum and Dad started arguing. Then, Alan began crying, frightened shitless by this demon who ruled over the house like something from the depths of 'Perdition' itself.

I then heard screams like a banshee echoing through the house; I wrapped Edward and Alan in a grey army blanket full of holes to try and block out the noise, which seemed to last for an eternity.

Then I heard the door knocker go with a heavy force, clunk-clunk; someone must have heard Mum screaming. A few moments passed, and I heard the door open, and then I couldn't help but listen to the bastard scream. "What do you fucking want, you nosey bitch?"

Then the front door banged shut, and with a shallow voice, my mum said, "Come on, boys, come down here. Your father has left."

Clasping my brother's hands, we walked downstairs together, only to see broken pottery all over the floor and Mum bleeding from her lip whilst trying desperately to hold back the tears on her etched face.

"I'm going to kill him! I don't know how? But I'm going to kill him," I stated as I ran into Mum's arms, hugging her with all the intensity in the world.

With gentle words, she said, "Everything will be okay, I promise."

Her words seemed reassuring to Edward and Alan, but I knew differently.

Ms Boyd came in through the scullery at the back of the house. Mum gave her a key to pop in for a cuppa. Ms Boyd was our next-door neighbour and an excellent friend to Mum. It was Ms Boyd that our ignorant brute of a dad called nosey before he left the house. Ms Boyd asked if we were all okay.

"Yes... for now," I said, "I will take Edward and Alan to the shop. Mum, do you need anything?"

"No, I am fine, darling, and thank you."

"Ms Boyd, do you need anything?" I asked.

"No, I am fine too, but here you are." Ms Boyd gave us a couple of shillings to spend on whatever we wanted.

"You don't have to do that, Ms Boyd." It was quite a lot of money, and we'd not seen two shillings together in all our lives. But we are poor through no fault of ours. It was all my bastard of a father's doing. He gambled or drank everything away with his cronies.

"Come on, you two." I grabbed my brother's hands and went out the back lane through the jungle, as I called it and up to Nantucket's. I'd spend both shillings on treats for my little brothers. When we returned to the house, I stood by the front room door and listened as Ms Boyd chatted to Mum, trying to give good advice without being too intrusive.

"You should leave him; you know it is the best thing to do," she said.

"He was so different, Agnes when we met and so handsome too. He was tall, with dark hair, charming and witty, and all the girls swooned after him; I was the lucky one."

"Joan, that was years ago; he is a beast now; he does not care about anybody or anything, just gambling and alcohol. What about when he won all that money and gave you two shillings to bathe his dogs and clean their cages, even though they stayed at Thomas Brown's? While he

25

spent hundreds of pounds in the casino with his cronies, plastering the walls with pound notes."

"I know, but I can't stop loving him, Agnes." Mum started to cry, and I couldn't help but enter the room to hug her.

"What's this bastard done to you?" I cried. "Ms Boyd's right, Mum; you don't deserve this."

Ms Boyd stood up and said, "I will leave you with your boys; I will ring the police next time, Joan. They can put him away for a while."

Mum nodded and thanked Agnes for her chat. Ms Boyd left, and we all cuddled each other. Alan cried for ages, and Mum struggled to settle him, so I took him to bed with me. We top and tail with coats for blankets. I didn't care; I just wanted him to settle. Finally, Mum went to bed as well. I heard her sobbing uncontrollably. All I could think about was how I'd kill the monster!

The next day was Sunday, and my dad had returned home through the night and slept on the couch. Mum was still in bed; I asked her if she was okay.

"Yes, I'm fine," she spoke. I told her dad was asleep on the couch.

"Okay, son, thank you."

I popped into Bernie's room and told her what had happened last night. She was angry but couldn't bring herself to say anything. She was a female, and it felt like this was the way of the world. Men would dictate what happens and when it happens.

I went downstairs and grabbed Edward from the kitchen table while he was trying to eat a slice of half-stale bread with beef dripping to take him up to Treebanks to see if we could swim in the pool. It was cold outside, but the sun was shining brightly.

"Just make sure you're back for tea, boys."

"Yes, Mum." We left the house and went to try and get into Treebanks, but the bitch, as I called her, was watching, so we gave up on our attempt and headed to Duke Street bombsite.

We played on the wasteland that stood bare of the opportunity to build more houses after the war. It was a grassy area with multiple mounds. Taking the mantle of adult, I had to engage Edward in childish games to take his mind off everything. We would see who could do the best dead man's fall. We ended up with mud-splattered clothes, but we were having fun; we knew we'd be in trouble, but we didn't care; we'd taken plenty of beatings before.

We got home as Mum was setting the table. Dad didn't even acknowledge us. He just sat there reading the newspaper as calmly as you like. I stared at him, wondering what had gone through his mind. Moments later, Mum put tea on the table. Chips and fried bread. Flat potato slices, fried in a pan and fried bread cooked with beef dripping. While looking at it, I could only believe that every day is potato day. Chips? Mash? Or boiled? Always the same. We couldn't afford fruit or vegetables; we were destitute. Dad never gave Mum any money; he spent it all gambling.

I just said, "Can we have something different than potato?"

A fist across the table caught me in the head, knocking me off the chair.

"You get what you are given! do you understand? You ungrateful git," he said as I climbed back onto the chair, refusing to start crying. Mum stared at me, afraid to speak for fear of a beating herself.

She worked for a gentleman in our street doing housework which paid her £1.12 shillings per week, but Mum told Dad she was getting £1.10. So, she would hide the two shillings away for a rainy day. Then Dad's tea came down on the table, a plate with a round purple thing on it.

"What's that?" I sneered.

Once again, the monster reared his ugly head. He went berserk. He stood up, screaming at Mum, "What the hell is that?" he asked. "I asked for Beetroot?"

Mum needed to be savvier in cooking, but she did her best.

"I don't know how to cook it," she said innocently.

Dad screamed, "You bloody useless woman!" He then threw the newspaper down on the table. I could feel Edward trembling like a leaf as he lay his leg on mine under the table. I gripped Bernie's hand tightly; I could tell she was petrified as her hands wouldn't stop shaking. Something was going to happen. I must admit I was scared too. Dad hastily left the kitchen, mumbling to himself but extremely angry with Mum.

"I am going to the pub," he shouted, then the door slammed behind him.

Mum grabbed the back of the chair, looked down at us all, and started crying,

"Come on, boys, eat up," she spoke. Bernie hugged Mum and took her into the front room until the tears dried.

"I'm sorry. I know I'm not a good mother," she said as she ran out of the room to go and freshen up; I looked across at the shivering wrecks of my brothers, who didn't understand a thing, and thought, *how long does this have to go on?* So, we sat and tried to eat tea, but every mouthful made me want to throw up. I was sick to the stomach with worry for Mum.

Mum returned to the kitchen and said, "Edward, Alan, you need to have an early night tonight and keep your door closed."

"I'll take them upstairs, Mum." So, I put them down to sleep, covered them as best as possible with some old coats, blew the candle out, and softly whistled a lullaby until they had both fallen asleep. I was so scared for Mum, afraid of what would happen when the monster came home, knowing he'd be drunk! She was sure to take a beating for the mishap with tea.

"Mum? Bonfire night is fast approaching, and we don't have any money for fireworks. So, I'm going to take Edward guying tomorrow."

"No, son!" she said sternly. "If your father found out you were begging, he would strip your hides."

"Mum, it's supposed to be a celebration. November the fifth is about bonfires and fireworks; it's a tradition."

"Tony, your father will kill you if he finds out."

"Mum, we'll go far away from here, and anything we get, we'll bring home to you. Dad will be at the racetrack, so he'll never know."

Mum hesitated; with good reason, the seriousness of what we'd do could disgrace the family. But some money would help with food as well.

"Tony, please make sure you're far away."

"I will, Mum I promise." I'd gather a pair of Dad's old trousers, an old brown jumper full of holes, and some newspapers to stuff it. I'd make a cardboard cut-out for a head and draw a face on it using Bernie's makeup. I had a grey cap to place on the makeshift head and would use Edward's broken shoes to make us look poorer than we already were. If that's possible?

I woke up quite early the next day. I hadn't heard any shouting or screaming throughout the night. I went into Edward's room and woke him up; we went downstairs, but Dad had come home and passed out at the bottom of the stairs, slumped and snoring, pissed as a newt. The smell of alcohol stanched the air. No wonder we didn't hear anything. He was so drunk that he couldn't even climb the stairs.

"We'll have to creep past him," I said.

"But what if he wakes up, Tony?"

"He won't, and he's too drunk, bro." So, we slowly crept around him and went out to the scullery. I grabbed our Guy Fawkes and went out through the back lane.

"Where are we going to go, Tony?"

"I know a place near the precinct, and plenty of people will be there."

"The guy looks so good, Tony; when did you make it?"

"Last night while you were sleeping. All that's left, bro, is to use your shoes."

"But Tony, I will not have anything to wear. And it's cold."

"Edward? The sole is hanging out; you'll get cold feet anyhow?"

The subway near the car park was perfect, and we were out of sight, of the police and our dad. So, I sat the guy up against the graffitied subway wall, and with an old biscuit tin, we started begging for a penny for the guy.

"Please, have you got a penny for the guy?" asked Edward as the first gentleman walked by. He put a couple of pennies into the biscuit tin. All day, we begged. We must have spoken a thousand times, most people were very generous, and our biscuit tin became full. We even had a shilling off some old lady who was very smart in appearance but wearing a cat fur around her neck. *Poor cat,* I thought.

But there were also three or four wankers who'd spit in our faces or kick the guy, forcing us to put it back together again. But most people pity Edward for not having any shoes on his feet.

It had gone seven o'clock, and the evening air was moist but cold, and we still had to get home as Edward was only twelve. We were both freezing. Very few people were coming through the subway. So, we stopped for the day. Edward took his shoes off the guy and put them back on his feet.

"My toes are freezing, Tony," he said, shaking from the cold. We grabbed the guy and raced across Duke Street bombsite, paper flying everywhere. We ditched it in Webb Street Lane; we knew it would be safe there. We then sat in a doorway, taking shelter from the cold and the rain, which started to fall.

"While we're here, let's try and count what we have, I said." I counted what we had made from standing in the cold all day. We had collected just shy of £17.12 shillings; Mum was going to be so pleased.

"You have a big grin on your face, Tony?"

"Come on, bro, let's get some sausage and chips from the chippy van." Edward's eyes lit up, and with a cheeky grin on his dirty face, he said, "Really?"

We stopped at the chippy van and got our sausage and chips. Edward scoffed his way through it in no time at all. I knew it was later than Edward would usually be allowed out, but this was the first time we had food like this.

"Let's go home, bro, and I'll give the rest of this money to Mum, and she'll get the fireworks when we're ready."

Dad hadn't returned when we arrived home, and Mum was preparing his supper, or food hell, as I called it.

"Mum, look how much money we've got?" As I emptied my bulging pockets.

Mum cried, "Oh, my boys, I love you boys so much." It was like all her Christmas's had come at once.

Giving us a big cuddle. Mum took the money and put it into an old black bag with a silver buckle to lock it tight, and then took the bag upstairs to hide it away from our dad.

When she returned, I asked, "Do you know when Dad will be home?"

"I'm expecting him through the door any moment. Now, boys, you have missed tea."

"Oh, it's okay, Mum; we're not hungry, are we Bro?" I nudged him to agree with me.

"But boys, you need something inside you; you've been out all day?"

"No, honestly, Mum, we're okay," I said.

Dad came in the door straight from another day at the racetrack in an ever-demanding mood.

"Where's my tea?" he asked in a concerned manner.

"Just coming, darling, just a few more minutes," Mum replied.

Mum then put tripe, this milky lining you get from animals, like cattle, sheep, goat, and deer, with onions. It gave me the urge to vomit.

"Have you kids had your tea?" the monster asked.

"Yes, we have," I answered.

"Yes, dad? Now what have you been up to?"

33

"Um, we went over to Michaels's house."

"What did you do there? Behave, I hope?"

"Of course, Dad, we helped take stuff into their nuclear bunker."

"Well, at least you were not getting into trouble."

"Trouble, Dad? As if?"

"Go out and play some more while I eat supper."

I scampered out the door with my brother in tow. "God, that was a close shave; I thought he cottoned on to what we did, bro."

"You were good, Tony."

"Yeah, I know." I rubbed Edward's hair and let him chase me around the street. "It's been a good day, hasn't it, bro?"

"Tony, if we do it tomorrow, will we have to go somewhere else?"

"Yes, I have it all planned out," I replied. With that, Colin came down from number fourteen.

"What have you two been up to?" he asked.

"Put it this way; I found a straightforward way of making good money,"

"How?" asked Colin.

"I'll tell you if you can get your sister to go out with me." I wanted to go out with Heather; she was gorgeous. Of course, I could use my charms on anybody, but Heather was different; I liked her, she was independent and working, and she was bright too. Colin, eager to find out how I get easy money, hurried back to his house, and told Heather I fancied her and would she go out with me.

She must have been interested because I saw her looking down the street towards me while standing in her doorway. I waved to her, and she smiled and waved back at me before she disappeared back into her house.

Colin came racing back. "I think she will, Tony; she likes you."

"Colin, meet us here tomorrow morning, no later than ten."

"Yes, okay, Tony." Colin returned to his house, wondering how he would make easy money.

"Come on, bro, let's go in." I could hear Mum and Dad talking about Bernie inside the house, but I could not get close enough. So, I whispered to my brother, "Come on, let's go upstairs."

I don't know what got into me that night, but all I'd think about was Heather, her gorgeous body, and what I'd like to do with it. I had to learn quickly about all that lovely stuff. I mean sex and all that. I had only ever kissed some girls. I was too shy to try anything else, but I wanted Heather. I wanted her forever. And although I was quite hard, I had a soft heart for girls. I started to feel different; something or someone was playing with my emotions, it felt weird it seemed like I had total control of my feelings.

Morning came, and Edward and I dressed as fast as possible and instantly ran out of the house. I had a plan in my head, and I was determined to see it through. Ten o'clock came, and I saw Colin and Heather heading down our street right on schedule. Heather was wearing a gorgeous red halter dress with black polka dots. Heather dressed her blonde hair in a bun style and painted her lips cherry red. I couldn't take my eyes off her; my crush on her was sending me nuts, and Heather knew it too. She beamed a huge smile; I had become extremely nervous and felt sick.

"How do we earn this easy money?" asked Colin.

"You'll see soon, mate," I replied arrogantly, trying to impress Heather.

We walked over to Webb Street Lane to retrieve the guy. "Go get the guy, bro," I said, pointing into the lane.

"A guy? That is how you can make lots of money? It is begging," said Colin.

Being from a well-to-do family, they wanted for nothing. Colin's parents put everything on a plate for him and Heather. However, I admired Heather; she was working and fending for herself. I told Colin he didn't have to come if he didn't want to. Heather smiled and told Colin he did not have to go anywhere, but she was coming with me.

"Come on then, let's start earning money," she said.

"Heather, what are you doing?" asked Colin, shaking his head.

"I am going; if you do not want to come, that's up to you, dear Brother." So, Colin decided that if Heather were going along, he would come along.

"Where are we going then, Tony?" asked Heather.

"The Dog and Bone over on Rathin Street."

"The pub?" said Colin. "We will get our fucking heads kicked in. My dad said it is always full of navy personnel; Matlow's?"

"Even better, they'll be pissed as newts; they could easily give us a good handout."

"You don't lack bottle, do you, Tony?" said Heather.

"No, I don't. But in my family, you've no choice but to be tough." We sat the guy next to the pub wall beside the main entrance; all four of us were standing around it. Then a man came out of the pub.

"Penny for the guy, mate?" asked Edward. The man gave a disdainful look,

"You are begging?" he said.

"Penny for the guy, sir? For our fireworks," I spoke.

"What about a penny for your young lady? I would not mind giving her a few pennies. I will even make it a shilling if she would repay in kind?" Slurring his words.

I was about to lamp him when Heather looked at him and said, "You couldn't afford me, sir; I do things that cost pounds, not shillings." Fluttering her eyes at him.

The man sighed, put his hand in his pocket, and threw four coins at us without even looking.

"Thank you, sir," I said politely.

Heather glanced at me, looking incredibly surprised at how easy it was to obtain money.

"If we're polite, we can make reasonable money," I said. Heather's stunning beauty was sure to attract anybody out the pub door.

"We could do this all day, couldn't we?" she asked.

"Let's see what happens?" I responded. Lots of men put money in our tins, and they filled quickly.

"It's so easy, Tony; why isn't everybody doing it?" asked Colin.

"Because I own it!" I remarked.

"What do you mean… you own it?"

"I started it, Colin. Now I have it. And it's mine," I responded. "Edward, take the tin. I handed the container to him and invited Heather around the lane at the back of the pub.

"What for?" she asked.

"Just come around here a minute." We went to the back of the pub and into the back lane. I moved her gently backwards up against the wall.

"What are you doing?" she asked as she gazed into my eyes.

I grabbed her by the hand and asked, "Are you going to kiss me then?"

"You are a bit presumptuous, aren't you? And a bit cocksure of yourself."

"It's only a kiss," I said. Then, with Heather leaning against the wall, I moved in to try and kiss her. Heather hesitated momentarily, and then her cherry red painted lips touched mine. They were soft and warm; they sent my heart racing. There was a sweetness I had never tasted before oozing from her lips. I was intoxicated with her warmth and tenderness; I paused momentarily and said, "How did you enjoy that kiss then?"

"It was all right." She smiled at me.

"Yeah, you know it was better than all right," I said adoringly as I looked at her. I had a self-belief, and with Heather by my side, I became more confident in who I was. Finally, everything started to go in the direction I had wished for most of my life.

We made our way back out of the lane and back to Colin and Edward. They caught us holding each other's hands and laughed. Heather said, "You're a real jack the lad, right?"

I just looked at her, assuming she would be mine forever. "I tend to get what I want; I want more out of life than this. But I'm determined to have a great future, and I want you to share it with me, Heather."

"Hang on a bit; we've only just got together; you will be asking me to marry you at this rate."

"Is that a proposal?" I jested. I just looked at her adoringly, wishing she were already mine.

"Tony, look! Someone put a pound note in our tin."

"It's a fake note, you idiot."

"No, it is not," said Heather, "it is a real one!"

My head was reeling. I didn't care whether it was real; I was so in love. A combination of Heather's beauty and Edward's boyish good lucks opened a doorway to much better things. The money was accumulating in the tins. But we only had a couple weeks before we'd have to stop because bonfire night was coming up.

I suggested we should all go to the arcade and have some fun once we finished. I was desperate to spend more time with Heather.

An hour or so had passed when two blokes came out of the pub.

"What are you lot doing here?" one spoke. Then he caught sight of our guy. He took the mick out of the guy and tried vainly to kick it. He then looked at Heather and asked: "What are you doing hanging around with these boys?"

Heather looked at me, then turned to the bloke and said, "He's, my boyfriend." Pointing at me.

The bloke giggled and replied, "You're jesting?"

Blessed by my father's preaching of never backing down from anyone, take a beating if you must, I confronted the weasel. I put my face in his face and said, "Leave it... Now, go away." Whilst eyeballing me, the drunken fool tried to throw a punch. I was quick in the movement to duck the attempted punch; I threw my head back and forcefully head-butted him. His nose burst as he fell backwards, leaving a blood-spattered face.

Stumbling whilst rising to his feet and holding his nose to stop the flow of blood, he shouted, "I'll have you for this."

"Yeah, all right," I said whilst nodding, I moved in his direction, and he scuppered off. I exhaled a sigh of relief. I thought I was going to get a kicking.

"Ooh, look at you, so brave and bolshie," Heather remarked.

"Nice to know you're impressed," I commented. My whole body was trembling, I didn't know if I was scared or if it was an adrenalin rush, but they were gone; that's all that mattered then. I took the tins of money and counted what we had earned.

"So, how much do we have?" Asked Heather.

Thinking quickly, because I had to make sure I put some of the cash back for Mum, I said, "It's about twenty pounds."

"You are joking? In just over four hours? Wow, we could be rich in no time. Pity we couldn't guy every day of the year?"

"Thanks for that, my love. I need to work twenty-four hours daily to make anything of myself."

"I was only joking, Tony. How is your head feeling?"

"It feels okay; however, a gentle hand rub wouldn't go amiss."

"Cheeky bugger," she replied.

Heather didn't know we had about forty-five pounds; the rest went to my mum. Heather came over and started to play with my hair, letting it run through her fingers, so soft and gentle, easing the aching. "How's that?"

"Wow, it feels good." Heather caressed my face and gently kissed me once again. I wished the moment would last forever, but life's not like that, "Come on, let's get moving; we've done enough today."

As I picked up the guy, a Panda car turned up, and a constable or a pig started to get out of the vehicle. I didn't know what to do, so I stood on the guy, trying to conceal it from him.

"We have had a call to say you kids are begging for money?" said the officer as he exited the Panda car.

"It's not begging. It's appealing to people's hearts and generosity. Have you not heard of Guy Fawkes, Constable?" I knew I was out of order and should've shut my mouth.

"Now, sonny boy, less of the attitude; it will not do you any favours. I want all your names and where you live."

The constable took out his little black book and a pen and started writing down our names. Then, finally, he confiscated our money and put us in the Panda car to take us home.

I couldn't help looking at the badge on his lapel and his funny-shaped hat resembling a giant dark bluebell. I looked out of the car window; the skies were turning grey.

Heather and Colin had never been in trouble before and were so scared. I could feel Heather's trembling hands on mine. I had no idea what her parents were like; all I knew was they were well-to-do people. I showed a calm exterior on the outside, but I was bricking it inside. I knew Edward and I were in big trouble. Our demon father was going to kill us.

We pulled up in our street outside Colin and Heather's front door, then watched as the officer knocked. I'll never forget that moment Heather's dad opened the door to be confronted by an officer of the local police force. He stood with shock on his face. Then the door closed. A little while later and it was our turn to face the consequences of our actions. I knew what was coming, so I gripped Edward's hand tightly and watched the blood disappear, leaving his hands white.

The constable pulled outside the door and told us to leave the car. The knock on our door sent shudders down my spine. I tried vainly to stay strong and stand up to him, my father, or the devil incarnate.

My father opened the door. "What's this, Officer?" he asked, his evil eyes wide open staring at me. Edward stood looking down at the floor, shuffling his feet in fear.

"Can I come in?" asked the Officer.

"Of course," replied my dad.

While the constable communicated why he was there, I heard my mum descending the stairs. As she entered the front room, she became frantic seeing the constable sitting with Edward and me. More would scar her ashen face.

What have I done? I thought. The look on my dad's face said it all. We had disgraced him, and my attitude was far from respectful to the constable.

"The boys have collected a lot of money which I have confiscated for the police fund," he spoke.

Police fund? I thought. "Bullshit!" I spoke. My father looked across at me, and I could feel his rush of blood inside my nervous stomach. I knew I was going to hell for speaking out.

Then the pig had the nerve to stand up and say, "Good luck, boys," as he walked out to the front door.

The constable left, and I heard the front door close. I braced myself for what was about to happen next. Dad walked into the front room with a face like thunder.

"Dad?" That was all I could manage to get out of my mouth. The next few seconds changed my life forever, from a boy into a man. The force of his fist against my head knocked me to the ground. Chaos ensued! Dad continued his onslaught on my body, Mum screaming and trying to pull the beast off me. Edward had peed himself with fright and was crying. Finally, my dad shouted, "How dare you bring the police to this house?"

I couldn't escape his onslaught; even Mum took a backhander trying to get him off me. Edward ran upstairs to hide from this demon.

"Get off him!" Mum screamed.

Bernie came down the stairs and jumped onto his back, screaming, "Leave him! Leave him!"

The door knocker clunked; someone was at the door. The bastard's relentless onslaught stopped momentarily as he hurried to the door. Mum and Bernie were trying desperately to see how bad I was. Mum arched her body over my bloodied and broken body to shield me from any more beating. He opened the door only to be confronted by Ms Boyd.

"Is everything okay?" she asked.

"Mind your own fucking business," he shouted and slammed the door in her face whilst walking away from the house, I heard Mum softly whisper the words under her breath through the waterfall of tears, "That's enough, you bastard! you'll have to kill me first." But he had left.

I lay on the floor, bloodied and broken, listening to the door slamming. I watched the front room door with my bloodied and bruised eyes, not knowing who would walk through it, Dad? Or the police? But it was Agnes.

"He's gone, hopefully never to return," she cried.

Mum knelt beside me in tears and asked if I was, okay? wrapping her gentle arms around me. The beating was a beating, but my mum's tears were more than I could bear. I struggled to stand upward and staggered into the kitchen to wipe away my blood-spattered face. I reiterated, "I'm going to kill him, Mum!" I went upstairs to my bedroom and sat contemplating my next actions. I was mad inside; at that moment, the beast in me I never knew I had, shone its ugly self. Looking into the mirror, all I could see was the face of a devil with thoughts only of killing my father. Mum went to Edward and Alan to check on them.

My poor kid brothers are going to be scarred for life. Mum gave them some milk and chocolate that Ms Boyd had given her earlier that day. She then came into my room,

"Are you all right, son?"

"Go away! Please go away!" Shielding my face from view. "All this time, you've stayed with him. You let him beat you, starve you, and treat you like shit. Why?"

"I love him." She then tried to put her arms around me.

"No, Mum, you love him more than you love us, kids…? I can't do this anymore, Mum. I'll get you out of here and far away from him, whether you love him or not?" I put some bits into a bag and made my way downstairs.

"Son, where are you going to go? What am I to do?"

"I don't know, Mum. But I must go. Leave him, Mum!"

I looked to the top of the stairs. Edward and Alan were standing there, sobbing their little hearts out. "I'll see you soon," I waved them goodbye. Then, with tears full of pain and torment, I walked out the door; I had nowhere to go, I didn't know what I would do, but I had to leave the house. I dare not look back. It was the hardest thing I'd ever done.

I drifted around the streets for days, sleeping in any dry place I could find. It was cold, and my body was bruised all over, which left me in crippling pain that was hard to bear. I knew not what to do. I lacked sleep and was very hungry. Then I heard someone say,

"Tony, is that you?" I then felt a hand on my shoulder. "Tony, it's me, Ms Boyd... Oh, look at you, my boy."

I stood up weary-eyed and shivering. "Hello, Ms Boyd." I could hardly see her. My eyes were so badly swollen.

"You are coming home with me right now; we need to get you sorted, my boy. I need to get a satisfying meal into you. You can stay with me until you decide what you will do."

I put my arm around her shoulder to help bare my weight, and together we made our way back to her house. I pleaded with Ms Boyd not to tell anyone I was staying with her, which meant my mum too.

A couple of days had passed, and my strength was returning; I just needed my bastard father to get out of the house to see the family.

"You know your dad is at the racetrack today?" said Ms Boyd, or Agnes, as she asked me to call her.

"Yes, I know, Agnes; I'll wait to see him get picked up."

Well, seven o'clock on the button, one of my dad's cronies pulled up in his car, and my father jumped in, and they drove off. I hurried to Mum's door and knocked. Mum opened the door and just burst into tears. She was ecstatic to see me, and then my little brothers raced to me, giving me hugs and kisses. I felt so vulnerable after building this façade.

"Are you home to stay?" asked Mum.

"No, Mum, I'm staying with Ms Boyd for tonight. She has been charming. She said Dad was getting worse. Where's Bernie?" I had so many questions to ask.

"Your sister is sleeping at her friend's house. Your dad's buying another greyhound, and we will keep it here. He is also buying another dog because the area has recently had break-ins. He wants some protection if they break into our house, not that they would get anything of value." Rolling her eyes.

"So, no doubt it means more work for you, Mum. I hate him, and he makes me sick. I still don't understand why you haven't left him?"

"Because marriage is for life, you will understand one day, son."

"Married or not, Mum, I wouldn't treat a lady as he treats you. He's just an evil bully and a pig." Time went quickly, and I had to leave. Mum pleaded with me to ask Ms Boyd if I could stay longer.

"Mum, can you send Edward to the local shop tomorrow morning? I'll meet him there. But I must go."

"Okay, son." Mum kissed my forehead and watched me whilst sobbing enter Ms Boyd's house.

I sat on my bed in Ms Boyd's house till the early hours, waiting to hear the shouting start next door, but there was a peaceful silence.

The following morning, I waited for my little brother to meet me at the shop. When he arrived, I asked him, "Where have you been? I have been waiting for ages, little bro."

"You didn't tell Mum what time, did you?"

"No, I didn't, cheeky little bugger." I smiled at him.

"It's bonfire night, Tony, and we don't have any sparklers or fireworks."

"I promise you, bro, we will have it by the time the bonfire starts tonight."

"Tony, will I be able to have a potato from the bonfire as well?"

"Yes, now we've all day to do some guying, and I've already made up a fantastic-looking guy. People are going to love it. We're going to the subway; we won't get caught there. What time is Dad back?"

"I think it's about five o'clock, Tony."

"Okay, go home and tell Mum, you are with me today. That applies to this evening as well. Tell Mum, if Dad asks where you are, to tell him you're with Ms Boyd. He wouldn't dare go to her house." Edward ran home, told Mum everything I said, and then hurried back to me.

We went to the subway, stopping off at Webb Street Lane to pick up the guy I had made the day before whilst nursing my bruises.

"Wow, the guy looks brilliant, Tony."

"I made it yesterday. Ms Boyd gave me some old black trousers, a black jacket and a pair of shoes belonging to a male friend. Then I found a jumper of mine in my bag, then I used my old school white t-shirt, filled it with paper to resemble the head and drew the face. Looks cracking, doesn't it?"

Edward was a cute kid who always drew people to him. Well, we spent the next six hours doing guying. In return for our endeavours, we collected lots of money. I looked older than I was and could buy fireworks, sparklers, and a few bangers. I also bought treats and still had loads of money left over. Edward was as happy as I'd ever seen him.

We made our way to the Duke Street bombsite, where the neighbourhood would come together to build a tall structure to celebrate the attempted plot to blow up the houses of parliament by Guy Fawkes. The community filled it with everything, from furniture to newspapers, anything everyone discarded.

I could smell the stench of burning coals from chimneys on the black-tiled roofs; trees were standing bare, uncloaked from their coloured leaves, after being ravaged by the winter weather. I felt snow falling as it tickled my hair. White flakes glisten through the beaming lampposts. Soft and velvety, as I let it fall on my tongue. Edward was skipping with delight as he sang, "It's snowing, it's snowing," excitedly.

My hands were freezing, so I buried them in my holy jacket pocket to the touch of Teddy bear fur. Trying to warm them. "Edward, keep your hands in your pocket; they will stay warm."

I could hear the clip-clop of metal studded shoes as they hit the cobbled floor. The sound of excited children filled the air. Long fur coats cloaked most adults, whilst winter coats, in a kaleidoscope of colour, wrapped many of the children.

I saw a German shepherd dog tied to a lamppost with a wet, dirty rope. The pitiful thing was shaking and quivering from the cold and noise. Then I heard the crackling and what sounded like the humming of killer bees as the fireworks whistled through the air. And the bang-bang of firecrackers. We hastily made our way to the bonfire, not wanting to miss anything of this annual extravaganza.

We turned onto Duke Street and marvelled at this impressive structure the locals had built together. The bonfire was lit and turned into a towering inferno whilst fireworks boomed overhead, illuminating the sky in a rainbow of colour.

I pulled a couple of sparklers out and had them lit by a gentleman wearing a cloth cap and smoking a cigar. We gently swirled our sparklers, listening intently to their gentle crackle. The smell reminded me of the stale odours of tobacco smoke. I glanced at a little girl beside me, looking at my sparkler, head resting against her mother's shoulder. I could hear dogs barking and people chattering. The blazing flames made the air warm and comfortable. I could see tinder's sparking high into the sky. It was ablaze for hours. The bonfire started to fizzle out as the night drew in, leaving grey and black ash on its border. People placed potatoes in foil on the embers to cook. I put Edward's and mine onto the embers as they were; I wanted the smoky flavours on the skin.

A giant Catherine wheel ignited, spinning, and gathering speed until it was like a cyclone. It was drawing you in, with its strobe-lighting effect, whilst whistling.

Back gardens came alive with fireworks that boomed and buzzed, drawing further on our excitement. I noticed a grey-haired old lady looking on from her window, arms folded on the ledge.

Children started to cry with discontent as the night air temperatures dropped. I grabbed a birch off the gravelly floor, which creaked beneath my trainers. I pulled out our dark-black potatoes with their velvety skin of burnt ash. Soft and fluffy on our tongues, I looked at Edward with his darkened ash lips and smiled as I wiped away the powdery feel of ash from my lips.

The fireworks eventually fell silent, so we returned to Mum's house.

"Tell me when you're coming home?" Edward begged.

"I'm not, little bro, but you'll see more of me." Edward buried his hands in his face and started to cry.

"I'm so sorry, little bro." I gently pulled his hands away from his face and gave him a piece of rag I had in my pocket to dry his tears. I could hear people chattering aloud from the wonder that was bonfire night. I left Edward at the door to Mum's and went into Ms Boyd's house.

For the next few days, I saw as much of the family as possible whilst that demon was at the bookies. I even got to pop up the street to Heather's house. I knocked on the door and got a rude welcome from Heather's mum.

"Go away! Heather has nothing to do with you. Just stay away from her." Then she slammed the door. So, I didn't even get the chance to see Heather.

Time moved quickly, and I felt indebted to Ms Boyd. I had to find a way to get some money; Ms Boyd was good to me.

I stayed with Ms Boyd for a few weeks, living off this wonderful lady. But the guilt of not paying my way was too much to bear. Christmas was just around the corner, and I had nothing, and the only thing I could think of was turning to crime.

I started breaking into shops and vans, anything to get money. Which slowly turned into houses, where I amassed many items to sell, I hid in an old tunnel that was boarded up, but I found a straightforward way in, and money started flowing in as I peddled my goods on the street, I knew it was wrong, but the benefits far outweighed the negatives. Nobody knew what I was doing, I found it easy to buy cigarettes and alcohol, and even drugs became easier. Marijuana, alcohol, and cigarettes had become a part of my life.

Dad brought a greyhound called Nugget and a mongrel named Penny home. The greyhound was a top racing dog and must be fed chicken, rice, and sheep heads. And the mongrel, Penny, was a black and brown crossbreed German shepherd and Labrador and needed regular dog food. She barks at anything and everything.

Mum had a small cooler in the pantry, solely for the sheep heads. The bastard even had the nerve to give Mum a few pennies for taking the dog out. However, unknown to Dad, I gave Mum money from my dishonest gains.

It was Christmas Eve, and I bought presents for the family and a gift for Ms Boyd.

I could smell the roasting of chestnuts wafting through the freezing air and the sickly smell of Christmas treats emanating from Nantucket's. I filled my cloth sack with plenty of goodies for all. I bought Mum a fluffy white jumper made from sheep wool, and Edward a new pair of shoes and a dark black suit. He loved them: new shorts and shoes and a catapult for Alan to use sensibly. I bought Bernie cosmetics and Ms Boyd some lady's puffs and creams. Well, Christmas came and went. I saw Mum twice; one of those occasions was Christmas day after Dad had gone to the pub.

I left Ms Boyd's soon after and moved into a crummy bedsit. It was not much, but it was my home for the near future.

My seventeenth birthday resulted in getting pissed as a newt, which ended in a pub fight where I started bare-knuckle fighting. After putting a few lads away, I got arrested for breaching the peace and underage drinking. I got eight weeks in prison, but the governor could reduce it to six with good behaviour.

The prison was far worse than I could've ever imagined. I tried to act tough inside; otherwise, I was sure I'd have not come out in one piece. I went in behaving like I was better than anyone else. Trying to front up to other inmates in their cells whilst two correctional officers took me to mine—a mistake I was made to pay for later.

I was inside for just two days when three members of a Jewish gang confronted me at the door of my prison cell. "Can I help you, lads?"

"Our boss wants to see you," said one of the lads sporting a jagged scar that ran down the right-hand side of his face. If I didn't know any better, it looked like he'd had a broken bottle pushed into his face. They marched me down to a cell occupied by someone who had to be well-connected.

I stepped inside the cell and watched as the door closed behind me, leaving me alone with whomever this person was. He had everything in the cell; it looked like he made it a home from home.

"Hello, you wanted to see me?" I asked.

"My name is Adalai Abrams. Do you know who I am?"

"How the fucking hell would I know you?" I said, "I was reading my book when three of your fucking goons rudely interrupted me. Where are you from, Iran, Israel, Pakistan?" I soon found myself pushed against the cell wall with an arm across my throat.

"I make everything happen in here. I can get anything you need or want."

I shook my head and said, "Don't need anything, and I don't expect to be here for very long."

"Is that right? There's talk about you getting sorted tonight?"

"What do you mean, sorted?" I asked.

"Tom Dockan, he did not like your persona when you arrived. However, he is a large guy and has not taken a shine to you."

"The guards will be around; I'm sure they'll put a stop to anything?" I spoke.

"What's your name, lad?"

"Tony."

"Tony, you have never been inside before, have you? This bravado is all front and could easily get you into trouble. I have seen people like yourself taken out of here after Tom has had a go at them, and they have not returned. But… I can help you."

"Why would you help me? You don't know me either."

"You're new to the facility; I need something done in return?" said Adalai.

"Like what?" My mind was blank for a moment. I could go out in a body bag or be protected if I do what Adalai wants. But I was scared and was not sure what to do. "What is it you need from me for your protection?" I asked.

Adalai pulled out a steel blade with no handle. Then said, "I need this pushed into an inmate's hand."

"No, no fucking way. I'll get more time and want to be out of here in six weeks."

"Well, I doubt we will see each other again." His eyes steered me to the cell door.

I knew extraordinarily little about these guys, I could manage myself, but I only saw a way out if I went to the governor. He would have to protect me. Or is he bent? What if I get caught? Who is going to protect me then?" I asked.

"You won't; the guards work for me."

I should've guessed, I hesitated for ages but knew I should do it if I wanted to be protected.

That evening, I was drawn by Adalai's men toward the inmate's cell. I concealed the blade in my hand; I watched him read his magazine as I drew up alongside his cell.

"Hi there, do you mind if I come in?" Acting as if I wanted to befriend him.

"What's your name?" he asked.

"I'm Tony, and I have a message for you."

"A message?" he replied. He looked perplexed. His hand rested on his thigh, so I sat beside the guy on the bottom bunk. I didn't even know his name. I pulled the knife and forcefully stabbed it down on his hand; it penetrated quickly and continued through his thigh. He screamed, but I put my hand over his mouth and said, "That was from Adalai for cheating at cards." I then swiftly left the cell. Adalai's lads confirmed what I did while I hastily returned to my cell, awaiting repercussions. But there would be none. A shallow cut on my hand which I dressed in a dirty hankey.

During the six weeks, I was there, I was untouched as promised, but I met many characters who would become part of my family. I also knew who was relevant outside the prison. Anybody else, according to Adalai, didn't matter. The knowledge I gained inside would see me grow in crime on the outside.

When I got out, I sought the friends and associates of the lads still inside. Months passed, and my reputation was growing. I started bare-knuckle fighting around the biggest shitholes in the city, but they kept coming for the fights; it was relentless. I was becoming harder and a nasty piece of work, hungry for more and more blood. I had guys rigging the odds of me winning, and as always, I might have been bloodied and broken at times, but winning became a habit. I took to raising myself above all others. Winning allowed me to get everything I wanted, tobacco, drugs, girls, and alcohol. I even started extorting money from lorry drivers, threatening them that their haulage could go missing and their vehicles could be damaged. They were so petrified of any loss of produce, contraband, or even the lorries themselves that they paid in full.

I had built up a gang of real characters and started to run much of the city.

Edward wanted me to take him under my wing; he was too young, and I loved him. I gave him money for new clothes, so he always wore new clothes at school. I didn't want him to become like me. He needed to be well educated so he could have a respectable job. So, I would catch up with him whenever I could, take him out for dinner and get him to choose the dessert. I would then give him money to give to Mum so she could buy some beautiful things.

I caught up with him one-day last week, "How's everything at home?" I asked.

"Dad treats Nugget like a Queen. She gets everything. I heard Mum say to Dad, 'You give that dog and your cronies everything while we live on the scraps.' He told Mum to, 'Shut up or else.'"

"Bastard! He'll get what he deserves one day," I said. "If anything happens, like he hits you or Mum, you get me. Got it, bro?" I wrapped my arms around him. "I don't suppose you've seen Heather?"

"Weeks ago, Tony, she was at the shops with her mum. She said hello to me behind her mum's back and asked how you were. I told her I didn't see you that often, but when I did, you were working and looking very smart."

"Thanks, bro." Moments of memories continued to occupy my thoughts, I couldn't stop having these strong feelings for her, but I'm not sure she'd like me now. I'm a different animal. Anyway, I left little Edward and returned to the bedsit.

I woke to the sound of a car engine revving outside my bedsit; an associate of mine had bought a car, no doubt, illegally. But he wanted to know if I was interested in buying it. A blue Ford Cortina MK1.

"How much do you want for it, Jack?" I liked this guy; he seemed quite intelligent. So, I offered him a price and a significant role in my criminal business. He accepted, and in time Jack became my accountant.

My illegal businesses gathered momentum. Jack was my driver and drove me everywhere in the Ford Cortina, Business meetings, dining, and girls. He was my right hand.

My reputation continued to grow alarmingly, and four years on, the city's illegal operations were all mine. I traded everything from drugs to alcohol and extortion. Everything came via my authorisation. I had moved into a sizeable four-bedroomed house, had multiple vehicles, and gained some of the best operators in the city.

One of the most significant businesses was exploiting haulage drivers in the city. Drivers were paying my lads through the nose to keep their haulage safe. The company was bringing in hundreds of pounds a day. Unfortunately for them, and fortunately for us, the police were not fast enough or clever enough to work out when or where we would be at any given moment.

Every time the lads clocked a police vehicle, they would take down the number plate. Even when the police were dealing with other situations, the lads took down the number plate. So, every police car had been marked: we were like shadows in the dark. Nobody outside the city knew who we were.

However, without my knowledge, the city's police force was setting up a task force to try a crackdown on the crime, causing significant grievances to all manner of businesses.

I had Michael as my new right hand; we had been friends since we were kids, but he spent most of his youth in and out of borstals and prisons. He was a real animal, with a large skull tattoo on the left-hand side of his face. Only the brainless would stand up to him. So, I gave him control of the extortion of money from the many lorry parks around the city. Jack continued to be my accountant, and for his safety, out of sight from the savage existence I started to live.

I would send money every week to the very poorest in the city; to the families that couldn't work through no fault of their own so there would be no starvation. The neighbourhoods were eternally grateful. I was protected by the city's poor. I felt like a modern-day Robin Hood taking from the wealthy, to give to the poor. The people of the city knew who I was. The poor would say nothing, and the rich dare does not say anything.

Some unaccustomed drivers came into the city and tried to park without paying so they would move on to another park, but somebody was always waiting to unload any money from their hefty pockets. Those who refused to pay must explain their lost products or how the vehicle was damaged.

Meanwhile, Jack and I were back at my house drawing up contracts for the independent pub proprietors agreeing to pay me and only me for their alcohol. We started importing Alcohol from France, Holland, and Belgium, including vast consignments of tobacco and marijuana. In addition, an American student movement gripped the country with its 'hippie movement,' and LSD, a drug that would send people into a faraway world, became available at a prohibitive cost. But as always, I bought to satisfy my connections.

"Jack, do you want a drink?"

"Thanks, boss."

I poured myself a cognac, a drink I got a taste for after visiting a club that couldn't sell any beer at the time through a lack of deliveries. "Jack, how many more lads do we need to employ to cover the contraband around the city?"

"Boss, you have your fingers in so many pies; it's hard to juggle everyone around."

"I didn't ask that, Jack," I barked. "I asked how many more lads we need?"

"Six, boss. But you have everybody worth having already working for you."

"Find them, Jack; we must address all the acquisitions, and if that means finding more employees, then find them, even if you must go outside the city. Search everywhere, and I only want the best!"

"I'll start first thing, boss."

"Take Jimmy and Richard in case there's any trouble."

"Trouble, boss? Why would there be trouble?"

"Don't worry, Jack, that's why Jimmy and Richard will go with you."

"Will do, boss." Jack left the house, and I took to a cognac bottle whilst sitting in my armchair in front of a roaring fire, contemplating whether I should visit Dixie's club to see Barbara, a local girl who was quite pretty but slightly slag. But I didn't care too much, as I was getting what I wanted and had no time for real love.

Then the thud of my door knocker went, and as I was not expecting anybody, I got up and moved to my window to see if I could see anyone outside. There was nothing suspicious, so I moved to open the door, withdrawing an army knife from my pocket, just in case.

"Who's there?" I asked.

"Tony, it's me, Edward."

I quickly opened the door. "Little bro, what are you doing here?" I asked, even though I was so glad to see him.

"I'm sixteen, Tony, and I want to work with you."

"Bro, I can't let you work with me; it's dangerous work I do."

"But you have everything, Tony; look at this place; it's like a palace full of lovely things."

"Never mind all that; how's Mum, Bernie, and Alan?"

"Mum misses you a lot, and Alan hates school apart from football, and Bernie, as usual, is working hard to give Mum some money to better ourselves."

"What about him?" Meaning the bastard demon that was supposed to be our father.

"Nothing changes there; still many arguments, and Mum cries a lot."

"Do you want a drink and some food, bro?"

"Yes, please; what have you got?"

"How about Swedish meatballs, followed by jelly, your favourite?"

"Really?"

"Yes, bro. Do you want a lager shandy as well?"

"Yes, please."

We sat talking for ages. Edward loved the food and the lager shandy, but it was time for him to go; he could not stay because Mum was expecting him home, but maybe next time. "I will speak to you in a couple of days. Tell everyone I love them." I took a wad of notes from my pocket and said, "Give this to Mum."

I went to bed, cradling the cognac bottle I consumed whilst listening to the Beatles on the radio. I woke up hours later with a bad hangover, so I bathed and submerged myself, embracing the warm water as it flowed over my head. Lying in the bath, smoking a cigarette, I seemed at peace with myself. Eventually, I got dressed into a pale blue shirt with a white collar, a black three-piece suit, a dark blue tie, gold cufflinks of oval shape and a tie pin in gold and black onyx. And a pair of black and white lace-up Oxfords.

I rang Michael and asked him to come around to the house. I needed to know how the extortion racket was going.

"Boss, I am a bit busy now; there was an issue last night at Megan Park. A lorry driver pulled a knife on Brendan and stabbed him in the arm. Brendan's had fourteen stitches up at the hospital. I have told him to say nothing, to go back home. So, I went to Megan Park, but the driver had fled."

"That's an inconvenience, Michael."

"What else could I do, boss?"

"You might need to find a more direct approach to the business. However, I can't afford any uneasiness; we must find that driver and who he works for."

"I am on it, boss."

There was a knock on the door within moments of putting the phone down. I opened it to Jack, who brought a gang of misfits back to my house. "What's this, Jack?" I barked. His naivety in bringing the lads to my home amazed me.

"These lads are the best I could find, boss."

"Jimmy, you and Richard look after these lads; I need a word with Jack."

"Indeed, boss," replied Jimmy.

I put my hand on Jack's shoulder and said, "Come inside, Jack." I closed the door behind me and led Jack into the back garden without saying anything.

"Is everything okay, boss?" he asked concernedly.

I turned to Jack and grabbed him by his shirt whilst pushing him against the wall,

"How fucking dare, you bring strangers into my place? They're fucking nobody who could easily bring my business down."

"I'm sorry, boss, I wasn't thinking."

"You are too fucking smart to make this kind of blunder. Now take the lads to the warehouse in Compton, and you fucking keep them there until I get there, got it?"

"Yes, boss." Jack returned to the guy's and told everyone they were going to Compton.

I was disturbed there might be a stooge in the gang of lads. I had been around the streets for years and had not seen any of these lads before. But of course, now they know where I live. So, I got on the phone to Michael, "Where are you?"

"Top of North Street, boss, I found who the driver was working for; it's a company called Long-steel. They make steel tubes in Leeds."

"That's brilliant, Michael. We'll deal with that later; I need you to come and pick me up from the house and take me over to Compton."

"Sure, boss, I will be with you in an hour."

I paced across the front room floor, coupling my hand around my chin, thoughtfully working out my next move.

Meanwhile, Jack and the lads were waiting for me to arrive in the warehouse.

"What's wrong, Jack?" asked Jimmy.

"I took the lads to the boss's house; like a fucking idiot; now he's in a bit of a panic."

A skinny bloke with buck teeth and one side of his head shaven asked, "Wh-Wh-What's on then, mate?" Stuttering his words.

"We're waiting for the boss to come over and check you guys out," said Jack, standing toe to toe, staring down at him.

"Well-well-well, he had better hurry up, as I have things to do," responded the bloke.

"You're here for a job, aren't you?" said Jack.

"Ye-Ye-Ye-Yes! of course, I am. I have A-A-babe-babe waiting for me at home."

"Where's that? Your home?" questioned Jack.

"Um, D-D-D-D-Dartford."

The bloke looked nervous, and his hands twitched; he wouldn't sit still.

"Are you okay?" asked Jimmy. "You look a bit nervous?"

"No-no-no I am okay."

Meanwhile, Michael and I arrived at the warehouse. We entered the warehouse; I had Michael to my right and Ambrose to my left.

"Do you know who I am?" I commented. The lads nodded as I heard the soft whispering. "So, you all want to work for me?"

"Aye, we do."

I walked over to the lads and looked them up and down. "I want to know where you live and what you have done before. If you have any family? Don't leave anything out. I'm not nice if you're not telling me everything. Am I making myself clear?" There were nods all around.

"Michael, I want to know everything."

"Yes, boss."

The lads spent the next few hours interrogating them while I sat at the desk in the warehouse, a glass of cognac in one hand and a cigarette in the other, feeling a little claustrophobic. "Come on, lads; I've other business to attend to." I stepped outside the warehouse overlooking the canal. I watched as a riverboat moved slowly along the water with a young couple laying prostrate on its front end near the bow, wearing costumes, catching the sun. I thought they looked happy together, something I craved in my life; I have money, but I wouldn't say I was delighted. I flicked my cigarette into the water and returned to the warehouse, "Come on then, lads, what's taking so bloody long?"

"Boss, most of these guys will be good assets. Unfortunately, we have a bit of a stutterer of words. However, one guy does not figure I cannot work him out."

"Where is he, Michael? Bring him to me."

"Yes, boss." Michael brought this guy over to me and sat him on the chair. He looked nervous. I caught sight of a knuckleduster on his hand.

I sat on the desk and looked down at him, searching for answers to any questions. "What's your story, mate?"

"My name is Paul Fisher; I have spent most of my life in borstal or prison. I don't have any family; I was brought up on the streets scrounging food and anything else I could get my hands on to make money."

"Still living on the streets, Paul?"

"Yes."

"Where are you from originally? Your accent sounds Irish."

"It is. I lived in Ireland until my parents brought me here. But they died a few years after in a car crash, and I was put in a home for neglected or orphaned children. I ran away from the home when I was fourteen and have been homeless ever since."

"What have you done to keep you going this long?" I asked.

"Pickpocketing, burglary, theft, anything."

"Can you handle yourself?"

"I'm always fighting, so I can handle myself."

"Do you carry a blade? I see you have a knuckleduster on your hand?"

"No blade." Paul held his hand out to show me his knuckleduster properly.

"What would you say if I told you to carry a blade and if you had to use it irrespective of the circumstances?"

"Then I would carry and use it, boss."

"You'll be working with Michael; you'll follow his orders. Any problem with that?"

"No, boss, and thank you for the opportunity."

"Jack, blade up the guys and put them to work, and make sure they know what they need to know, and no more."

"Boss."

"Michael? Tell me about this Long-steel company, and how can we track the driver down?"

"I know they are based in Leeds and have four drivers. So, I am sure we can find out which one came down. I had a description off Brendan."

"Send up a couple of guys and get this driver back to me. Send Paul and Ray."

"Yes, boss."

"Michael? Can you take me over to Dixie's club? I need a good drink."

"Yes, boss," Michael opened the door to the Ford Cortina MK1. I took my flat grey cap off and lit another cigarette. "Mike, can you drop me at my mother's house first."

"Sure, boss."

We took the fifteen-minute drive over to Mum's house. I had never told my mother what I do for a living; she believes I work as a supervisor in a factory. I couldn't tell her the truth.

Once we pulled up outside the house, I asked Michael to knock. I didn't want to leave the car if my father answered the door. Michael knocked on the door, and my mother opened it,

"Hello, how can I help?" she asked.

"I am Michael, a good friend of Tony's. Is your husband in?"

"No, why?" she asked. Michael opened the passenger door of the car, and I climbed out.

"Hello, Mum; I didn't know if Dad would be home, so I got Michael to knock first."

"Hello, son; it's so nice to see you." Giving me a massive cuddle. "What a nice car."

"Yes, it is. I've come to take Edward out for a ride. Is he in?"

"Is it your car?"

"Yes, Mum, I picked it up cheaply, and Michael drives it for me, you know, for work and that."

"Tony? You are not doing anything you shouldn't do, are you?"

With that, Edward approached the front door. "Wow, what a nice car."

"Yes, bro, and you're going for a ride in it."

"Really?"

"Yes, Mum, I'll drop him back at the house later. Bro, get into the car. And stop saying really!"

"Where are we going?" he asked.

"Just for a quick ride around the block, and then I've work to do." So, Michael drove us around the block while Edward played with the winding handle, which made the window go up and down, letting the soft, warm air of the spring sunshine blow against his face. He loved every minute.

"I'm going to get me a car, soon." Said bro. We dropped him back home, and Michael drove me to Dixie's club.

"Michael, I'll be a couple of hours; can you pick me up then?"

"Sure, boss."

I stepped inside Dixie's to the sound of 'The Loco-Motion' by Little Eva, playing quite loudly on the Wurlitzer.

"Evening, Tony," was the voice I heard as I stood at the bar with a cognac in hand, listening to the vibrant music playing on the Wurlitzer. I recognised the voice, which belonged to Barbara.

She put her arm around my shoulders and asked, "How's your day been, honey?"

"Long but interesting," I responded as I inhaled the smoke from my cigarette whilst looking her up and down. She had shoulder-length brunette hair and wore a lime green knee-length dress with white polka-dots cut to just below the shoulder and silver heels.

"Are you going to get me a drink, love?"

"Viv, can I have a whiskey sour for Barbara, please?" Viv put the drink on the bar, and we moved to a table by the window.

"I've missed you; you haven't been in for days."

"Sorry, Barbara, I've been swamped and, to tell you the truth, a bit knackered."

"Can I ease away your tiredness tonight?"

"No, maybe another time, Barbara." I sat with a cigarette in hand, staring out the window, watching a couple of young lads playing hopscotch on the cobbled stones. Finally, Barbara stood up, grabbed her whisky sour, and said, "I'll leave you to it, then."

"Yeah, maybe another time, Barbara." She walked to the bar to talk to the gentleman who sat alone, minding his business. I stubbed my cigarette into the ashtray and took a sip of cognac from my glass. I was looking out the window when a young lady caught my attention; she seemed familiar, so I hurried out the door as I looked down the street; this blonde-haired beauty was walking into the distance. I raced after her. Something had stirred inside my chest, my heart pounding as I struggled to breathe. Finally, I caught up with this stunning bird dressed in a vivid red dress. "Heather? Is that you?" She turned around, and I couldn't believe it. "Heather, it is you."

"Tony?" she said with a huge grin.

"Heather, I can't believe it's you." I smiled as I offered my hand to hold hers. "You look stunning; where are you off to?" I asked.

"Just to a friend's house," she responded, gazing into my eyes.

"Have you time for a drink? Unfortunately, it's only Dixie's, but as you can see, it's just here," I pointed to the club.

"Why not?" she replied.

I offered my hand to hold hers, and when she grabbed it, my heart almost burst with joy. I had so much I wanted to tell her, and I didn't know how she would react. But I was sure of my heart; I was in love with her and always have been.

We entered Dixie's, and silence filled the air as people looked stunned at what I could only believe was Heather's beauty. Heather was dressed in a puff-sleeved sheath dress in red with a back zip and eight white buttons, four on each side running horizontally with each other on the front of the dress made of wool. With her beautiful blonde hair in a flipped bob hairstyle and bright red ruby shoes, she could have been a descendant of Aphrodite herself.

Holding hands, we walked to the bar. "Viv, can I have my usual, and what would you like, Heather?"

"Why don't you surprise me?" she replied.

"Viv, can I have a Babycham for Heather?"

Barbara stared at me with contempt and then opened her mouth. "Who's this then?" she asked, in a bold tone, staring at Heather with a look of jealousy.

Before I could respond, Heather politely said, "I am Heather, an old acquaintance of Tony's. How do you do?" Then, she offered Barbara her hand to shake. Barbara turned away and went to a table where a couple of gentlemen sat quietly, having a pint of ale, and admiring Heather. Viv brought the Babycham over in its dainty depth glass, bubbles still bursting as they erupted inside the glass.

"How do you do, Heather? I am Vivienne, but my friends call me Viv, so please call me Viv. I own the club, and let me tell you, you have a real charmer in him," she pointed at me.

"I know he's a real charmer," responded Heather.

I felt slightly uncomfortable at any praise; it was just me, especially in front of Heather. We went and sat down at the table by the window. I had so much to say but didn't know where to start. We both went to start a conversation at the same time.

"Please, Heather, you go first," I said with a smile.

"Okay then, how are you?"

"All the better for seeing you."

"It has been four years, Tony. I had not moved anywhere. Where have you been?"

I offered Heather a cigarette whilst I wrestled with my conscience to find a way of telling Heather what I'd been doing and why I stayed away.

"I don't smoke, Tony."

I nodded in approval, lighting my cigarette, puffing, and exhaling the smoke. "I've... My life has changed,

Heather, and I'm not the same person I was a few years ago." Then, in haste to change the subject, I asked, "Are you still working in the factory?"

"Yes, I have been promoted, and the pay is good, and I can get the clothes that I like at discounted prices."

I stared adoringly into her bright blue eyes. "You're more gorgeous now than you have ever been. And believe me, you were stunning when we first kissed."

"You have not lost any of your charms, have you? So, who is this, Barbara?"

"I'll not lie to you; she's lovely. We have spent some nights together, but that's it."

Heather turned and looked at Barbara, sat with the two gentlemen and gave her a gentle smile.

"So, as you evaded my question somewhat by changing the subject, why wouldn't I like you?"

"I run a dodgy business, which is going well."

"What do you call dodgy? It must be bad if I would not like you?"

"Well, I don't want for anything, Heather. I have a large house, multiple cars, and sixty employees. Most of them are from the neighbourhood. I have pushed, beaten, fought and grafted my way to where I am. I have respect from many, and I look after whoever is important to me."

"Wow, that is impressive." Heather grasped my hand and pulled it towards her, forcing me to stand and lean across the table without losing balance. She stood and leaned toward me, caressing my face. She kissed me gently, and my chest fluttered like a thousand butterflies trying to escape. The taste of her lips was soft and warm as they caressed mine, a memory I had not forgotten. Then I heard, "Get on, son," as it echoed through the air from a young man sitting at the table. Heather turned and smiled at the young gentleman. I sat down from the warmth of her kiss, overwhelmed by my emotions.

"Where's this house of yours, Tony?"

"Down by the water, on canal street, why?"

"They're lovely houses down there. I would like to see it, Tony?" She gazed into my eyes. It was strange, but it was like the first time we met, and nothing had changed.

"Just waiting for my driver, Michael. He'll not be long. Shall we wait outside?" We got up and started walking out of the club when the chants began,

"You have a great one there, Tony."

"Thank you, guys. Catch you later, Viv."

We exited Dixie's and strolled southbound down the street, holding hands. I knew Michael would come from that direction. "What about your friend? Won't she be worried about you?" I asked. "It's been over two hours," I said, looking at my watch.

"She is all right. I have often bailed out before, depending on what happens." Heather gazed into my eyes and said, "You have got 'come to bed eyes, Tony. Do you know that?"

"I've not been told that before. But of course, everybody is different, aren't they? But thank you for the compliment."

Heather pushed me gently against the wall and started another kiss. I responded by kissing her cheek, and then I softly nibbled on her ear and moved gently to her neck. Heather sighed with enjoyment as I put my arms around her waist and pulled her closer. Her hands rested against my chest; I could only assume she must have felt my heart pounding because it sounded like a battalion of drummers trying to get out. Once we stopped kissing, we stood with our backs against the wall while waiting for the car to arrive. I lit another cigarette and asked Heather, "How are your parents?"

"They are fine, both working hard."

"What about Colin? What's he up to nowadays?"

"He works in a car showroom selling cars."

"I must catch up with him; it's been a long time."

"Well, I am sure you will see him soon."

I spotted Michael coming up the street in the Ford Cortina. "Here he is, Heather." As he pulled up, Michael hastily got out of the car with a face of concern. I walked over to him and introduced Heather.

"Nice to meet you, Michael."

I helped Heather into the back seat of the car. "I'll not be a moment, sweetheart. Michael, what is it?"

"They've got the driver who knifed Brendon."

"Where?"

"They're holding him in the warehouse in Compton. He has been blindfolded all the time."

"Thank you, Michael. I want him held there until tomorrow; I need you to take me and my young lady home.

Would you pick me up in the morning? And then I'll deal with him."

"Yes, boss. Wow, she's a doll, boss."

We climbed into the car, and Heather asked if everything was all right.

"Yes, of course, just some business that can wait until tomorrow." Heather clutched my hand and placed them on her lap whilst we were being driven back to my house overlooking the canal.

We arrived at my house, six Bayswater Road. A red-brick Georgian house with four windows at the front: two up and two down, with a black tiled roof and a chimney set to the south side of the house—a white front porchway with white glass doors as the entrance. Sitting so proud with a sizeable lawn at the front and back with views over the canal, it's a perfect setting for romantic sunsets.

"Tony, this is beautiful. But I'm aghast. It looks like a huge version of my doll's house."

"That's a wonderful way to describe my home. Michael, I will see you tomorrow."

"Yes, boss."

"After you, sweetheart," I said as I let her walk through the front door.

Heather walked straight into the living room, "Wow, it's light in here," she complimented. Heather's eyes were everywhere. The electric chandelier gave plenty of light, as did the two double bay windows adorned in gold and red drapes, offering a subtle but warm touch to the décor. The giant oak hearth was ablaze from hot red coals recently ignited by my cleaner, Sue, who helps with the housework every few days, bringing warmth and a soft glow to the room. A long orange couch left plenty of room for relaxing, and a sizeable wool rug patterned in roses, with dahlias on a red and cream background with hints of greens, adorned the floor. Heather touched everything from the Georgian coffee table to the white China Irish wolfhound sitting under the tall brass mirror on the wall. Even the silver ashtray sat on a Georgian side table alongside a blue and white China vase filled with roses.

"Can I get you a drink, Heather?"

"Surprise me. You have done an excellent job up until now."

"How about a Bloody Mary?"

"You are making it?" She smiled; the house continued to amaze her. "I will chill on your couch if that is, okay?" Heather sat down on the couch with one knee over the other, feeling the texture of the sofa with her fingers. "You have done so well for yourself, love."

That word at the end of her last sentence, love, had me in rapture. I don't know if she was trying to get some inclination toward what I did for a living. I rimmed the glass with salt, poured the vodka and tomato juice into the tall glass, and added salt, pepper, and ice. I poured myself a cognac and moved to the couch next to Heather.

"That Bloody Mary looks amazing. I hope it tastes as good as it looks."

I put the tall glass in Heather's hand and put my cognac on the side table.

"Oh, that is very good," she expressed after sipping the Bloody Mary. The drink moistened her deep red lips. We sat with my right arm and her left arm resting on the back of the couch whilst I gently put my left hand on her right thigh, gazing into her piercing blue eyes. Her right hand moulded around her glass as she moved closer to my lips.

"Just a moment," she whispered as she turned and put the glass on the side table. I moved closer to get comfortable; she turned back and shuffled closer to me. My heart pounded as I put my left arm around her neck to draw her lips close to mine; she put her right arm around me as we embraced each other tightly. Then, with the flickering of flames reflecting in her eyes, I closed mine, and we gently kissed. I could feel her gently trembling in my arms as our kissing intensified. My tongue searched for hers as our lips locked as if never to be opened. It seemed like another world I lived in, if only for those moments.

"I need some air," she said as she sat up, inhaling a deep breath.

I grabbed her drink from the side table and offered it up to her.

"Oh, thank you."

She took a mouthful. "Are you okay?" I asked as I grinned a little.

"Oh, yes! Where is the bathroom?" she asked in a flutter.

"Just up the flight of stairs on your left." Heather went upstairs in a hurried manner. I took a sip of my cognac and sat back down, patiently waiting for Heather to return. A few moments passed, so I started stoking the fire to keep the room temperature warm whilst waiting. I began to undo the buttons on my shirt as my body temperature rose at the thought of spending tonight with Heather. I couldn't help but look to the flight of stairs wondering why Heather had not returned yet; it had been fifteen minutes. I moved to the bottom of the staircase and shouted, "Heather, Are you okay?" But there was no reply. I hurried up the stairs and knocked gently on the bathroom door. "Heather, are you okay in there?" But again, there was no response. Panicking, I opened the door to find Heather lying unconscious beside the bath. "What the…?" I quickly knelt and raised her head with my arm. "Heather…? Heather…?" I tried to wake her, but she was not responding, although she was breathing. Finally, I sat her up against the bath and raced downstairs to dial 999.

"Hello, what service do you require?" asked the lady on the other end of the phone.

"Ambulance! Please, hurry. She is unconscious, and I don't know what to do. Please, hurry!"

"I need your address and need you to hold on the line. Can you do that for me?" she asked.

"It's number six Bayswater Road."

"I've got that, sir; you did say six Bayswater Road?"

"Yes! Now, please hurry. I've told you where I live! What more do you need?" I said condescendingly.

"Sir, we are here to help. Can you tell me what has happened? The ambulance is on its way."

"We had a couple of drinks, she went to the bathroom, and then I found her unconscious."

"Has she taken any pills or any drugs?"

"How do I know? Not whilst with me."

"Are you with her?"

"No! I'm on the phone."

"Sir, please can you go and check on her, see if she has a temperature? Can you do that for me?"

I returned to the bathroom and felt Heather's head to see if she had a temperature. It felt lukewarm; I assumed that was okay, but she was still unconscious. I raced down to the phone, breathless; I said, "She feels lukewarm to the touch but still unconscious." Then, still panicking, I asked again, "Where's this ambulance?"

"They will be with you, sir. You do need to calm down, sir."

Moments later, I heard the siren from the ambulance. "They're here!" I said to the operator, and then just slammed the phone down. I hurried to the door to give directions as the pale blue ambulance pulled up outside. The ambulance crew hurried upstairs to Heather; the crew had no idea what was wrong. "What do we do next?" I asked. We found ourselves on the way to the hospital. I held her hand, praying for her to wake up.

We arrived at Freedom Fields Hospital after what seemed an eternity. First, they rushed her through the doors where a doctor was waiting, and then they swiftly moved to the emergency department.

"What's wrong, Doctor?" I asked.

"We don't know yet; we need to do some tests. So please, sir, you must wait out here in the waiting area and let us get on with our job."

I looked at the reception desk, where a nurse was looking in my direction. She saw my anxiety when she asked me if I was okay.

"I don't know; I found her unconscious in my bathroom; she was fine fifteen minutes earlier."

"I'm sure she will be okay; she's in good hands."

I sat in the waiting room next to a mother and child. The child looked as if he hurt his arm as he held it tight to his belly. He could not have been any more than seven years old. "What did you do?" I asked.

"I tripped over the curb and fell on it." He replied.

I lit a cigarette to ease my anxiety.

"Sir, you cannot smoke that here; you must take it outside." Said the nurse.

I got up hastily and went outside to smoke my cigarette. I then rang Michael and asked him to come to the hospital.

I paced up and down the waiting area whilst waiting for the doctor. Finally, Michael arrived, and I told him what had happened.

"Are you okay, boss?"

"I don't know what they're doing. Why is it taking so long?" I puffed away on my cigarette whilst looking through the glass doors, desperate to see the doctor appear. Finally, I returned to the waiting area; the child who had hurt his arm and his mother had disappeared. I approached the nurse at the desk and asked, "Why is it taking so long? Why can't I be with her?"

"The doctor will let you know as soon as possible, sir." Two hours passed, and the doctor, dressed in his white coat with a stethoscope around his neck, eventually came out.

"Sorry, doc, I'm Tony; what's the news? Is Heather, okay?"

"Heather's awake; she is feeling a little disorientated. Can I ask a couple of questions of you?"

"Yes, whatever? When can I see her?"

"In a few minutes, we will get her more comfortable. Tony, has Heather taken any drugs?"

"No! Heather's not that sort of girl."

"We have taken blood to do some tests and given her some antihistamines, which seem to have worked. Do you know if she has any allergies?"

"No, not that I'm aware. Now can I please see Heather?"

"Come this way, Tony."

The doctor took me to the emergency room, where Heather was being treated. I was overwhelmed by all the machines and tubes everywhere. Heather had a saline bag attached to her arm and looked as white as a ghost.

"Tony," Heather said in a shallow voice.

"Thank God you're all right. I was so scared; I didn't know what to do." I could feel myself welling up, as I leaned over to kiss her gently.

"My mum and dad will be frantic with worry if I do not return home tonight. Can you please let them know I am, okay?"

"I'll get Michael to take me around once I know you're settled. Until then, I'm staying here with you."

"I feel so weird, Tony. My head is spinning, and I imagine all kinds of things."

"Like what, Heather?"

"Different colours and strange sensations."

I was familiar with the drug that made you feel extremely weird and would give you hallucinations. It was LSD. "Heather, have you taken any drugs?"

"Yes, I have; please don't tell anybody; my father would kill me!" and started crying.

I tried to get as comfortable as possible on the bed to cuddle her. "What have you taken? And have you taken it before?"

"No, I have never taken it before; the lad said it was LSD; I only took it because I was a bit nervous with you. The lad I got it from said it would relax me and make me feel like I had a few drinks. I am so sorry."

"Heather, it looks like you've reacted to it." I felt so guilty that she thought she had to take it when she was with me. But more importantly, it opened my eyes to the dangers of selling this drug on the streets. Yes, there was a fortune to be made by selling the drug but seeing Heather in here and giving me the fright of my life, I had no choice. I'd stop the sale of this drug in my city.

I sat with Heather for over an hour, and eventually, she fell asleep. So, I went to Heather's house and told her parents what had happened, only in my version.

It was eleven-thirty when Michael and I arrived at Heather's house. It was dark, with fading light coming from the street lampposts. I knocked, predicting an uncomfortable conversation as they disliked me intensely and told me to stay away from Heather over three years ago. Instead, Mr Bray answered the door with a crowbar, dressed in striped pyjamas underneath a long grey night coat. He did not recognize me. But when I started the conversation, he realized who I was.

"What do you want?" he asked.

"It's Heather. She's in Freedom Fields hospital after collapsing from an allergic reaction to something she ate." Mr Brady started to panic and called for his wife to hurry down.

"I have seen you before, haven't I? Where do I know you from?" His eyes squint in the darkness.

"I'm Tony; I lived down the street. I haven't been around for a long time, Mr Brady."

"That's it!" he said, raising his voice. "You... You better not have anything to do with this?"

"Heather has asked me to tell you not to worry and that she's okay. I've done as she's asked, Mr Brady." I looked down the dark street towards Mum's house, wondering if I should knock on the door. But I came to my senses and would enquire about things in a few days. But first, I needed to get back to Heather and ensure she knew what I'd communicated to her father.

I eventually got home. "Thank you, Michael! I'm not sure what I'd have done without you tonight."

"You're welcome, boss. But remember boss, we are still holding that driver at the warehouse."

"Yeah, a problem. I'll sort it out tomorrow if you can pick me up?"

"Of course, boss."

Michael left, and I poured myself a cognac while contemplating what must be done tomorrow. A restless sleep ensued. My thoughts towards Heather left me disturbed by the events of last night.

It was damp and misty outside as I drew the curtains open. My body was ravaged by the cold that infested itself through the night in the house. I bathed, took a Grey pinstriped suit from my mahogany wardrobe and a blue and white pinstripe shirt, and dressed. I wrote a note for Sue to ask if she could set the fire aglow before leaving. Michael beeped the horn to let me know he was outside waiting. I picked up my blade, placed it in my jacket pocket, and joined Michael in the car.

"Morning, boss."

"Morning, Michael, let's get this over and done with?" Michael drove towards Compton. I was prepared to do anything to protect my business. But my thoughts were still with Heather. Michael and I didn't speak much in the car; I had to set myself to the task.

When we arrived at the warehouse, Paul and Ambrose sat opposite this weasel who stabbed Brendon. They'd tied his hands behind his back and gagged him with twine.

"Boss? He's been tied up all night," said Ambrose.

The weasel looked petrified. Sweating like a pig trying to wriggle free from the bindings whilst trying to muffle something. "Seems he has something to say. Take the gag off, Ambrose." Ambrose untied the twine gagging the weasel, who then tried to speak.

"Don't fucking speak! You haven't the right to speak in my presence. You used a knife on one of my associates rather than pay your dues. Why would you be so stupid?" I said, shaking my head. "I'm going to ask some questions. You'll nod or shake your head to answer, do you understand?" The weasel nodded. I then pulled my blade from within my jacket pocket. I played with the handle made of bone whilst I started my questioning of the weasel.

"What's your name?"

"Barry, Barry Drake."

"Do you have a family?" The weasel nodded.

"What? A wife and children?" Again, he nodded, as the tears rolled down his face, and trembling uncontrollably. No doubt wondering what I might do to him.

"You know we have your home address?" Again, he nodded, "Please, Please, I'm so sorry."

My conscience told me to do one thing, but my heart another. "I'm going to give you a memento to take home with you." His eyes widened in surprise at my statement. "If there are any repercussions from this, I'll kill your family! Do you understand?" He nodded again, head bowed on his chest, crying.

"Ambrose, take his shirt off." Ambrose ripped open his shirt and cut the vest underneath with his blade, baring the weasel's chest to me.

"Hold him down," I said to Ambrose and Michael.

"No! please don't hurt me?" he squealed.

Ambrose and Michael held his shoulders; hungry for blood, I took my blade to his chest and gently pierced his chest with the knife, not too deep, just deep enough to hear him wince in pain. "I told you I will leave you a reminder of what happens when you don't pay your dues. And then I moved it slowly down his sternum, but this time I cut more deeply, and enjoyed every inch I pierced whilst his hollow screams echoed around the warehouse. "If you think this is bad, any repercussions will see your family to the afterlife." I pulled my blade away and wiped it in his vest. "Ambrose, Jimmy, clean him up, take him back, and drop him at his front door." I put the blade back in my pocket and promptly left the warehouse with Michael.

We got back in the car, where I told Michael to tell our associates that we wouldn't be buying LSD from them.

"They are not going to like that, boss?"

"If they disagree, tell them we'll look elsewhere for our business. Take some of the lads in case there's any trouble."

"Yes, boss. Hospital, boss?"

"Michael, you read my mind. Thank you."

"I thought you were going to kill that weasel, boss?"

"Another day I might of, I'm too worried about Heather. There shouldn't be any repercussions. At least that was my thought process, Michael, we can't afford taking chances it would bring a different element to the safety of the businesses."

"Do you think he will talk, boss?"

"He won't talk; he knows we know where he lives, he'd endanger his whole family. I don't know how long I'll be in the hospital, Michael but hopefully, I can have Heather out of there today and see her back at my house. So, I might call you later after you've taken care of that other business."

"Sure, boss."

Michael dropped me off at the hospital, and I hurried to Heather's bedside. On arriving, I peered through the room's glass window only to see her father sitting beside the bed. A moment passed as I thought about whether to enter or not. Heather would be part of my life, and he couldn't do anything about it. She's twenty now.

I politely knocked before entering. Mr Brady stood and glared at me. "Hello, Mr Brady... Hi, sweetheart." I turned to look at Heather, beaming a huge smile back at me.

"I am popping out for a bit, Heather," said Mr Brady. He walked past me without as much as a look. He left the room, and I leaned over and kissed Heather. "How are you feeling?"

"Much better; the doctor said I should be able to go home today."

"That's fantastic! I'd love it if you came back to my house."

"I told dad I was going home with him. He does not like you, and he now blames you for me being here."

"I've done nothing. So how can your father blame me?" I was angry inside, but I couldn't let Heather see. I shrugged my shoulders.

"It is just dad. It is because I was with you, and now I am here. Think about what that looks like, my love. The last time we were together, I had the police take me home, and he never forgot it. I am sure one day he will."

I gently held Heather's hand and said, "I love you and want you in my life forever."

"I love you too. Let us give it a few weeks and see how everything stands. I do not want to rush into anything; I know little about you. You have gained so much in four years? But you will not tell me what you do for a living?"

"Isn't it enough to know that I love you? And I want you in my life?"

"No! How can I trust you if you cannot tell me what you do?"

"I'll tell you, but not just yet."

"Dad is bringing in some bits for me to change into; I feel uncomfortable after being here all night. Thank you for last night; I enjoyed our time together, even if it was a bit short-lived, and I am sorry for taking that drug."

I started to feel guilty and ashamed of myself, one of my lads would've sold her the LSD tablet, and I had this uncontrollable accountability trying to burst out of me to tell Heather it was my fault.

"Do you have something I can use to write a telephone number down?" Heather asked.

"Of course, sweetheart," I took a pen and a slip of paper from my pocket and handed them to Heather.

"Here is a telephone number, it belongs to my friend, please do not ring home. I do not want Mum and Dad stressing because of our relationship."

"But Heather, you're twenty; you're old enough to make your own decisions?"

I put the slip of paper back into my pocket and sat down next to the bed. *What a horrible place this is? It was clinical in its colour,* I thought. Then the doctor came in and asked Heather how she was feeling,

"Fine, Doctor, I am ready to go home."

"You can go as soon as your father arrives with your things."

"Thank you, Doctor," I said as he left the room.

"Well, I suppose I had better get moving. I'll ring this number in a couple of days or so; that will give you time to settle back home." I kissed Heather and walked out of the room. I then called Gary, another associate who drives one of my vans to France and Belgium for contraband and liquor, to come and pick me up. I was leaving the hospital much quicker than expected.

I walked down the street to the newspaper stand to pick up my local paper. "What the fuck!" I opened the folded newspaper only to see the headline:

'Crime! Crime! Crime!'

The article states that a task force is being set up in the city to deal with the vast number of crimes. An Inspector Blakely of CID. (Criminal Investigation Department) was determined to stamp out crimes committed by Gangs on the businesses and bring those involved to justice. The local newspaper gave detail about the companies I had put together. Inspector Blakely's pale but aged face was splattered all over the front page of the local *Herald*, informing the public:

Haulage vehicle drivers are extorted! Gangs on street corners and in parks are turning our city into a drug capital! It has even been brought to our attention, alcohol and other contraband are being smuggled into our city. Let me assure the city's people, I will not rest until these criminals are brought to justice and our streets are clean once again! If anybody knows who any of these criminals are? I urge you to ring the police emergency number: 01742 668668. This is the number that we have set up for these crimes only. Please do not be afraid; all conversations will be kept confidential!"

I folded my newspaper and put it under my arm while waiting for Gary. I knew I'd have to be even more innovative than ever before. It was time to call a meeting to unite all the gang and seek new distribution methods!

We worked as shadows unseen by the local law enforcement. Now we'd have to go deeper than ever before. I knew the city like the back of my hand; there were places the Gods themselves wouldn't go. Hiding would never be a problem; it was physical bodies on the streets. My entire business was in jeopardy. It depended on the physicality of lads manipulating the cities' Pubs and clubs and the drug scene. Cigarettes were easy to offload; I could sell them from any house if we rotated every house we owned. Customers didn't care where they had to pick it up; the cheaper they were, the faster I would sell out. All I had to do was bring each carton of two hundred down from fifty shillings to forty shillings. I knew this would eat into the profits; However, the country saw a rise of ten per cent in people smoking, meaning fifty-six per cent of the country was now smoking. So, although my profits would decrease through offloading quickly, I would see gains balanced by increased distribution.

Gary pulled up, and I jumped into the car. "We have an issue?"

"What's that, boss?"

"I've sent Michael and Paul out of town to bring the Hendricks for a meeting."

"Is everything okay there, boss?"

"Oh, it's fine, Gary. It's about the drugs we sell. Michael will engage them to come over tomorrow. More around not selling LSD, to be truthful."

"But boss, it's a favourite among the younger generation?"

"We're not going to be dealing LSD; that's all that matters. However, I do need you to track the others down, Michael, Ray, Joe, Richard, Ambrose Paul, and Leroy, to meet me at my house tomorrow at ten a.m. Can you get around and tell them all?"

"Of course, boss."

Gary dropped me at my door, where Edward was waiting for me. "Bro, what are you doing here? What's wrong?"

"It's Mum; Dad came home last night and started arguing with her. I heard Mum screaming. Bernie entered our room to get Alan and me out of the house. I swear, Tony, I wanted to hit him. We ended up in Ms Boyd's. She rang the police, and minutes later, we heard a police siren, and then the noise stopped, and they took him away. Once he had been taken away, we returned to Mum; she'd taken a beating from this demon of a man. She was also frantic; she didn't see Bernie take us out of the house. I looked at her face; Tony, it was swollen and bleeding. Dad hit her, and extremely hard too."

Edward welled up; I was enraged. "That fucking bastard, I'll kill him," I screamed in front of him. "Go home, and don't tell Mum you've been to see me; I'll deal with him in my way." Edward left my house whilst I took stock of what I needed to do to overcome some of today's events. But first, I needed sleep, so I took to my bed, hoping to wake up with a clearer head.

Morning came, and I was up early, weighing my expectations for the day. I knew the Hendricks would pose a problem. LSD was a considerable investment by the Hendrick brothers and me. The police task force headed by Inspector Blakely was forever at the forefront of my mind after seeing his statement in the local *Herald*.

It was nine fifty a.m., and the first knock on my door came from the Hendrick's. Brian and Timothy together ran the drug scene in the city. Their invaluable investment of funds enabled me to set up the drug scene and giving them control meant all I had to do was talk to my contacts in the drug trade which were given to me by Adalai, and ensure the correct amounts were brought into the city.

"Morning, boss," said Brian.

I reciprocated as I showed them to my living room. "There are drinks in the cabinet if you wish. We'll wait for the rest of the lads to get here, and then we'll continue with a business plan I have."

I sat in my armchair and watched Brian, the eldest Hendrick, scan my living room. Brian was thirty-four and Timothy thirty-one. They came down from London looking to set up a business in the city. However, when I went inside, I was warned of these guys by chance, so I knew exactly how to manage them. They brought significant investment opportunities and were desperate to deal in drugs: marijuana, heroin, and LSD. But they had no idea how to get themselves set up, and that's where I came in; I had contacts arranged through Adalai in prison.

"You look as if you have done well for yourself. This is a nice gaff," said Brian.

"Yep, I like it. Suits fine," I responded. Michael, Ray, Joe and Richard, Ambrose, Leroy, and Paul turned up a few minutes later. "Come in, Michael… lads," I said as I nodded to them. We moved to the living room, where Brian and Timothy Hendrick were comfortable. "Grab yourselves a drink, lads; there's plenty to discuss." We sat around the Georgian coffee table, where I stubbed my cigarette into the silver ashtray. "Do you all know why you're here?" I asked.

"Well, it appears you don't want to deal in LSD anymore?" said Brian.

"That's correct! I don't want to be part of dealing with that drug anymore. But we're not just here for that; so much is happening, and I pay you guys lots of money to protect my interests. including any complications that arise? Does anyone disagree with that?" There was unbroken silence, just a gentle crackle of the fire from the embers of a log on the fire. "Has anybody read the local papers recently?"

"We don't bother with the local papers; there's no point?" replied Timothy.

I nodded in response and then walked over to the chair where Timothy was sitting and pulled my blade quickly from my pocket, and held it up against Timothy's throat; Brian jumped up and said, "What the fucking hell's going on?"

Timothy was scared. I could feel him trembling through the vibration of the knife I held against his throat. "Sit down, Brian!" I said sternly. There was anguish amongst the lads. "Sit down! I will not ask again." Brian sat back in his chair, giving me an intense glare. I stabbed the knife from Timothy's throat into the Georgian table. Timothy slumped back into the chair. "I feel like my throat is being cut," I spoke.

"I do not understand, boss. What has happened?" questioned Michael.

I put the local *Herald* newspaper on the table, revealing the front-page news: 'Crime! Crime! Crime!' "So, none of you have seen the local press?" The room went silent as I strolled over to sit in my armchair.

"Boss, we have evaded the police for years. What are you worried about?" said Michael.

"We've not had a task force set up specifically to rid the streets of crime, which does not take too much to work out; I own the city! Haulage, pubs, and clubs, the drug scene and contraband? I have made you all wealthy by sticking my fingers up to the police. Now I'm worried because there are lots at stake, and if we don't react quickly, I can see everything crashing around us."

"What's your plan, boss?" asked Ray.

"I want this Inspector Blakely watched. I want to know where he lives, who he's close to and even what he eats."

"Boss, he's a copper; it's going to be hard to get close to him?" said Michael.

"I'll not let everything I've built fall to ruin because of a copper. Do I make myself clear?"

"I don't want any part of this; it's going too far," said Brian.

I rose from my chair and confronted Brian in front of everyone. "I fucking made you," I said, prodding my finger into Brian's chest. "You are fucking nothing without me. I made you, and you'll follow what needs to be done." Brian sat down, looking sheepish, not uttering another word. "We have hunted for years, lads. Now I think we may be the hunted." I set out my plans to keep the businesses safe or as safe as possible.

"Brian, no more LSD on my streets; for all other drugs, keep it corner to corner until it's safe."

"I do not understand, boss. LSD has been so profitable, everyone wants it," said Brian.

"No LSD! That's the end of the matter. Joe: please hit the pubs and clubs and inform them of the situation. Michael, your haulage? I want the reins pulled in for a few weeks. Leave the drivers be for a few weeks; it will not make that much difference."

"Sorted, boss."

"Ray, take some of the lads, Colin Bray for one, team up and get the contraband to the warehouse. I want this distributed on rotation from each of the properties we own. We're less likely to draw attention this way." Ray acknowledged with a nod. "Lads, if we cooperate by following the plan, we can get through this." So, Brian, Timothy, Ray, Richard, Joe, and Leroy took off, leaving me with Michael.

"Boss, do you not think putting a blade to Timothy's throat was a bit extreme?"

"Maybe? I'm just not sure if I can trust them anymore. I had to stamp my authority. They are from the East End, Michael. I've never liked Londoners, but their investment was important then. I couldn't have built this business without it." But Michael struck a chord that left me with dark thoughts. "Michael, can you take me to my mother's house?"

"Is everything all right, boss?"

"Not really, but I'll need to deal with it." So, we left my house and drove to Hobart Street. As we cruised down the street, I looked out of the window, and seeing the young kids mired in shit, pricked my conscious once again we pulled outside the door, and I got out of the car and knocked on Mum's door as I glanced down the street, looking for any sign of Heather. Mum opened the door to see me standing before her, welling up as she wrapped her arms around me, a feeling I hadn't felt for ages, forgetting how vulnerable it always made me feel, "Is that bastard here!?"

"No, he was out all-night last night."

"Is it okay if Michael comes in, Mum?"

"Of course, it's all right."

"Michael? Take this first, and share it amongst the kids?" I took a wad of notes from my pocket and handed it to Michael. It was a gesture I frequently did to give to those in need.

I entered the hallway on the way to the living room. I could still smell the stench of dripping, which would haunt me forever. Then I caught the smell of something different, an odour I recognized, but it was more subtle amid the stench of dripping. We sat down, and I asked Mum if Dad had hit her.

"Yes, he did a couple of nights ago."

"He's dead!" I spoke. My blood started to boil as I struggled to hold my rage in.

"It's my fault, Tony. I threw a pot of pee over him from the stairs."

"What?"

Michael walked in as Mum made the statement; he smirked. I couldn't help but look at him with daggers. "What do you mean, Mum? You threw piss over him?"

"Yes, he was screaming for his tea, and I was still cleaning the house; I was about to empty the pee pot, and he screamed at me from the bottom of the stairs, and I don't know what came over me, but I just threw the pee over him. He raced up over the stairs and struck my face."

I sat on the chair, clenching my fist, boiling inside with rage, but at the same time, all I could picture was this man drenched in piss at the bottom of the stairs. I could see Michael from the corner of my eye, head bowed, staring at the floor, his shoulders shrugging quietly and laughing. I then burst into laughter. I don't know where the emotion came from, but Michael looked up at me and chuckled. Even Mum gave a wry smile. "I want you to return with me, Mum, and stay for a while."

"I cannot, Tony. It will make things worse."

"He'll not enter my house; I promise you, Mum."

"What about your brothers and your sister?"

"They can move in too. For as long as it takes."

"What do you mean, Tony? For as long as what takes?"

"To bring him to heel for all the years of shit he has put us all through."

"I will be okay, Tony, but I will consider it. Changing the subject, you couldn't do me a favour, could you?"

"Anything, Mum. What is it?"

"You couldn't pop up to Nantucket's and grab me a sack of potatoes?"

"Of course, Mum." What Mum said next had both Michael and me rolling with laughter.

"Can you ensure they're small potatoes as you get more for your money?"

"Mum, bless you. I know you are not the most switched-on person in the world, but small potatoes because you get more for your money?" I laughed again. "They are in a twenty-five-kilo sack, big or small; it's the same weight."

"I didn't realize that; I thought you naturally had more because they were smaller." Mum laughed for the first time in years.

"Michael and I will get them for you. Shall we make it big potatoes? It will make them easier to peel." Mum nodded with embarrassment. I stood up and asked, "How's Bernie nowadays? I've not seen her for ages."

"Your sister has a boyfriend, Rob, who seems quite nice."

"No fucking way! I didn't think she would ever get a boyfriend. Wow! And Edward and Alan?"

"Edward wants a job with you, and Alan's fine. But you know what it's like? None of you liked school, Alan enjoys playing football, but I have told him he needs an education."

"Michael, let's get these, um, big potatoes." Mum slapped me on the upper arm,

"All right," she said, "you do not have to take the mickey. Oh, I have not shown you the dogs. I will show you them when you get back."

"Okay, Mum." We left to go to Nantucket's. On our way, I glanced toward the window of number fourteen, hoping I might get a glance at Heather. *I thought she must be at home*, but then again, it may not be the right time to pressure her into coming home with me.

We were in and out of Nantucket's in a flash and back at Mum's; Michael carried the sack of potatoes into the pantry whilst I went out to the courtyard with Mum to see the new dogs, Penny the crossbreed and Nugget, the greyhound. Penny growled at me as I approached her, showing me her teeth whilst tied to an iron hook which protruded from the wall, "She won't bite me, will she, Mum?" as I hesitated to put my hand down to stroke her.

"No, Tony. Edward and Alan play with her all the time."

"She's beautiful, Mum," she was dark black and tan, with large paws and some large teeth. I eventually petted her head and caressed her ears which she loved. "And that's Nugget, I assume?" Sitting quietly in a cage, she was golden and so skinny you could see all her bones, but then she was a racing dog.

"She has raced twice and won both times; she is swift. She almost pulls my arms out when I take her for a walk, and I cannot take her into the park. She tries to chase everything," said Mum.

Michael put his fingers in the cage to try and greet her, but she just lay still with her head resting on her front legs, looking incredibly sad. "Hello, girl," he said, but her response was not forthcoming. "Well, it's time for us to leave, and I want to say a quick hello to Agnes before I take off. Please consider moving in with me, even if it is just for a while."

"I will, I promise."

I hugged Mum and said, "Tell the guys I love them, and I will see them soon." Then, I walked out the door and blew Mum a kiss. Michael jumped in the car whilst I knocked on Agnes's door. She, too, was surprised and gave me a big hug.

"I am so happy to see you. It has been a while," she spoke.

"Sorry, I've just been swamped with work and other things. I promise I won't leave it that long again." I told Agnes what I'd said to Mum about moving in.

"I wish she would, Tony."

"Well, she's going to think about it; that's the best I can hope for now." We had a lovely five-minute chat, but I needed to get going. Michael was sitting in the car. "Goodbye, Agnes. I'll see you soon, I promise." I then jumped in the car, and Michael drove off.

Meanwhile, Detective Blakely's task force grew as he pulled in favours from everywhere. There was a more substantial presence on the streets of police officers walking the beat. This slowed down our activity on the streets. The pubs and clubs had to pay the total price for alcohol from the breweries, which also started to hurt them.

Weeks had passed, and the lads grew ever more impatient as they sat idle, awaiting instruction. Finally, I rang Michael and asked him over. I'd need to be bold in my decisions. I felt uncomfortable with the restrictions enforced on my business, and I had no choice but to re-engage with the publicans and the club owners who were desperate for cheaper alcohol. If I didn't move forward now, I would surely lose out to any other wannabe crime syndicates outside the city. The loyalty of the lads was of utmost priority in my mind.

Michael arrived, and we sat and discussed the business operation and how we could move forward without putting anybody at risk of being caught. Inspector Blakely was a thorn in my side and needed to be dealt with, as word on the streets were of Blakely's task force questioning everyone all over the city; he was forever drawing near. "Michael? We need to halt Blakely; I need him to know he is playing with fire and that he needs to break this task force down or suffer the consequences to his family."

"Boss?" said Michael, as he frowned. "Dealing with a lorry driver differs from dealing with a police force?"

"Michael, my hands are tied. I have no choice, the lads are impatient, and the publicans are struggling as the breweries inflate prices. People are looking outside the city for recreational drugs, so we must bring everything back under control. I need to go over to the prison and see Adalai. He knows everyone. We'll need to know if anybody tries to trespass on our turf. Michael, be careful to choose the right lads."

"Will do, boss." Michael left the house to pick up the lads.

I made my way into the prison to see Adalai and seek advice.

When I arrived at the prison, which I'm thankful for being outside, as it was much more comfortable than the inside. I sat at the table, waiting for Adalai. I peered around the room, observing the screws. Adalai arrived and sat down at the table. "I'm under pressure, Adalai. I have a task force hunting me down led by Inspector Blakely; I have had to shut down most operations to keep a low profile."

"Tony, word on the street, is that the Hendrick brothers are selling LSD, amongst other drugs, on the city's border. You will need to get rid of them. They're both extremely dangerous. I have ears and eyes out there watching everyone. There is also talk they are going to bring you down," said Adalai. "Oh, and this Detective Blakely? He is a real piece of work. He leaves nothing to chance. He's busted crime rings around the country. So, you will need to watch your back."

"How can I get rid of him? I've already got somebody watching him."

"If I were on the outside, Tony, I would have him killed. But this is Blakely; he's intellectual and ruthless. Oh, and Tony, get rid of the Hendricks, or see your business ruined."

"Thank you, Adalai. I'll send in what you need. It's a small price to pay."

I had been given a chance by Adalai to work and profit from the world outside; when he called in a favour, someone was always available to carry it out. "I'll have it in by Thursday." So, we both got up, and I left the prison and went over to my Compton warehouse.

I walked alongside the canal, taking in the sights and sounds of the factories that billowed smoke out of their vast chimneys. I could hear birds twittering away in the trees and the soft water dappling as small boats moved up and down the canal. Then, moments later, I saw Heather talking to one of her friends whilst sitting on the grassy bank overlooking the canal. My heart was all a flutter with excitement. But Heather said she needed time to think about what she wanted to do with our relationship at the hospital. Should I tell her I was here or try to evade her until she has decided? I turned to walk back the way I came when I heard Heather shout my name, I made out I didn't hear, but again she called, "Tony!"

I turned around and watched as she raced towards me, dressed in a bright yellow knee-length skirt and a red poppy blouse. "How are you?" she asked.

"Fine, better off for seeing you, sweetheart." She then caressed my face and gave me a lingering kiss on the lips. Her warmth to the touch never wavered.

"You are not usually up around this way; what are you doing here?" Heather asked.

My heart ruled my head, and I said, "Just looking in on the warehouse just up there." I pointed to my dark grey warehouse.

"What is in it?" Heather inquired.

I could see she was very curious, and the time had come for me to tell her what I did for a living. I wanted her in my life so much that it hurt.

I decided it must be now or never. "I'll show you, Heather; all I ask of you is to try and not be too judgmental?" I unlocked the warehouse and turned the lights on.

"Wow! This is amazing. You could fit three houses in here; it is that big."

A green canvas covered the contraband in the corner of the warehouse. But Heather's curiosity asked what was under the canvas as it was so large. I pulled the canvas back, which revealed the contraband.

"So, this is your job! You sell cigarettes! And you could not tell me that?"

"It's not just selling contraband; it's done through the black market, as are most of my businesses." I waited for her response, but it was not immediate.

"What else do you do on the black market?"

"Alcohol, drugs, extortion, anything that will make me money. I have a team of seventy-one, including your brother, Colin! You knew what I was like when we started guying those few years ago. But Heather, sweetheart, I have a gift for this type of business." Heather sat down on an old wooden crate, crossing her legs to try and get comfortable.

"You can sit at my desk? You know now what I do for a living. I would love you to be part of it, but I utterly understand if you don't, and we can part ways here. I have loved you for so long, but if it's not meant to be, then there's no more I can do. It sounds like I am giving you an ultimatum, but that's because I must do what I think is right."

"What would happen if you got caught?"

"I'd probably spend a long time in prison."

"You do not hurt anybody, do you? I have heard so much about gangs and criminals on the radio."

I could hardly swallow my spit as the lump swelled in my throat. "Only if I must, I must keep my business safe. And the jobs of the families that work for me are safe too. This is because they are so dependent on what I do."

"So, this is how you got rich quick?" she said as she stood and walked over to me. "You want me to be part of this? Gangs and crime?"

"Oh, Heather. I want you to be a huge part of me and my business." Before I could speak another word, Heather threw her arms around my neck and kissed me passionately. She pawed at my shirt and started ripping it off me hastily; I undid the buttons on her poppy-printed blouse, baring her white bra. I unfastened her bra and bent down to caress and fondle her breasts. Cupping each one gently whilst tasting the warmth of her plump lips as they tingled on mine. I gently kissed her neck and shoulders as I moved down her tanned body to roll my tongue across her nipples which stood firm. Her arousal heightened as she nibbled gently on my nipples. We then hurried to remove the rest of our clothes. We lay on the floor butt naked as I caressed her thighs; she pulled me closer to her with arms around my midriff. I moved up and down slowly and passionately, touching and caressing every inch of her body with my tongue. Whilst enjoying her hand on my head, directing me to where her greatest pleasures were. After some passionate foreplay, we engaged in ecstasy, which seemed like the gods of love had given us the knowledge of their carnal desire. Sometime later, Heather released a big shrill and gentle sigh as she exhaled; she just lay there in her world as if she had never been pleasured.

"Are you okay, sweetheart?" I asked.

"Oh, yes," she sighed, caressing my lips again.

I lay there with immense satisfaction as I lit a cigarette and inhaled the smoke deeply.

"I want to move in with you, Tony."

I looked deeply into her blue eyes and said, "That's fantastic. When are you thinking of?"

"As soon as you want, my love."

We got dressed after a while and started to plan the move. I was so excited, happy, and in love, and most importantly, Heather knew what I did for a living too. Everything I dreamed about was coming true. I never thought negatively, but things were going so well that I couldn't help but feel a little scared.

Heather and I walked along the canal holding each other's hands. We were drawn in by the canal's water which glistened as the sun shone its light on its water.

"Isn't this romantic?" I spoke. We locked ourselves in an embrace, passionately kissing, not caring who or what was watching. We walked back to my house overlooking the river. I had a call from Michael. His voice had an element of fear as he said, "Boss, I took Paul and Vic to Blakely's house. We wore masks to cover our identities, we knocked on his door in the early hours, and when he opened it, we placed a sack over his head and forced him into the car. The bedroom lights came on his wife looked out of the window. It was dark; she could not have seen anything apart from a car driving off."

"Then what?" I asked.

Michael had no idea what I intended after speaking to Adalai.

"I told him to disband the task force, or he and his family would suffer the consequences. We then drove around and around, and finally, we kicked him out of the car at his own home. We're now nearing the warehouse in Compton."

"Do you think he got the message, Michael?"

"I don't know, boss. He is a fucking copper."

"Okay, Michael, leave the car in the warehouse and go home. I need you in the morning."

"Will do, boss."

My head was all over the place. What should I do? Adalai said to kill him. And yet Michael might have scared him enough to leave us alone. Or would this have just made things worse? I could only wait until something happened; the press might be involved. God knows. Heather stayed over, and we made love all night. She intended to move in next week. I couldn't wait.

Michael picked me up in the morning on a bloody rainy day, and we started out to deal with the Hendricks. "Michael, we must eliminate these brothers before they impact the businesses."

"But boss, they're doing their job, right?"

"Trust me, Michael they have become an inconvenience." Michael looked at me in a concerned manner. I pulled my blade from my inside jacket pocket and pushed it up my sleeve.

"Boss… really?"

"You don't have to be part of this, Michael, but I have to do it."

"Boss, we've worked together for a few years now, and my life is entirely different; I have money, a house, cars and a beautiful wife and daughter all because of you. I'll stick by you for the rest of my life, and whatever you say, I'll do."

"Thank you, Michael; you're like a brother to me." We pulled outside Brian's house, and I knocked on the door, and Brian answered. He looked dismayed at our presence at his house. "Is Timothy here as well?" I asked as I pushed passed Brian.

"Why, yes, but he is sleeping. What has happened?"

"It's been brought to my attention that you are selling LSD on my streets after I specifically said, not on my streets anymore!"

"But boss? It's easy money, and the kids are frantic for it out there."

Michael grabbed Brian's arms, holding them locked so that Brian couldn't move, only struggling to try and free himself.

"What are you going to do to me? You cannot touch me. I know too many people!" he commented, raising his voice.

"That's why?" I said as I moved up close, staring Brian in the eyes; as I pulled the blade down from my arm and punched it under his arm, perforating his armpit four times. I could feel his wet warm blood on my hand before it started to drip onto the floor, His blood spattered everywhere as he dropped to the floor. I dropped the blade and put my hands to my head, smearing my face with his blood, wondering what I'd just done. I wiped my mouth with my hand, trying to wipe away the blood. "Timothy?" I said as I stared at Michael. He raced upstairs, where he found Timothy fast asleep. Michael took a pillow, and within a few minutes, he had asphyxiated Timothy. I sat in a chair, wiping myself with a tablecloth, smiling. Michael said, "I've done it, boss; I've killed Timothy."

I left a message written in blood on the mirror: *My town. My rules!* "Make sure everything's clear outside, Michael. We need to move quickly?"

"Are we going to just leave them here like this, boss?"

"No, we need to get them into the boot of the car and get rid of it; clean up here so there's no trace of any evidence that could bring it back to us."

"There is a forest over Lowes's croft where I can burn the car. It is so dense nobody would tread anywhere near it," said Michael.

"Let's get it done! First, let's put the bodies in the car, Michael. Then, I'll start cleaning the floor to remove the bloodstains. Did you touch anything upstairs, Michael?"

"Only the pillow, boss."

"Put that in the car along with the tablecloth too. We can't leave anything?"

After scrubbing thoroughly, we took the car to my Compton warehouse. I called Brendan and asked him to meet us in his car, so we had transport out of the forest. My hands were trembling, and my head was dizzy with thoughts. I stooped so low now even to committing murder. But there was a part of me enjoying what I was doing. So, it didn't matter what I did from now on; murder was as low as I could ever go. I was out of control. I was so desperate to keep my businesses afloat that I started to neglect my natural family, Mum, Bernie, Edward, and Alan—even Agnes. I wasn't my dad or the demon I called him. I'd become much worse, a murderer, a drug dealer, an extortionist, a dealer of contraband and a fence, and I loved it so much. But parts of my head fought for dominance against my malice other side.

A life behind bars is what I deserve—locked away in a cage where beasts belong. Then, I'd be out of everyone's reach where I couldn't do damage. But I was not behind bars, and as time passed, I went to all lengths to get what I wanted.

Inspector Blakeney was not the kind of copper who would lie down without a fight. So, his task force grew, and the city was being stretched in all directions. But the business was booming with the loyalty of my gang. My alcohol, cigarettes, and drugs were competitively priced, and life was like a walk in the park.

Heather had moved into our house and soon became pregnant. The demon? Well, he continued to be the bastard he was behind closed doors. Bernie? Well, she was set to marry her fiancé, Rob. So, there were exciting times ahead. Edward and Alan were forever growing. Edward had become sharp-witted and a math genius. He could do things with numbers only I could dream about. And Alan was in his last year at school, hoping a football scout would seek him out. The estate watched him grow and develop his skills as a football player. Edward was on my payroll and getting to know the business very well. We always ensured Mum had money, which Dad never knew about, hidden in her secret place. Big Colin, Heather's brother, had trained to become a police officer, but this was his second job. I needed somebody on the inside to keep me one step ahead of Inspector Blakeley and his task force.

Colin and I worked discreetly together to ensure he made the grade in the police force. At considerable cost for those cops on the take. I had a little insight from the inside as Colin tried to get closer to any conversations around my business. In time, Colin, astute as he was, would eventually be drawn in by the task force for all the clever work he did over the months he had been there. We were bang in the middle of the middle of the 1970's with the help of the bent cops. Colin was right where I needed him.

We were racing through the seventies, and business was booming, and new innovative technology would change the world. The seventies saw the age of majority for legal purposes came down from twenty-one to eighteen, providing everybody over eighteen the right to vote.

The Rolling Stones lead singer, Mick Jagger, was fined for using cannabis. There was even an outbreak of rabies in Newmarket, some ravenous disease imported into the country by cats and dogs. People worried about everything. Even the greatest band on the planet, the Beatles, had talked about disbanding, to the horror of music fans worldwide. Demonstrations ravaged the world over Vietnam and the ever-growing nuclear arsenals. Colleges became of ill disrepute: drugs and alcohol and bell-bottom trousers. Communicating was made easy by the introduction of the mobile phone. Disco clubs started opening around the country, and these dancing clubs were jammed tight with the youth of the day and the considerable expansion in profits from our drug market. I wanted it all. My inner thoughts were simple, *if I could get away with murder, I could get away with anything?*

It was Monday morning, and the sun shone as I pulled back the drapes in the living room. Looking out my window, I noticed a blue escort car sitting outside the drive with two gentlemen inside. *Peculiar*, I thought. So, I popped outside to see who they were. The gentlemen became agitated as I approached the car, so I knocked on the vehicle's window. The gentleman sitting on the passenger side was a broad-shouldered man with red hair and a red beard. He then wound the window down.

"Can I help you, gentlemen?" I asked.

"No!" said the red-haired gentleman in a Scottish accent.

"Why are you parked here? It's a private road, and I don't like you parked at the bottom of my drive." I stared at the driver, who was about thirty years old. "Answer my question?" I asked with an intense stare into his face.

"We're just looking for a house to buy on this road for our mother, somewhere tranquil, so she can gaze upon the river."

He, too, was Scottish, "Well, this one isn't for sale. So, I'd kindly like you to move along, okay?" The driver started the car and drove off slowly. I waited until it was far from sight, then hastily moved back inside the house. I took notice of the number plate; I wrote it down. PNW 315J and placed the piece of paper in my drawer.

"Darling are you okay?" questioned Heather as she came down the stairs in a pink dressing gown, holding her tummy and cradling her baby, looking exhausted.

"I'm fine, sweetheart; I must get to work."

"Oh, can't you take the day off? It seems like forever since we spent some time together that wasn't in bed."

"You know that's impossible, sweetheart."

"But I feel so frumpy and fat."

"You're eight months pregnant; how do you expect to feel, sweetheart? Just rest. You will be glad of it once you've had our baby."

Michael arrived to pick me up for work over at Compton. "Look, sweetheart, it won't be long, and when the baby comes, I promise we'll spend more time together." I kissed her on the lips and walked out the door. "Morning, Michael," I said positively.

"Morning, boss. You're very chirpy this morning."

"Why not? The sun's shining, I will be a father soon, and everything's going well." I then pulled the paper from the top pocket of my striped suit.

"Michael, see what you can find out about that number Plate? I'll ring Colin and see if he can track down to whom it belongs."

"Any reason, boss?"

"It was parked outside the drive this morning, and when I confronted them, they told me they were looking to buy a property in the area for their mother. They were Scottish; quite frankly, I didn't believe them."

"Do you want me to return to the house once we finish business?"

"No, you're all right. I'll sort it if anything happens."

Nightclubs and boozers were opening all around the city. So naturally, I visited these new establishments to ensure they abided by my rules.

I took a phone call from Mum; she was distressed; my father had beaten her again. I was enraged; Michael tried his best to calm me down as we drove to my mum's house.

"Boss, you need to calm down."

"I'll kill the bastard!" Finally, we arrived at Mum's house, where Agnes was comforting her outside the front door. Jumping out of the car, I raced into the house, but he had fled. I returned to Mum and told her she and my brothers would stay at mine for now. "Grab some things, Mum. You're coming with me now."

Agnes cuddled me and said, "At last, I know your mum will be safe."

"Can you tell Alan when he gets home to meet me at the church on Stipple Street at four p.m.?"

"Of course, Tony, look after her. She needs some real love."

"You can be sure she'll get plenty of love at mine." Mum had bagged up a few things and hugged Agnes before she reluctantly got into the car.

"I'll be seeing you soon, Agnes, and thank you for everything," I said. We drove off with Mum staring out the rear window, tears rolling down her face waving goodbye to Agnes, not knowing if she'd ever return to the house. "You'll be okay, Mum. I promise." She nodded, at me, and said, "The dogs, they're on their own?"

"They'll be okay. That bastard can look after them and see what it feels like." We arrived back at my house, and Mum was stunned when we pulled into the front drive. I had a large water fountain with cherubs and dolphins installed on the front lawn; I watched as she gently put her hand in the water, caressing it in her palm. I opened the door and called for Heather, who greeted us in the hallway. "Sweetheart, Mum, Edward, and Alan will stay with us. So, Mum put your bag down, and enter the living room, and get comfortable. We'll get a pot of tea on."

"I'll leave you to it, boss, unless you need me for anything else?" said Michael.

"Thank you, Michael; I'll see you in the morning." I put the kettle on the stove and brewed tea for Mum.

Heather entered the kitchen and asked, "Where will we put everybody, darling?"

"Mum will have the guest bedroom, and Edward and Alan can share the double bedroom."

"Darling, I am going to have our baby very soon. It's only two weeks to go."

"It'll be fine, sweetheart. I promise we'll deal with everything as it comes."

"Okay, if you are sure, darling."

We made tea and talked about what lay ahead; Mum was a little anxious her hands were shaking, and she started to well up, but I was determined not to let her emotions get to me. So, she was staying here until I could get something else sorted out.

"Edward will be here briefly, and I'll pick Alan up at four o'clock."

"But Alan won't have any clothes, not that he's got a lot anyhow," said Mum.

"Mum, please don't worry. I'll outfit him from top to toe at Debenhams. Just changing the subject, a minute; how's Bernie? She still looking forward to getting married?"

"They've decided to get married in a registry office as it's much cheaper."

"They're not getting married in a registry office. I'll help with the wedding costs. Bernie's my sister, and it'll be the biggest day of her life. Even if I did believe she would never have a boyfriend." Chuckling to myself.

"She'll have a lovely wedding, I can't wait to be a bridesmaid, and I won't be pregnant," said Heather.

"What about you two? When are you going to get married?"

"When we're ready, Mum," I swiftly changed the conversation to discuss what we could have for tea. "I fancy fish and chips. What do you fancy, Mum?"

"Oh, I am not sure; I'm not hungry?"

"Shall we all have fish and chips?"

"That sounds nice, and I'm not putting you into too much trouble, am I?"

"No, Mum," said Heather. "It will be lovely having you here, and if I'm honest, it would be nice to talk to somebody else outside the cleaner, Sue. She is beautiful; she comes in every day. I get so tired, and I am not allowed to move because I am pregnant, and according to your son, he thinks it's too much. I keep telling him it's a baby, and I am not ill. I am pregnant."

"I heard that, sweetheart," I said as I walked back into the living room after having a quick shower. "It's not like that! You have two weeks before giving birth, and I want to ensure you do as little as possible. I looked at my watch, "It's half past three, and I need to walk down to St Peter's Church to meet Alan; I'll see you ladies later."

So, I left the house to go to St Peter's Church; as I turned right out of the driveway, I noticed the car that was outside my house just up the road. As I neared the car, I could see both driver and passenger sitting and waiting in the car. I pulled my blade out of my pocket and knocked on the car window. I got a glare from the red-headed Scotsman seated in the passenger seat. So, I struck again; this time, he wound down the window. "You guys still here?" I questioned. "I did tell you there were no properties for sale on this road. So, what are you doing here?" I moved my head closer to the window with my blade clenched in my hand.

The driver responded sarcastically, "I told you, looking for a property for our mother."

I knew something wasn't right; my gut instinct told me they were here for me, so I swiftly put my hand in through the car window, and with my blade clenched tightly, I pushed it into the Scotsman's throat. I took them by surprise. The redhead trembled in fear for his life. The driver went to turn the ignition on to try and drive off.

"Leave it! Or I'll cut his throat." I slowly pierced the redhead's throat.

"Okay!" said the driver, pulling his hands away from the ignition.

"Any movement and I'll cut his fucking throat!" I pulled the mobile phone from my pocket and rested it on the car window as I punched in Michael's number, with some difficulty; I needed support as I didn't know how long I could hold them. "Where are you from?" I asked.

"Glasgow," replied the driver.

"Why are you here?" I questioned.

"Property, looking for property."

"But I told you there weren't any properties available this morning?"

The driver looked at his redhead passenger and then looked to me and said, "Okay, we are thieves. We rob houses like these because they are stinking rich. That's the truth, I swear."

I penetrated the redhead a little more with my blade.

"I swear, we are telling the truth. Look in the back of the car; you will see some tools for breaking in." Moments later, Michael arrived, screeching the car to a stop behind their vehicle.

"Boss, are you okay?"

"Yes, Michael. Get out of the car," I said to the driver. He slowly got out, and Michael put his massive hand around his throat and pushed him up against the car. The guy was petrified. Michael was a monster of a man with tattoos down one side of his face. With his hand around the guy's throat, the Scottish wanker was always going to tell me what I needed to know. So, I took the redhead to the car's boot with my blade against his throat.

"Open it!" The redhead opened the car's boot. It was full of jemmy bars, hammers, glass cutters, gloves, and overalls. "There's no work here for you, so try your luck somewhere else… like London. If I see you back here, I'll ensure you'll not be able to loot any more. I fucking own this city, now fuck off."

The guys jumped back into the car and sped away. "Thank you once again, Michael. I'm running late for my little brother, Alan. Can you drop me at the church and bring us home?"

"Of course, boss."

"Michael, I need bodyguards. On a few occasions, I've needed help, even relying on you to get me around. And you know when you get a feeling, I keep feeling it, and I'm concerned with the baby due."

"Of course, boss."

"Anyhow, how's Nora and the kids?"

"Loving life, boss, all thanks to you; we owe you a huge debt of gratitude."

"Don't be silly, Michael; I love you like a brother."

We got to the church, where Alan waited patiently, dressed in his black shorts, white T-shirt, and football boots, and holding a brown leather ball. "Hi, little one," I said.

"I'm not little; I'm sixteen," he replied.

"Yes, you are, but you're still little, but one day you'll grow into a fine man like me." I smiled at him.

"I've been told I'm coming to live with you in your big house overlooking the water?"

"That's right, little one."

"Is Mum, okay?"

"Yes, Mum's fine and warm too now; let's get you back." Alan jumped into the car, and we made our way home.

"How did school go today?" I asked.

"Okay, did some English, RE, spellings, and art and then played some football ready for next week's match against St. John's School, who are unbeaten."

"How many games have you won?"

"Four out of five. If we can beat St John's, we'll go top on goal difference, which could get us into the southwest finals."

"Wow, little one, didn't realise you were that good?"

"I'm only as good as the team."

I looked at Michael and gave a wry smile. I was impressed by my littlest brother. We quickly done some shopping and then returned to the house, and Alan went to see Mum. "Michael, get me five men you can trust one hundred per cent to protect the house and me when I'm active? Even if you're in the car, the extra bodies will come in useful it also shows my status in the city."

"Boss, are you worried about something or someone?"

"I've had a few altercations recently. I don't want to feel isolated anymore. I'm starting to feel like I might have a target on my back; there's a lot at stake."

"It will be our best men, Ray, Joe, Dexter, Leroy and Ambrose." Leroy and Ambrose were of Jamaican descent. They came to our country in 1963.

"What about the haulage, Michael?"

"I think as Edward wants to take over, we could hand that over to Edward; you want him to learn more about the business. This would allow him to show you what he can do."

I nodded to Michael; it made sense, and Michael was a colossal bodyguard to have around. "I'll let him know later when he gets here. Thanks, Michael."

Michael left, and I went into my house, gagging for a drink and a cigarette. Then, sitting in front of the open fire watching the flames, I started contemplating how and where I could set mum up in a house close to me.

"Are you okay, darling?" asked Heather. I looked at her smooth-skinned face and said, "Yes, but there needs to be a few changes around here."

"But why, darling? The house is fine."

"Protection!"

"Protection from what?" questioned Heather.

"I've had a few altercations lately, so I'm bringing Michael, Ray, Joe, Dexter, the guy with long curly hair, and Leroy and Ambrose to use as bodyguards and protect the house."

"I do not understand, darling. Why do we need all this protection? What have you done?"

"It's the business we're in; it will always be a bit dangerous; that's why it pays so well." But Heather had a concerned look on her face. I took a drag of my cigarette before I flicked it into the flames. Heather went out to the kitchen to finish making tea. I looked over at Mum and Alan sitting beside each other on the couch, looking warm and cosy.

"Heather?" Mum shouted. "Can I help you with anything?"

"No, I am fine. Everything is under control; I will dish up when Edward arrives."

Mum and I were chatting about Agnes, and when she took me in and looked after me for Christmas, I think I'd have been in the gutter dead if she hadn't found me when she did. I remember being wet, cold, and hungry in that doorway.

Suddenly there was a crash from the crockery in the kitchen. I shouted, "Everything okay, sweetheart?"

"No! No! Darling, I need you."

I hurried through to the kitchen, where I found Heather standing in a pool of water, holding her tummy with broken crockery all around her.

"It's the baby; my waters have broken."

"Don't panic, sweetheart; everything will be okay, Mum... I need you," I hollered. I quickly called an ambulance. "Quick! Quick! She's having a baby," I shouted down the phone. "It's six Bayswater Road; you've been here before a couple of years ago."

"Please do not panic, sir. I need to take some details while the ambulance is on its way to you."

After giving her the details, I put the phone down and returned to the kitchen. Mum had Heather sat down, leaning up against the kitchen wall.

"Breath slowly, Heather, slowly," Mum whispered calmly.

"Darling, get my overnight bag; it's in the cupboard at the top of the stairs," she said, panting heavily.

How could she be so calm, I thought? *While I'm rushing around like a headless chicken.*

"How often are your pains, Heather?" asked Mum as she put a cushion behind Heather's head.

"Every five or six minutes," she replied, gripping Mum's hand tightly with every contraction. Ten minutes had passed, and there was still no sign of an ambulance. The contractions were every four minutes. "Mum, can you deliver a baby?" I asked, "I don't know what to do." I thought the baby was going to be born in the house.

"Alan, wait outside for the ambulance," I yelled. Alan rushed out to the drive and waited for the arrival of the ambulance. Heather was bellowing swear words out in pain while Mum tried to calm her. I was a shivering wreck. All my anxieties had come to the fore, leaving me guilty because I didn't know what to do but hold Heather's hand and wipe her brow. Then, another contraction came, and I was getting apprehensive. "Where's is that fucking ambulance?" I stared at Mum, trembling uncontrollably.

"It'll be here soon, son."

Moments later, I heard the siren of the ambulance. "It's here, sweetheart; the ambulance is here; you're going to be okay."

The paramedics took Heather to Freedom Fields Hospital, to the maternity ward, and a couple of hours later, Heather gave birth to our beautiful daughter. I sat beside Heather, looking at this miracle we had made—a child with fine blonde hair, a tiny nose, and green eyes. I put my baby finger into the palm of this miracle, and she half clasped it gently.

"She's so beautiful," I cried, kissing her on her soft forehead as I took her into my arms, wrapped in a crochet blanket. Then, cradling and rocking her so gently. "You're going to have many admirers," I whispered. I then handed her gently back to Mummy. I kissed Heather on her lips and said, "You're an amazing woman, and I love you so much."

"I love you too, darling, but I am so tired I just want to sleep."

The nurse came over to put our beautiful little miracle into a crib in the baby ward with other babies. I peered through the window and blew her a kiss to wish her goodnight, and then I went home to sort some things to take back into the hospital—the following day.

I arrived home and told Mum, Alan, and Edward the excellent news. As you can imagine, there was a lot of excitement. Mum has her first grandchild. I rang every one of importance to us. And to tell Michael he'll need to take over the businesses for a few days. Word got around of our new addition to the family. We had cards galore coming through the door. Over the next few days, I would set up a party for family, friends, and colleagues. Heather and I sat and discussed what we could call this miracle baby, and we produced Zilah, a Hebrew name meaning shadow. Everybody said it was very unusual. But we loved it.

Heather was on her feet after a week and could get around comfortably. So, we dressed Zilah in a white dress over the top of a white baby grow and a little white bonnet; she looked beautiful. We then walked her to Hobart Street to see Agnes. If a thousand people didn't stop to look at the baby, then I must have been dreaming. Everybody wanted to hold her and compliment her on how beautiful she looked. Eventually, we got to Agnes's house. Before we knocked, I asked Heather, "I know she'll be so deliriously happy for us, and would it be okay if she could be a godparent to Zilah?"

"That's a great idea, darling."

I knocked on the door, but there was no answer, so I struck again.

"She must be shopping. She doesn't go out anywhere else; I will visit Nantucket's. That's the only place she shops."

"I will wait here, darling,"

I raced up to Nantucket's, but they said they hadn't seen her for days, which was strange because Agnes spent half her life in Nantucket's. So, I hurried back to Heather, who waited patiently outside Agnes's.

"Nobody has seen her for days, sweetheart?" I was concerned. This was peculiar and strange; it was not her routine. I knocked once more, but again there was no reply. I peered through her front room window, but it was dark inside. I could hardly make out any shapes. "I'm going around the back lane to see if I can see anything in the kitchen window."

"How are you going to do that, darling?"

"I'll climb over the back wall." I went over the wall and looked through the kitchen window, and my heart stopped as I saw her lying face down on the kitchen floor. I kicked in the scullery door from the garden which led straight into the kitchen. "Agnes, it's Tony," I said as I knelt beside her. But there was no movement. I tried to find a pulse on her neck and wrist, but nothing, I then placed my head on her back to see if I could hear her breathing, but it was to no avail. I turned her over, and She was cold and bluish grey. Our Lord God had taken her. I was heartbroken at my loss; I forgot that Heather was outside.

I managed to conjure up the strength to ring for an ambulance and then contacted the police. I walked to the front door to Heather, who had no idea. I burst into tears. Heather looked scared and shocked as I buried my head in her shoulders. "She's dead! Agnes is dead!" What seemed like moments later, the police and ambulance crew arrived.

In no time, there were people everywhere coppers, doctors, paramedics, and the street residents looking shocked. Everyone respected Agnes Boyd. She was a significant loss to all. I sat on the pavement outside my mum's house; Dad was not there as usual. Then a copper came out of the house and asked me some questions,

"How did you find her, son?" The copper questioned. I told him everything, and he took everything down in his notebook. Then the doctor came out, I then watched as two gentlemen took a trolley into Agnes's house.

"How did she die?" I asked.

"Heart attack," we think.

"What happens now?"

"We will take her to the hospital morgue. Do you know if she had any family?"

"She didn't have any family. She was a single child, and her parents died years ago." I then watched as they came out of the house, with Agnes wrapped in a black bag on the trolley they took inside; they put her in the ambulance and drove away. The copper shut the door, and he, too, drove off. I had to return home and tell Mum Agnes was dead. I knew she would be distraught. I gave

Heather a big cuddle, and we started to walk home to give Mum the grave news.

Whilst walking home, Heather asked me if I thought Mum would be all right.

"I don't know; they were best friends for so long; Agnes had always been there for her through thick and thin, and someone Mum would always use when she needed a shoulder to cry on." We got home; Mum was sitting on the couch watching the flames in the fire.

"Hi, son, go on; tell me how excited Agnes was?"

"Mum... You need to stay sat down for a bit; sweetheart, could you make a pot of tea?"

"What is it, Tony? You have a face like thunder. What is going on?" mum said, frowning and concerned.

I took her hand and held it tightly. "Mum," I paused momentarily. "Agnes is dead! She had a heart attack."

"No! No! She cannot be dead," she said as she shook her head. She then burst into tears. "It can't be true." Heather brought the tea in with lots of sugar. She poured Mum a cup of tea and put three sugars in the cup. They say it helps with shock. You could hear the chinking of the cup and saucer as Mum's hands trembled. Heather comforted Mum whilst I tried to ring the hospital to see if Mum could see Agnes before she was taken away for good. That proved a little troublesome, but eventually, as she had no family, they allowed Mum to see her, but it would not be until tomorrow.

"You can visit tomorrow, Mum."

Zilah started crying, so Heather took her to another room to breastfeed. Mum was so upset I couldn't calm her down; it didn't matter what I tried to do. Finally, I had to go outside for a cigarette. I was struggling with all the grief in the house. Then to top it all, I got a phone call from Colin.

"Tony? Inspector Blakely is closing in."

"What, Colin? What do you mean he is closing in?"

"Somebody reported the Hendricks were missing?"

"Shit! Do we know who called the police?"

"An anonymous caller also gave the inspector the full address. This morning's brief was about Sergeant Keel getting a warrant from the court to enter the premises."

"So! What difference does that make? They'll never find out where they are. They could be on holiday or moved to a different district. Could be anything, Colin."

"I am just worried if they find anything at the house, like fingerprints. Did you and Michael clean everything?"

"Of course, we did. We're not idiots. We cleaned and then burned everything; you're worrying over nothing." Dismissing it.

"I hope so, Tony, for your sake."

"Agnes, Ms Boyd... I found her dead today. Heart attack, they say. I'm going to miss her so much." I struggled to utter the words over the phone.

"I will miss the old dear too; may she rest in peace... Tony, the Phoenix pub on Phoenix Street, is under observation. The inspector believes it is taking in illegal alcohol, so you must get somebody over there and warn them."

"Thank you, Colin." I rang Michael and told him we needed to get over to the Phoenix pub.

"Certainly, boss."

When he arrived, I updated Michael on the Hendrick situation. "You didn't touch anything else upstairs apart from that pillow, did you?"

"No! Nothing at all."

We arrived around the back of the Phoenix pub, where nobody could be seen. The pub was quite busy. We went to the bar where John, the proprietor, served this beautiful blonde-haired lady wearing a two-piece grey suit. She wasn't the sort that would drink in this place. The lady looked classy and well-educated; I looked her up and down. She just stared right back at me with a smile.

"Sorry, miss, but I must take this gentleman away from you for a few minutes."

"What is it, Tony?" asked John.

"Michael, can you keep this lovely lady entertained for a few minutes."

"The pleasure will be all mine, boss."

"Ooh, is that your boss?" I heard her ask Michael whilst I was still in earshot range as I walked behind the bar and into the back room with John.

"You're being observed by the police, John. They think you're getting your alcohol from someone else and not the brewery."

"But how would they know? And how do you know they know, Tony? Your alcohol is brought in overnight, and your lookouts ensure we are always clear," said John.

"I don't know, John, but they're watching anyhow. First, you must buy through the brewery for a few months; that might eliminate any scent. After that, you need to find out if there's someone you trust putting you at risk, and I'd find out quickly!"

"Thank you, Tony."

I went into the bar for Michael, who was still chatting with this lovely lady. "Can I buy you a drink?" I asked.

"Why not?"

"Same again for this lovely lady, John, and I'll have my usual. Michael, did you want another?"

"No thanks, boss; I must return to my wife and kids."

"Once again, thank you, Michael."

"I will see you tomorrow, boss, unless you need me urgently. Oh, miss, get him to have a few. He's had devastating news today."

"Thanks for that, Michael. So, what brings a girl like you into this pit house? No offence, John, it's not like some of the nightclubs that have recently opened." John shook his head and put his tea towel on the bar to serve a gentleman.

"So, you still haven't answered my question?" I pulled a cigarette out of my pocket and put it into my mouth whilst offering one to the lady. She took one out of the packet whilst staring into my eyes.

"Don't mind if I do," she responded. I lit her cigarette with my lighter, then lit mine and took a slug of my cognac.

"Cheers." As she raised her glass towards me, I reciprocated.

"I am so sorry to hear you have had devastating news today. Do you want to talk about it?"

"Not really but thank you anyway."

"I am a reporter for the local *Herald*, and my name is Beryl."

Initially taken aback, I hesitantly said, "Nice to meet you, Beryl. So, what would a classy lady like you be doing here?"

"Just getting to know some of the locals, I tend to be stuck behind a desk most of the time writing columns. But I have been allowed to spread my wings, so here I am."

I started to wonder whether this was coincidence with the pub being observed.

"So, what sort of things do you write in your column?" I asked.

"Could be anything? Whatever's worth's reporting."

"But as a columnist, wouldn't you look for specifics for your column?"

"Depends? Enough about my work. I deal with that all day. So, what do you do for a living? No, let me guess. A smart suit, striped tie, and wicked black and white shoes, looking dapper! So, you must be a businessman?"

"Yes, I am." I nodded my head whilst grinning.

"So, what kind of business do you do?"

"Oh, you know, this and that." I tried to move away from that conversation. Then her hand touched my knee as she leaned in a bit closer. I could smell the aroma wafting from her perfume.

"So, you haven't even told me your name?" She closed right up to my face to kiss me. I pulled away from the attempted kiss. She looked a bit perplexed, but I was with Heather, a father, and I was happy.

"My name is Tony, and I'm sure we'll meet again. I hope you get what you are looking for in your reporting. But I must go, business and all. Hope we meet again."

She smiled at me and said, "I cannot wait," as she brushed her hand along my forearm. I exited the Phoenix and wandered up to the picture house to see what was on, *Cromwell,* a biopic of Oliver Cromwell, who led the parliamentary forces during the latter stages of the civil war.

He turned lord protector of England in the 1850s. I scrolled down the window to see if anything else interested me, but nothing did. After what happened this morning, I was desperate to get out of the house and spend some intimate time with Heather. So, I arranged for Mum to look after Zilah while Heather and I sat and cuddled in the back row of the picture house watching *Cromwell.*

We couldn't have been more than ten minutes into the film when we were all over each other, kissing away like crazy. You would've thought we'd just been together for weeks. We didn't even give ourselves that much time to eat our popcorn.

"I love you, sweetheart," I said as I came up for air.

"I love you so much too, darling, but aren't we supposed to be here for the film?"

The film finished, and we moved next door to Monroe's nightclub, owned by me and a friend called Zakaria. He came over from Jamaica in the 1960s, too. We met in a club outside the city, looking for a business. I helped finance the club for fifty per cent of the profits, which was a sound investment. I sold drugs, alcohol, and contraband through the club.

"Good evening, boss," said Devon, the bouncer, as we moved through the doors past all the youngsters waiting to dance the night away. I put Heather's coat behind the cloakroom. "Put it somewhere away from the stale smoke, please, Mary?"

Mary took Heather's coat and told me it was on peg number one, my favourite number. "Thank you, Mary." We stepped inside the club to a kaleidoscope of coloured walls and silver balls dangling from the ceilings giving a sparkling effect of silver specs on the dance floor. I was amazed.

I took Heather to the private sitting area with burnt orange leather chairs and mahogany tables on a beautiful gold carpet. Deana, one of the servers, brought some drinks for Heather and me, and said Zakaria would join us shortly.

"Wow, this place is lovely. How come you have not brought me here before?" asked Heather.

"Well, the baby and all that; made it difficult, but you're here now." It was one of those moments where you wish you'd waited a moment before you responded.

"What do you mean the baby and all that? Or were you too ashamed as I would have looked a bit fat, carrying 'our' baby?"

"I didn't mean it like that, you're beautiful, and the place didn't look like this before; it was a bit run down, so I let Zakaria update the décor and a bloody excellent job he has done." Heather turned away and put her glass down on the table. I could feel myself getting annoyed as I let out a loud sigh. "Bloody women," I said under my breath.

"Wah Gwaan, Tony," said Zakaria as he tapped me on the shoulder.

His greeting perplexed Heather, so I told her, "It means hello in Jamaica."

"Hi, Zakaria." I shook his hand. "You've done an amazing job with this place." I nodded in approval.

"You must be Heather? You are very 'criss,' that means pretty, Heather."

"Why, thank you, Zakaria," replied Heather. "This place is terrific."

"Bringing the customers in is the most important thing," said Zakaria.

"Any troubles?" I asked.

"Nothing, the odd fight here and there, but Devon and the lads always sort it out."

"Great; anything you need from me, Zakaria?"

"No, all good and profitable. Well, I will catch up with you a little later."

I lit a cigarette whilst admiring what Zakaria had done to the place—listening to Elvis Presley's 'The Wonder of You' playing through some prominent boxed speakers hung in each corner of the dancefloor. I sat doing that people-watching thing. What were people wearing? What made them laugh? What made them dance until they could not dance anymore? I had so many questions I wanted answered. Heather was the manager of a clothing retailer, so she was always on trend with the latest fashions; long gone were the miniskirts and thigh-high boots of the sixties, for maxi dresses, which came down to ladies' heels. It certainly stopped the youngsters from jumping everywhere trying to interpret their dance choice.

Instead, it was mellow and smoochy, everyone holding each other, listening to the changes in the music of the last decade to some great songs. Then 'Hey Jude' came on, and I asked Heather to dance to one of my favourite songs. So, we walked to the dance floor, me in a striped shirt and black slacks and Heather in a pale green maxi dress. Her beautiful long curls and wavy blonde hair made people look at her everywhere she went.

I held her with one hand around her waist and the other outstretched as if we were going to waltz through the record, whispering sweet nothings to each other. Then, a man had too much to drink and bumped into Heather, wasting his drink over her dress.

I saw red, grabbed him by the throat, threw a punch into his face with great intensity, and knocked him out cold as he fell to the floor. People screamed in horror as I stood there looking down, smiling at him, enraged over a spilt drink. Finally, Devon and another bouncer came over and asked if I was all right.

"Yes, now get the tosser out of here." I said abruptly.

"Yes, boss." They picked up the man and threw him out of the club. Heather was mortified by my behaviour and wanted to go home.

"There was no need for that! It was just a drink! What is the matter with you? I've not seen such rage!"

"I'm sorry, sweetheart; I overreacted."

"I want to go home now. That poor guy will feel the effects of that tomorrow."

"Well, I'm going to stay here for a bit; I'll call you a cab." I know I blew our night out; Heather jumped into the cab without saying anything.

"I'll see you back home." But Heather was upset and said, "Don't bother; I do not want to be disturbed." And the cab drove off. So, I returned to the club, grabbed a bottle of cognac and a glass, and sat back down in the private seating area, trying to console myself through alcohol. What a fucking horrible day.

What a fucking idiot I am, I thought to myself. When I heard my name, "Tony?" whilst I sat with my eyes closed, listening appropriately to 'Bridge over Trouble Waters' by Simon and Garfunkel.

142

I opened them to see Beryl, the reporter from the Phoenix. "Following me?" I asked.

"I just came out for a few drinks with friends when I witnessed this brutal incident. What did he do to deserve that?"

"I overreacted; it was as simple as that. Is that the sort of thing you put in your column?" I said arrogantly.

"Oh, we are a bit touchy, aren't we?"

"Don't patronise me. I didn't ask for your company, did I?" I took another slug of cognac. Then Beryl put her elbows on the table, leaned forward and asked if I wanted a dance.

Sulking like a kid, I snapped, "No, thank you!"

Beryl got up and walked over to the bar. I couldn't help but let my eyes follow her, she was a hot babe, and blond-haired babes made me horny. Beryl wore a peach-coloured maxi dress in a pinafore style with slits that went right up to her thighs, high-heel-wedged shoes with two thick gold bands holding her feet in, and a gold-coloured shoulder handbag. She came back in my direction, enjoying a glass of alcohol. She glanced at me, and using my hand, I gestured for her to sit at my table.

"I'm sorry; I was rude I didn't want to be. I was compelled to say go away, but that's not normally my nature."

"It's okay; please do not worry about it. I am not."

"It seems you have a forgiving nature," I said. Beryl just shrugged her shoulders and smiled.

"What's in the glass?" I asked.

"Vodka and orange, would you like to try some?"

I took a sip and found it disgusting. It was best described as turps. It was something I didn't want to taste again "That's disgusting!" I spoke. We sat there for ages, and the night moved on swiftly as we talked, and laughed about anything and everything. The club was busy, and she was taking my mind off the day's earlier events Time was moving on, and I needed to get back home. Then before I could say anything, Beryl asked me to dance again.

I hesitated. "No, I'm not in the mood to dance." But Beryl was having none of it. She insisted, grabbed my hand, and pulled me out of my chair.

"Just one, then." We walked onto the dance floor to 'A Whiter Shade of Pale' by Procol Harum.

She put my hands around her waist and moved tight to me as we moved gracefully on the floor, catching the light from the silver glitter balls as they flickered in her face. Her eyes and the subtle scent emanating from her body drew me in. I felt relaxed and at one with her, but I don't know why? I questioned myself, *Was this just the drink and a bit of flirtation?* Everything felt so weird. My emotions were spiralling out of control. "Come on, Beryl; I need to go."

"Are you not enjoying yourself?" she asked.

"Too much. It has been delightful."

"One more song, come on, you can manage that," she said, smiling but tipsy and giggling like a teenager. Again, I found her deliciously exciting and beautiful.

I said, "Last one, and I mean it." Trying to talk sternly to her.

"Ooh, okay then, better make this the last one." She wrapped her arms around my neck, puckered her lips and planted them on mine. I didn't resist because I was enjoying it. But as the song continued to play, we clutched each other closely and kissed again. I knew this was all wrong, but I felt compelled somehow; she had taken me under her spell.

"Where are your friends?" I asked.

"Oops, they left me on my own." She gave me a sympathetic look.

"Well, we'd better get you home, hadn't we?"

"Oh yes, please," she replied seductively. I put my arm around her to help keep her balanced as we slowly walked out of the club. Once we hit the fresh air, she asked me for a cigarette, so we sat on the steps outside the club while I lit her cigarette. It had turned fresh outside, and Beryl had not bothered with a coat, so I put my suit jacket around her to help take the chill away.

"My place or yours?" Beryl asked.

"Yours," I said. "We'll get a cab. What's your address?"

"Wouldn't you like to know?" she said, slurring her words.

"Of course, I would; how else will I get you home?"

"Carnegie... Carnegie Road, number eleven," she said as she held my arm with hers, smiling and hiccupping simultaneously. I noticed a cab pull up and let some youngsters out to come into the club, so I grabbed Beryl's hand and put her in the cab's backseat. I jumped in and asked the driver to take us to Carnegie Road.

"You're such a gentleman, aren't you?" said Beryl.

"I can be, but not all the time. I get by in what I do and who I am."

We pulled up outside Beryl's house. I paid the driver while Beryl was trying to unlock her front door. I guess the cocktails had left her a bit intoxicated. I grabbed the keys from her hand and opened her door to this ghastly decorated hallway. Dark green with brown wooden doors, you couldn't see where or how to turn any lighting on.

"Where are the lights?" I asked.

"There, just there on the wall." She pointed.

I couldn't see it. "I can't see it. It's so dark?" Beryl moved to the hallway wall feeling her way to the switch that she would be the only one to ever find in the dark.

"There you go; I told you it was there. Could not see it," she said, slurring her words whilst looking so innocent.

"Do you want to drink, Tony?"

"Have you got any cognac?"

"Umm… No! Vodka? Oh no, you do-do not like that, do you." Stuttering her words.

"Give me anything; it doesn't matter." While Beryl was trying to find me a drink, I stood up and scanned everything around the room. There were photos of Beryl collecting awards for her journalism—one with a man much older than her. A teak-effect coffee table with a notepad and pen was placed openly on a page detailing the

Phoenix pub. *So, she is up to something? Was she part of the task force?* I thought.

"Here you are try this one. I made it up myself." Beryl offered a tall glass of what looked like an ale with a lemon wedge hanging off the top.

"What is it?" I asked.

"It is a pale ale with a squirt of lemon and a lemon wedge for decorating. It is my drink I made up; go on, taste it? Taste it if you dare?"
It was revolting, but I praised it for keeping her happy. She looked at the pad on the table and discretely closed it.

"My work is boring, and my life is shit!" Whilst swigging her vodka, feeling sorry for herself.

"Who's the gentleman in the photograph?" I pointed to the photograph on the wall.

"That's my father. He lives up north. I don't see him very much, just once in three years. We didn't get on too well. He didn't care about me." She said whilst welling up.

"What about your mother? Is she still around?"

"No, she died when I was two."

"Sorry to hear that; I'm unsure what I'd do if I lost my mother." I had to be careful what I said. I couldn't let my guard down. Beryl grabbed my hand and practically dragged me upstairs to the bedroom after falling on the stairs twice, which Beryl thought was hilarious as I fell on top of her on one of the occasions.

We moved towards the bed, and Beryl started to undo my shirt buttons as I gently pulled down her zip from around her back. Whilst we were embracing and kissing. I undid my trousers and let them drop to the floor. Beryl's maxi dress dropped to the floor moments later. Standing in my underwear, I watched her struggle with her white bra. Eventually, the bra fell, and she was left in her panties. I admired her curvy body and perfectly formed breasts for a fleeting moment. She pulled me onto her bed. And I quickly lay over her. I quickly turned her over onto her front so I could kiss her back, using my tongue to taste every pore on her body. She sighed quietly moving her body as I continued to arouse her. I caressed her buttocks as my tongue moved with haste to the pleasures of her body. My tongue raced to lick every piece of her skin whilst she oohed and aahed. She turned over, and I started kissing her forehead and nose and gently caressing her lips; her arms wrapped me gently as she scratched her nails. The neck was the next area to be stroked by my tongue, and down her side, it went. She pulled at my hair as she became more aroused. I kissed her belly button and said softly, "Now, do I go north to the mountains and their peaks?" I looked at her perfectly formed breast with nipples erect. "Or do I go south on man's perilous journey in search of Beryl's clitoris to heighten her senses even more?" Beryl stretched her arms above her, and I started caressing and playing with her breast; I moved my tongue back and forth over her nipples as Beryl cried, "Oh, yes." She then grabbed my head, moved it down to men's most challenging journey, and let my tongue ravage her moist clitoris.

"Oh, God." she cried. Up and down, my tongue went foresting for new delights. I eventually moved on top as my penis swelled, ready to succumb to Beryl's inner secrets. I held Beryl's arms as I thrust my penis inside her. It was warm and comforting as I moved as hard as possible whilst Beryl gripped my buttocks. I began to sweat, as did Beryl. I turned her over so she could straddle me on my back, where we moved in rhythm to our erotic emotions. A few minutes later, I turned her back into the missionary position; I held her legs high and thrust with eagerness to bring her to climax.

"Yes, yes, yes," she bellowed out. "Aww..." I continued to thrust until I exploded inside her. Beryl yelped even more. I turned onto my back, exhausted from the physical effort.

I lay there full of guilt as Beryl fell off to sleep. What have I done? I love Heather so much. How could I be such a fool? I swiftly sorted myself out and called a cab. I left a note on the bedside box just saying, 'Thank you xx.'

The cab pulled outside my home, and I got out, staring at my bedroom window, wondering what I'd done. The immense guilt I felt was crushing in my head. I unlocked the door and went into the front room, where I lay on the sofa to try and sleep. I then heard footsteps coming down the stairs. I sat up expecting Edward or Alan, but it was Heather's figure when the light came on.

"Where have you been? It is four o'clock in the morning."

I had to think quickly, so I said, "With Zakaria, we had a lot to get through. You didn't want disturbing, honestly, I neglected the time."

"Zilah was unhappy last night; she cried a lot. Your mum struggled to get her settled. I gave her a feed from me, when I got home, and she eventually went off to sleep and will undoubtedly be awake soon. Are you coming to bed?"

"No, I need sleep, and if Zilah is due to wake up, I'm better off down here." Heather shook her head and went back to bed. My head was banging. All I could think about was last night, and as good as it was, I'll now have to carry this overwhelming guilt I'm feeling for the rest of my life.

It felt like five minutes had passed when I awoke to see everybody sitting at the breakfast table.

"Good night, bro?" asked Edward.

I just went upstairs to shower and get ready for work without replying to him.

Mum asked Heather if I was alright; Heather told her what time I had got in last night. Mum told Heather that four o'clock in the morning was unacceptable.

I returned down the stairs to a squalling Zilah and everyone else yapping at the table. I thought about how long I'd have to endure all this noise. I know I sounded horrible, but it's all becoming too much. I called Michael to do some business outside of the house. "I'll see you later, Heather." I kissed her goodbye.

"What time will you be home, darling?"

"Five… maybe six?" I left the house and lit a cigarette while waiting for Michael and the lads. Autumn was here. You could smell the air from the coals burning, bellowing out smoke through the chimneys. I sat there thinking of Bernie's wedding, and why would you hold it in the Autumn? It was three weeks away, and I needed to catch up with her and her fiancé, Rob.

Michael turned up with a car full of bodyguards. Two bodyguards, Leroy, and Ray, stayed around the house while we took off in the car. A lot of muscle with good sense, I hoped. They were there to protect me.

"Michael? We have some jobs which involve running around; first, I want to visit Rob's house, then to Compton and then to my old street to see my father."

"Woah, boss. Your father?"

"Yes, Michael, my father."

We arrived at Rob's house on Cremyl Street. Small and compact, it stood on cobbled stones that looked as if they needed a good clean as the weeds were taking over. I knocked on the door, and Rob answered.

"Hiya, Tony, please come in; Bernie is upstairs doing her hair."

"Is it okay if the lads come in too?" I asked.

"Of course, come in, gentleman."

We went inside and found seating for all. Rob put the kettle on to make some tea whilst I went up to see Bernie.

"Sis, you look more amazing every time I see you."

"Wow, which is praise from you. Normally you are slagging me off."

"Yeah, I know, but I love you. So where are we at for the wedding?" I questioned.

"My dress and Rob's suit are ready, the rings are both ready, and we have rehearsed at the church. Which you didn't turn up to! The reception? That is at your nightclub, Monroe's."

"That's great, sis, and I've got the cars sorted. What about bridesmaids? Are you having any? Besides Heather.

"Yes, and they are sorted. My flowers are prepared."

"I'm sorry I couldn't make the rehearsal; the business was the priority at the time. What's Mum wearing?"

"Mum's wearing a long dress with a pretty flower design and a wide-brimmed pale blue and white hat to match. What about the honeymoon? Have you sorted out where you're going?"

"No, we are going to wait. We cannot afford a honeymoon just yet. But Tony, I cannot thank you enough for all you have done for Rob and me and this wedding."

"Sis, I love you. But you know me, I'm all about family. So, if you're going to have a honeymoon, where would you have gone?"

"Rob and I were talking about Hawaii, which is why we're going to save?"

"Wow! That would be nice." She gave me a massive cuddle; it made me so happy to see her happy. "I have to ask the question, so I'll get it out as fast as possible." She turned to look at me with a look of concern.

"Who's walking you down the aisle?" I asked.

"I want you to give me away, Tony."

"What about him?" Implying the demon. "Do you want him at the wedding or not?"

"No! I don't care if I ever see him again. I don't love him."

"I'll be delighted and proud to give you away, sis." I went downstairs to chat with Rob, and he, too, could not thank me enough.

"You ensure you look after and treat her right, or you'll bear my wrath. Come on, lads; we've still got work to do. Be seeing you, sis, on your wedding day, most probably. I'll try and get around before if I can."

"Love you, Bro." Bernie shouted.

Out to the car we went, and off we drove. "Michael, let's get over to the warehouse."

When we got to the warehouse, I laid out some plans; it would be a busy few weeks ahead I needed to leave the business in Michael's hands. "I need you to take over the businesses, Michael, for a few weeks. I've places to go and people to see, I've also got the wedding, and I need to find a house close to me."

"Well, you know everything is safe with me, boss."

I handed Michael the keys to the warehouse, amongst other places. "It's all yours now, Michael. Now to my father's house."

"Boss are you sure this is a clever idea?" Questioned Michael.

"I'm sure." We pulled outside the house, and I got out of the car; Michael was getting out too. "No, Michael, I will deal with this."

I knocked on the door, shaking as I didn't know what to expect. The demon had been home for a while on his own. The door opened, and he appeared wearing pale green pyjamas in the middle of the day; I was surprised to see him even at the house; considering racing was on, he'd typically be at the track.

"What do you want?" he asked sternly.

"Can I come in?" He left the door ajar and turned to walk back through the house; I looked at Michael in the car and gestured for five minutes with my hand. Then, finally, I walked in and closed the door behind me. He sat in the front room on his chair, so I sat on the couch. I knew this was going to be a complicated conversation.

"What do you want?" he asked abruptly.

"I came here to tell you Mum is okay and smiling for the first time in years. And she will not return if I have anything to do with it." I took out a cigarette and waited for his response. But there was dead silence in the air for a few moments whilst I inhaled the nicotine in my cigarette.

"Who do you think you are talking to; you piece of shit? Who do you think you are? Look at the way you dress. You look like a fucking ponce."

"Is that so, I grew up with you, getting beaten at any slight comment, we all prayed there would be a day you would never return. You were never a father; you were a demon and a bully. You practically starved us to death. Listening to Mum scream through the beatings you gave her. Now she's safe and away from you, living a better life with me. So, I can say what I like and look the way I look because I keep the family safe and well. Something you couldn't do or wouldn't do?"

"She will come back… I know she will," he spoke.

"You arrogant piece of filth. It will be over my dead body," I replied.

"Really? Your illegal work and your bullies do not frighten me. You are just a fucking drug dealer, a thief, and a racketeer?"

I stood up and threw my fist at him catching him in the face, he rocked back, and I continued to let fly with my fists. I then screamed, "Yes, that may be true. But I support the family as the head of the household. You're just nothing. Go and live with your cronies. You'll not like living alone, and you won't be able to beat or shout at anyone. What's life been like for the last few months?" I shouted, wanting him to hurt inside without the family being around.

He got up with his blood-spattered face and said, "Mind your own fucking business. At least I do not have to put up with that fucking nosey bitch that used to live next door."

The animal inside me took over and although I struggled to swallow my spit as my throat tightened. I laid into him once again. Beating and shouting, "Agnes was a person, you bastard, who cared about people and someone I loved because I couldn't love you. I'm fucking telling you; you'll die a lonely old man." I made my way out of the house, leaving him bloodied and cleaved on the floor, swearing never to go back again. He can die where he lay.

"You okay, boss?"

"Yes, I'm okay; if you can drop me down to the town centre, I need a large drink."

"Boss, what have you done? Your hands are covered in blood?"

"It's okay, Michael; I haven't killed him, yet. Ambrose, you come with me. Joe, I need you to stick with Michael, okay, lads?" We stopped at the Bristol Castle pub, and Ambrose and I jumped out of the car.

"Michael? Any issues, ring me." We entered the pub. I was still shaking from beating the Demon; I asked Arthur, the owner, to give me a bottle of cognac and a glass.

"There you go, Tony." He put the bottle on the bar.

"Out! Everyone out! Now!" I shouted. Everyone scattered, and I sat at a table drinking cognac. Three glasses, I downed quickly. "Ambrose, do you want a drink?"

"No, boss, I'll stand at the door, so nobody comes in."

I drank three-quarters of the bottle whilst sat in solitude. I then got a call from Colin. "What can I do for you, Colin?" As I fiddled with the glass tumbler.

"Inspector Blakely has found some blood at the house that belonged to the Hendricks?"

"Colin, that's impossible? We cleaned everything?"

"There were bloodstains on a mirror with the words: '*My Town. My Rules!*' They have forensics taking blood samples and fingerprints from everywhere."

"Fucking hell, Colin, I did write that; I forgot about it. How fucking stupid of me?" I threw the glass tumbler at the bar in my frustration.

"I have other news, which is not good for you, Tony. I have been offered a new position within the Metropolitan Police in London."

I was angered as I tossed the table over. I started to feel uncomfortable and anxious, twiddling my fingers, worried about the world I'd built, which could crumble around me. Without Colin down here, I've nobody on the inside. I buried my hands in my face, closed my eyes, and tried to think briefly.

"Are you okay, Tony?"

"Colin? Congratulations, when do you move?"

"Four weeks, Tony. I will do everything possible to get you as much information as possible before moving."

"Colin? I would still like you to work for me; I'll guarantee a higher wage than you'll ever earn working for the police?" But it wasn't about money; it didn't matter how much I could offer; Colin enjoyed his work. So, I put the phone down, knowing that I would have to tread carefully without Colin and the safety of his networking on the inside.

"Come on, Ambrose, let's get a cab. Thank you, Arthur." I left him some money for the damages, then put an added hundred pounds on the bar and told him to split it between the households with children in the street. It was dirty, and the kids wore next to nothing. And if he needed any more to contact me." We left the Bristol Castle and went back to my house.

Meanwhile, Michael communicated with all the lads in the business to tell them he'd be taking over the company for a few weeks, and everything needed to go through him.

I arrived home to hear Edward moaning because Michael was taking over the business and not him.

"Bro, you're not ready for that kind of responsibility. Michael has been with me from the start, he knows the business well, and has the respect of all the lads."

"What is that supposed to mean? Are you telling me I don't have respect?"

"No, bro. I'm telling you Michael is running the business whilst I concentrate on other matters for the next few weeks. So now I don't want to hear anything more about it."

"Well, I know where I stand, boss." With that, he walked out of the house.

"Hi, darling, how's your day been?" asked Heather.

"Did you know your brother has a job lined up with the Metropolitan Police?"

"Yes, that's great news. I am so chuffed for Colin."

"You do know he works for me, too, right? Or are you just being stupid?" Heather looked at me, disgust written all over her face. I had never said anything like that before to her. She stormed out of the room and ran up the stairs crying. My head started to hurt as I tried to pull myself together. I went upstairs a few moments later and caught

Heather crying into her pillow and Zilah sleeping in the cradle.

"I'm so sorry. I didn't mean what I said. I've just had a horrible day."

"You do not have to take it out on me. I have done nothing wrong?"

"I know, and I said I was sorry."

"What is going on with you lately? You seem different somehow; you do not seem yourself. Can I help?"

"If you can convince your brother to stay down here rather than go to London, that would be the best help I can get now."

"Why do you need him here? He is getting promoted. We're all so proud of him; why can't you be?"

Heather never had a clue. She'd have a fit if she found out Colin was giving me criminal investigation information. Not alone, I've maliciously hurt someone and even killed them.

"I don't get you anymore?" She stared at my hand, which had swelled after punching my father. "Where did that come from? What have you done?" She took my hand and gazed at me, shaking her head.

"What's with the interrogation? I don't fucking need this. I need to go over to Miller Way. I might be an hour or two." I walked out the door for the first time, feeling much better than I did inside the house.

"Do whatever," Heather screamed.

I waited outside for a few minutes trying to clear my head. Then, finally, I re-entered the house and told

Heather, "Look, if I can get back before eight, do you fancy going for a drink? We couldn't have a better babysitter, could we, with Mum here?"

"I will think about it. But I am not in the mood now; let's see what happens if you can get back here before eight."

"Okay, sweetheart, maybe you'll be in a better mood?" I replied sarcastically, I grabbed my jacket and called Michael for transport to Miller Way to look at a four-bedroom house which had been up for sale for quite a while. It was not too far from me, accessible to some shops and close to the river.

We pulled up outside. The description in the paper didn't match what we were staring at. It seemed creepy. I noticed an old swing right back in the corner of the front garden. We walked up the overgrown path leading to the house's front door, where the number sixty-six hung upside down on the door. I peeked through the window; it was dark, but some boxes were in the middle of what I assumed was the reception room. There was no door knocker, so I banged on the door a few times, but no one answered. Finally, I took a cigarette out and lit it with my lighter. The for-sale signpost said: 'If anyone is interested, do not hesitate to contact the estate agent on this number.' I tried the number, but nobody bloody answered.

"Great! Come on, Michael, I have the details. I'll try again tomorrow. Can you return to the house and let Heather know I'll be back shortly? I've some shopping to do."

"Certainly, boss."

I wasn't too far from the city centre, so I took a stroll. There was a full moon, and as I looked up at the night sky I could see the darker shades on the moon, like majestic mountains. The clear skies made the stars in their multitudes so bright. The North Star was visible, and you could make out the group of stars that shaped Orion's belt. Two squares that looked deformed whilst joined together. I enjoyed Astronomy but there were no teachings out there. I then found myself standing outside the travel agents Thompson. I entered and was greeted by a lovely lady in a blue uniform.

"Hello, can I help?"

"Hopefully, my darling? I'm looking for a holiday in Hawaii for my sister, who is getting married in a couple of weeks. It's for their honeymoon; please help me out?"

"I'm sure we can find something for you even at this late notice; please take a seat."

I sat down opposite the lovely lady called Fiona. That's what it said on her badge. Fiona was scrolling down her computer, checking the world for holidays; it took ages, but she found me a week for two in Hawaii, which I set out to book, so my job was done.

"Thank you, Fiona." I left and went back to the house. "I'm home," I shouted. Mum was sitting cosying up near the fire. "Are you okay, Mum?"

"Yes, lovely and cosy; Heather has cooked a beautiful tea. I thought it was scrumptious."

"What is it?" I asked.

"Boeuf bourgon? Or something like that."

"Sounds good." I popped into the kitchen, where Heather plated up my tea—already dressed to go out. "You beautiful thing. You look stunning, sweetheart." My mood had changed, and I complimented her on her outfit. She was wearing a white polyester midi-dress with a multi-coloured flower pattern, a V-neck with tight waist fitting, and gold-coloured stiletto shoes.

"Food smells lovely, sweetheart?"

"It's Boeuf bourguignon?"

"I know; Mum made me laugh when she tried pronouncing it." I chuckled while kissing Heather's neck.

"Get off me; there's no time for that."

"I can always find time for some of that, sweetheart. You know you want to?"

"It has taken me ages to cook dinner, so you will sit and eat it. When you have finished, you can get dressed, and then we will go out for a few drinks. So, behave yourself. I do not want to spill anything on my dress."

"Is that me being told off?" I jested. Heather gave me that look, head bowed on her chest with eyebrows raised. I consumed the delicious meal Heather had cooked and went upstairs to get ready to go out.

I put on my purple shirt, black trousers, and black and white spats. I splashed on some aftershave and went back downstairs. "I'm ready, sweetheart; let's get some drinks?"

"You have not even picked up your daughter today. Don't you think you should cuddle her before we go out?"

"Yep." I went over to the crib, but she was sleeping; I touched her face with my index finger knuckle, which wasn't the best idea because it woke her up. I plucked her out of the crib and held her, talking daddy language, only to fall foul of her throwing up all over my shirt. "No! I don't believe it." Heather and Mum thought it was hysterical.

Heather then said, "I didn't like that shirt." Whilst still laughing. "Give her to me; I will sort her out."

"There you go, sweetheart, mind she doesn't throw up over you!" I changed into a black shirt whilst Heather changed Zilah's Babygro. "Alan and Edward shouldn't be too long, Mum," I said as we walked out the door.

"You two have a good night!" she shouted.

Once we got downtown, I told Ambrose to go home until the morning. "There is a new bar opening tonight next to Diamond Lil's called the Woodhouse. Shall we try it, sweetheart?"

"Why not? It might be better than some of the shitty pubs around here," expressed Heather.

Well, it was eight forty-five p.m. and quite dark. All you could see were the lamppost's dim lights shining on the cobbled floors. An eerie fog fell in the centre of town, making it difficult to see anything more than a few yards in front of us. Then suddenly, I felt something heavy hit the side of my head, and Heather screamed as I felt myself falling to the floor. My stomach felt as if it had been hit by a car. My face exploded like I had dropped from a window with such ferocity. The faintest of sound came from

Heather; I must have fallen unconscious because I don't remember anything else.

When I eventually woke, I was in the hospital with an oxygen mask and tubes coming from everywhere. I saw Heather sitting in a vinyl chair next to the bed, reading a book, from the corner of my eye. I tried to move my right arm to reach her, but it was sore, and I could hardly move it. My left arm was in a sling; I couldn't grasp the mask to speak out. I lifted my right leg, hoping Heather would catch a sight; it worked; Heather turned to look at me. She hastily got up and shouted for the nurse. She rushed back to my side, gently grabbed my hand, and said,

"Thank God you're awake," tears started rolling down her face. Then the nurse approached the bed, and a doctor entered the room.

"How are you feeling?" asked the nurse.

I tried to speak but struggled under the mask. Then the doctor came beside the bed and removed the mask from my face.

"How are you feeling, Tony?"

With a shallow voice, I said, "Like I have been run over by a train. What happened?"

"It appears you and your good wife were viciously attacked by a couple of thugs," said the doctor.

I felt mortified. I looked at Heather in fear of what had happened to her.

"I am okay; the guys just pushed me to the ground. Honestly, I am okay."

Then the nurse escorted Heather for a cup of tea, leaving the doctor beside me at my bed.

"What's the damage, doc?"

"They left you with a cracked skull, your right arm has some severe bruising, and your left arm is badly sprained. You have bruising on your ribs which feels very painful? Generally, how are you feeling?"

"Groggy, my head hurts, my arms hurt, and my ribs are very sore?"

"We will get some pain relief to ease the pain. Can you remember anything?"

"No! not really. When will I be able to get out of here, doc?"

"A couple weeks? If your recovery goes to plan. Try and enjoy your time with us, Tony."

The doctor left the room whilst I lay there in pain and disbelief. Worried about Heather and the businesses, giving me no rest, I couldn't wait for Heather to return to the room. My mind was full of dark thoughts: *Who? And why?*

The door opened, and Heather walked in with red puffy eyes where she had been crying. "Please tell me what happened, sweetheart?"

"It all happened so quickly. First, two men came from behind us. One of them had a red brick in his hands and smashed it against your head, pushing me to the floor. I watched as they kicked and kicked and kicked you repeatedly. Then, finally, I screamed aloud, and people came running out of the fog to help."

"Did you see who they were? Did you recognise them?"

"No, darling. But one of them was shouting in a Scottish voice."

I lay there holding Heather's hand whilst thinking back to the Scottish guys we thought were burglars looking for properties to rob. "Heather, I need Michael; you must ring him and get him here quickly."

"Of course, I will ring him. There's something else I need to tell you, darling?"

"What is it, sweetheart?"

"I am pregnant! I hurt my back when they pushed me to the floor, so the doctor did precautionary scans."

I didn't know whether to be happy or sad; I was in so much pain, and in truth, I was petrified; all I could think of was my family was alone without my protection. "Michael, I need Michael. Please ring him, sweetheart."

Heather went out to ring Michael and must have gone out one door whilst Colin entered the front entrance because he came into the room with a uniformed police officer.

"How are you, Tony?" he asked.

"Colin, I'm okay. Some bruised bones and ribs and a cracked skull are not helping my breathing."

"Well, this is Constable John Brown, and we are here to investigate this vicious attack. Oh, Officer Brown, Tony is Heather's other half."

"It's nice to meet you, Tony," said the constable.

"Okay, Tony can you tell me what happened in your own time?" asked Colin.

"Not a lot. Heather and I were walking to the new bar by Diamond Lil's when something hard hit my head. That's all I know, Colin. You might get more from Heather; I was out cold."

"That's no real help; I'll catch up with Heather later and see if she can shed more light on the attack."

"Heather's here, Colin; she popped out to make a call." We had a chit-chat together whilst waiting for Heather. I asked Colin how he was doing.

"All right," he said. Then Heather walked into the room.

"Hello, Colin; what are you doing here?" Heather asked.

"I have popped in to see you, sis," He then kissed her. "This is Constable John Brown."

"How do you do, Officer?" she replied to Colin's introduction.

"I have been put in charge of this investigation to find the bastards who viciously attacked you. But Tony does not remember anything of worth."

"We were on our way to that new bar opening next to Diamond Lil's when two guys came from behind us and hit Tony with a red brick in the head and then attacked him, kicking and shouting at Tony. They pushed me over and continued to kick him until a gentleman who must have heard me screaming came out of the fog with a significant other in tow, and then they ran off."

"Did you get a look at them, Heather?"

"No, not really, one had ginger hair, and he spoke with a Scottish accent. But that is it. The next minute, we were both in an ambulance."

"Would you mind getting some tea, Officer Brown?"

"Of course, sir. I will see what I can do." The officer exited the room to fetch tea.

"Right, Tony, tell me what happened?" said Colin.

"Not here, Colin; I'll get Heather to ring you when it's easy to speak."

Colin shook his head. "Are you both okay?"

"Brother, I am pregnant!"

"Congratulations, Sis. That's fantastic news. Hoping for a boy this time?"

"It would be nice to have one of each. I think that would be our perfect family," said Heather.

"Colin? I need you to be close to Heather until I leave. We are both in danger. I have Michael on his way over."

"You need to be more forthcoming with your information, Tony, if it's likely to put Heather in danger?" With that, the officer came in with tea for all of us.

"I don't feel great. Would you mind if Heather and I could have some privacy?"

"Of course, Tony. Sis, let me know if you can remember anything else?"

"I will do, Colin. Thank you, Officer," said Heather.

"You're welcome, Mom," said the officer. Colin and the officer left the room. The nurse walked in with some pain relief and to take some ops.

Being sarcastic, I asked the nurse, "Is there was any chance we can be left alone?"

"We need to stop the pain, Mr Bell. We must also monitor your vital signs; you have been in a coma for days," she said calmly. I rolled my eyes; I just wanted some private time with Heather. The nurse left, and I quickly engaged in a conversation with Heather. "You're going to be all right, sweetheart."

"Why? Why would they attack you in such a violent way? You must have done something awful?"

"I've done nothing, sweetheart. Michael will be here soon, and you'll be fully protected."

"I do not want protection; I want to live normally. I do not know if I can do this. I do not want to be worried every time I walk out the door."

With that, Michael entered the room. "Thank heavens you are okay, boss."

"Michael, I want six guys around the house. Listen to me!" I tried to grab him by the hand. "I want them armed! A guy hangs around Duke Street in a black Anglia car. He can get what you need at whatever cost."

"Boss, why wasn't Ambrose with you?"

"I told him to go home; it's my fault. But Michael, it was the Scots?"

"What, those two ginger fuckers we sent on their way?"

"Yes, Michael. Colin is overseeing the investigation."

"That is good, boss. Isn't it?"

"Michael, take Heather home and get the lads around the house for her protection; the police officers will sniff around. I will keep you informed if they are due to come around to see Heather. It would help if you tightened the business. Let Edward take some responsibility. Now, get Heather home."

"I'll see you tomorrow, sweetheart." Heather leaned over to kiss me on the forehead. "I love you, darling, and I will see you tomorrow, try and get some sleep."

"In this place? You're laughing." I blew her a kiss, and they both left the room. I was conscious Bernie's wedding was only a couple of weeks away; I had to be fit enough to walk Bernie down that aisle. I needed to do whatever it took.

Over the next few days, Michael took charge of everything, even to tracking down the Scottish guys' car while they were looking for places to rob. Heather continued to try and have the protection removed. But I was insistent we had the protection at home for everybody's safety.

Mum came into the hospital to see me, which was lovely. She sat beside the bed and told me all the gossip. We did laugh. The beauty of it all was she never once mentioned my father. Then she said she had something to tell me, but I had to swear not to tell anyone else:

"Swear to me you won't say a thing to anyone, swear it!" she demanded.

"Okay, Mum. I'll never tell anyone what you're about to tell me."

"Not even Heather."

"Not even Heather, Mum?"

"No! Not even Heather… I've just been told I have lung cancer…."

I lay there stunned, feeling sick, knots twisting in my stomach. I couldn't quite grasp the reality of what Mum had just said. Those few moments in the deaf silence we were sharing were cutting me up. Was this God getting me back for all those sins I had committed? I looked across at Mum, tears rolling down her etched face. I couldn't speak. The lump in my throat was slowly choking me. Mum's tears were more than I could bear, but she had a look on her face as though she had known for a while; I gripped her hand tightly. I just wanted to hit out at everything as the pain increased inside my head. "No! No! This can't be happening?" Between the pain and tears, I asked Mum how long she had known and her life expectancy.

"Three months? I have a year at best."

"What can I do, Mum? How can I help you?"

"There is nothing anybody can do for me, son. It is all down to God now. I can have treatment out there, but it is unlikely to benefit me, given the cancer is quite aggressive. It is also a painful process, and that bothers me when you are sick. So, I have told them I do not want treatment. My God will take me when he is ready. I want to live as normal a life as possible."

"There must be doctors worldwide that can treat you, Mum; doesn't matter how much it costs?"

"I did ask the question, but they said it's just a waste of money."

"No, Mum!" I screamed. A doctor rushed into the room to see if everything was all right.

What is it?" asked the doctor, "Is everything okay?"

"I said no! It's personal." The doctor could see there was a moment we were sharing. He turned and left the room.

"I love you, son, more than anything in the world, and I'm so sorry to give you this sad news."

Mum kissed me and said she would return in a couple of days. I lay there shocked; this couldn't be happening to my mum. Waves of emotion came over me. I'd cry one moment, and the next, I'd be angrily punching the wall. I tried to think of everything; there must be something I could do. Have I explored every avenue? My thoughts led me nowhere. I then started to question God. Why would he take this beautiful lady? How would I keep a secret as massive as this? It was far more than I could bear. What was I to do?

A week later, I was making excellent progress from my injuries and looking forward to leaving the hospital. However, Bernie's wedding was just nine days away. I couldn't wait for it. The doctor told me I would make the wedding, but I still had to protect my ribs and my arm.

"I don't care, doc. It's the right arm that's important." Then, the doctor left the room, and Michael walked in. "Update me, Michael, please?"

"Everything is going well, boss. Business is flying. Your brother is doing a fantastic job. We have not had any visits from the police, and there's little media around us now. You are looking so much better, boss. The only thing I have not finished is those fucking Scots. I have sent Paul, Joe, Boris, and Micky up to Glasgow to ask for information to try and find these Bastards! Even to the extent of giving a significant reward."

"I want those bastards found, and who they work for?"

"Yes, boss."

"Business apart, Michael, are you looking forward to the wedding? It will be a great piss-up."

"Yes, after everything that's been going on, I will need a good drink."

"Can you bring me a bottle of cognac and some cigarettes, please?"

"Boss, you are not supposed to drink or smoke here."

"Michael, bring in what I've asked for, and don't say anything to Heather. She'll kill me."

"Okay, boss. If Heather does catch you, you will not be coming out of here before the wedding," chuckled Michael.

"Just get them in here; the quicker, the better," I said.

"I could always ask Heather to bring them in?"

"Hahaha… Get out of here; you wind up merchant." Michael hurried out the door.

It was the wedding day, and everyone was dressed in fine clothes. There were suits and ties for all the gentlemen and the ladies—what a pretty picture. Bernie looked so beautiful in her long white wedding dress with a lace top and veil. The bouquet was red and white roses with an odd carnation. I was so proud to be taking her down that aisle. I was so full of nerves people would've thought I was about to get married. I knocked on Mum's door,

"Who is it?"

"It's Tony, Mum."

"Come in, son." I opened the door, and Mum was standing in front of the long mirror, trying to adjust her hat to fit comfortably, standing in this long blue and white dress with a white bow tied on the front and a large blue and white hat with a peacock feather in it looking stunningly gorgeous.

"Can you help me with my hat, son?"

"Of course, Mum." Whilst pinning Mum's hat on, all my thoughts were of Mum and how long it would be before God would take her from me. My Zilah will not remember her because she's just a baby. I wept a few tears; Mum asked if I was okay.

"Yes, Mum." I made out the tears were for Bernie when they were for Mum.

Everybody set off for St Peter's Church apart from Bernie, the other bridesmaids, Heather, and me. We all looked fabulous. There were lots of family and friends making their way into the church. "You need to go around the block, please, driver. We're not ready."

We took a turn and arrived back at the church a few minutes later. This time the priest came over to the window of our car and said the organist still needed to turn up.

"What do you mean the organist hasn't turned up?" I said abruptly.

"He must be held up. But I can play the organ?" said the priest.

"Well, that's great. I need you to do the service," I said sarcastically.

"Sir, I can play the organ and then rush down to perform the service."

"What a fuck-up. Sorry, Father, we'd better do that then, hadn't we?" The bridesmaids exited the car, followed by Bernie and me with her veil down. She wrapped her arm in mine, and we slowly walked down the aisle. Everybody stared at us, and there was quite a lot of chit-chat in every row we passed. Eventually, we found our place, and after a few moments, the priest returned from playing the organ, and after a few words from the priest, I handed Bernie over to Robert.

I then sat between Mum and Heather for the rest of the service. Mum was an emotional wreck; the immense joy of seeing her daughter marry was tainted with the sadness of the reality of what she was facing in the coming months.

We thanked the priest for the beautiful service and went to Monroe's for the reception. Colin said he had something to tell me, but this was not the time; it was my sister's day, and nothing would spoil it.

When the cars started pulling up outside Monroe's, I'd have imagined the talk between the guests would've been something like, "What the fuck? Who are these other men?"

I had been attacked recently and ensured it wouldn't happen today. So, there were three exits, and I had two men in grey suits and black ties at each door to look like some of the wedding party. But they were all carrying guns underneath their jackets.

"Tony, who are these people?" asked Robert.

"Some assholes had robbed the club a couple of weeks ago, so I wanted to make sure people knew there was a reception inside, hoping that would deter anybody trying to break in as it's daytime."

"Oh, I see; it just looks a bit heavy, Tony?" said Robert.

"It's my business. I must take care and look after it."

Sat on the top table, white linen adorned in red and white roses, I stood firstly to toast the bride and groom and then tried extremely hard to give a father speech as her brother; I found it difficult and strikingly weird. But I got through it and left the best man, Edward, to do his speech. It dragged on for a bit but with all good intentions. They looked delighted together. As the day wore on, the fluids flowed, as did the drugs. I swapped the guys outside to enjoy a couple of drinks as well.

Cognac after cognac, bottles flowed, and the guests started dancing. Of course, there was beer everywhere, but I didn't give a fuck; I wouldn't be cleaning it up.

"Tony, Tony, come sit down. I have something to tell you?" said Colin.

"What is it, Colin? Can't you see I'm trying to enjoy my sister's wedding day?"

"I think you might want to hear what I have to say."

We sat down at the table whilst everybody was dancing or gabbling away. "Tell me what's so important then, Colin?"

"I'm not going to London to join the Metropolitan; I'm staying here."

I just stared with disbelief, "You're fucking joking, aren't you?" I said as I put my arm around his shoulder. "Why have you changed your mind?"

"I fear for my sister. She is carrying another baby, and you have gotten into serious situations. I am better off down here where I can also track Inspector Blakely."

"You have helped make this an unforgettable day. Come on, have one of these." I poured two cognacs into two tumblers and handed one to Colin. "Cheers, Colin." I offered up my glass. Heather walked over to see what we were chatting about, and I gave her the good news. She looked at Colin and then squeezed him tightly.

"Thank you, Brother." Heather then turned to me, gave me a sloppy kiss with a huge hug, and then shuffled back to Mum's table.

"Come on, Colin, let's go and have a few drinks with my brothers." We walked up to the bar where Edward was talking about his nerves doing the best man speech to Alan.

"Donna, can we have a round of drinks here, please?" I shouted as she was some distance from my seat at the bar, and the music was loud.

She went to walk down toward me when this guy, who didn't know who the fuck I was, stopped her and said,

"I was here first; you serve me, darling?"

Donna looked at me and then touched the guy's arm. "I will be right back to you, sir. Do you not know who he is?" as she looked in my direction.

"I couldn't give a fucking toss; who is he, the one-arm bandit?" His mistake was saying it too loud and taking the piss out of my arm, which was still in a sling.

Edward and Alan followed me down.

The prick looked over my shoulder and said, "Brought your babysitters with you, aye?"

I turned away from him and shouted, "Does anybody know who this prick is and why he's here?"

Robert came over and said, "Yeah, I know him, he's Peter an acquaintance of mine?"

"Get rid of him, Rob, before he comes to any harm."

Robert tried to reason with him, but he had none of it. Meanwhile, one of the other bartenders called upon two of the door attendants. They came up behind him as he started to look a bit threatening.

I was determined not to get into a fight, especially on my sister's wedding day. I instructed them to remove this prick and whispered to them to kick his fucking head in. That would ensure he did not come back in. My lads grabbed him and started marching him out of the building.

"I'm sorry, Tony, I haven't known him that long," said Rob.

"No, Rob, don't say sorry to me; this is your day as well as my sister's; now come on, everyone, let's keep the booze and the dancing flowing." The lads later came in to tell me they gave the twat a good beating. I appreciated it and told them to get a drink.

We were well into the evening when Heather and I managed to sit Bernie and Rob down. "How are we doing, guys? I hope the day has been brilliant, Bern, but Heather and I just wanted to put the cherry on the cake."

"My darling, do you want me to tell them, or do you want to?" Heather handed Bernie an envelope and said, "This is your wedding gift from us."

Bernie took the envelope out of Heather's hands and opened it. To her surprise, she saw it was tickets to Honolulu, Hawaii. "That's your honeymoon, guys; I hope you get the best out of it?"

Heather put her arms around my shoulders whilst looking at Bernie and Rob's faces at our wedding gift and gave me a huge kiss. Bernie and Rob were overwhelmed.

"It's for tomorrow?" said Bernie in an excited tone.

"Yeah, so you guys need to get your skates on." Bernie wanted to say something, but I said, "Not now; pack quickly for your honeymoon."

Bernie and Rob said thank you and disappeared. Zakaria took care of the club whilst we all made our way home. Apart from the odd moment, some of us had too much libation after a lovely wedding.

Heather put some nibbles together at our house and made Mum a cup of tea; Edward and Alan were in the games room playing American pool. Mum was tearful. The day was all too much. I tried to comfort her until Heather came in. She said she wished Dad had been there to see his daughter get married. I was astonished; by all the pain and hurt he caused over the years, and she says she wished he were there. So, I told Mum bluntly, everybody else didn't want him there, including Bernie, and it was her wedding.

The following day, it was back to the day job; Edward had disappeared to continue extorting lorry drivers. Michael continued to track down my attackers. I returned to Hobart Street to the old house to see if my dad was in. I knocked. Bang… bang… bang. Dad opened the door, saw it was me and slammed it shut in my face. So, I hit again.

"What do you want?" he snapped.
"I need to come in. I have a few things I need to tell you. I thought you might be interested. I followed him into the kitchen; the place was a shit house. There was dirty laundry on the floor in the scullery, empty packets, and some corned beef tins on the side in the kitchen, and the bed was filthy. "I take it you haven't found a skivvy, then?" He glared at me, but he knew he couldn't hurt me. "Bernie got married yesterday; she didn't want you there?"

It was the first time I saw him look disappointed; he put his head down on his chest. I could see that it hurt him. I then inflicted more pain than he could bear when I told him Mum had lung cancer and had just months to live.

He became enraged, lifted the table, and threw it to one side as the bits of pottery smashed to the floor. He screamed at me as his tears rolled down his face, "Get out! Get out!" he cried.

I laughed and left him broken and angry, which I wanted to achieve; he had hurt the family so much over the years.

Although I've always been about family, I didn't see him as family; he was cruel, selfish, a bully, and a chauvinist pig.

The weeks and months passed by, and my business was booming. Colin had reported that the investigation into the murders of the Hendrick brothers was going nowhere; they had no leads. Michael had found the car with no tyres on it in Glasgow Street.

This led to all the businesses using more human resources for protection. There was no weakness in the operations at all. After weeks of trying to get hold of the estate agents for the house on Miller Way I was trying to buy for Mum. I eventually had a return call.

"Hello, Mr Bell? I apologise for not getting back to you, but I have been out of the country for a few weeks. However, the Miller Way property is still available, and the buyers are looking to sell quickly."

"What will they take for the property?" I asked.

"They're asking for £3,720."

"No! That's too much for around here? I will offer £3,200, which is my best, and it will be cash; they can take it or leave it? I need an answer in the next twenty-four hours." I then hung up.

Two hours later, I had a call accepting my offer, which was good in one way but surprising in another; I thought *there would be some haggling before the agreed price*. I arranged to meet the estate agent the following day at the house to sign the paperwork and take the keys.

He drove to the house in a red sports car with a big bonnet. It looked smart. "Hello, there, Mr Bell." He offered his hand to shake mine, Michael looked at me and then screwed his face up as if to say, who is this? I knew what Michael was thinking, *He's a person with dwarfism?* He was short and skinny, wearing a blue suit that looked too big on him and brown shoes, which was not today's look.

"Where are the owners?" I asked.

"They are now living in San Diego. It is nice if you are rich, isn't it?"

The agent drew the dusty curtains open in each of the rooms.

"For a large house, there's very little light coming in?" I then grasped the Balan stair, and it practically collapsed.

"This is a dump," said Michael.

Then the agent got a little defensive, "You have got it cheap. What do you expect? Look how big the back garden is?" He opened the back door.

"That's a tip as well?" said Michael. "What are you trying to offload here?"

Michael and I walked up the garden path to get an idea of how big the garden was. It was severely overgrown, so bad you needed a digger to move the bushes. There was an old shed at the top of the garden.

"What's in there?" I asked.

"I do not know, Mr Bell, I have never seen it opened. The glass window has always been painted."

"Do you have the keys for the lock?" I asked.

"Yes, but I left them at the office, sorry?"

"And the tree, is that something I can pull down?"

"No, Mr Bell, it has a preservation order on it," stated the agent.

I smirked and then pulled a cigarette out of the packet and lit it, then said, "There's a lot of work to be done to get the property into an inhabitable place. Michael, how long do you think before I get the family in?"

"Two to three weeks, boss. Providing we put enough men on the job."

"Okay, pay the man the money and get some decorators in." I signed the paperwork and then set Michael to fix the house up. "Oh, I'll need the keys for the shed?"

"I will get them for you now, Mr Bell." We shook hands, and the agent disappeared. Michael and I moved through the house again to share ideas on what I wanted for Mum. I entered the bedroom on the second floor, which must have been a child's bedroom, as there were minor handprint marks about two feet up the wall, and further into the room was a dolls head with coarse blonde hair with a dent on her cheek. It had to belong to a little girl, once upon a time. Michael was jotting down rough estimates of the room sizes. I opened a cupboard door only to be hit with an awful stench.

"God, Michael, take a smell of this. It's rank!" Michael knelt and put his head in the cupboard.

"Hell! That is rank, and look, there is a hole in the back?"

"It must be coming from inside the hole," I said. "Wonder where it leads?" I started to pull away at the plaster around the hole. "Fucking hell! Michael. There is a small passageway in behind here." I popped my head through the hole.

"Leave it, boss. Let the estate agent deal with it."

My curiosity grew, so I started to hack away with my hands through the soft plaster. "The stench is awful, Michael; we'll have to find out what's causing it before we start getting the house ready for the family."

We eventually broke through to the passageway; I flicked on my lighter to see if I could see anything as we neared the awful stench. Handkerchief against my nose, I stepped upon a dead rat. I turned to Michael and shook my head. Then a rat, which I swear was the size of a cat, ran over my foot. I jumped back and yelped, "Shit!" I decided to continue down the narrow passageway when something creaked behind us. I tried to see what it was with the flame from the lighter, but there was nothing. Then the passage became much colder, but I couldn't see where this cold originated from.

"Boss, we need to explore no more. Let the builders do their job?"

"Michael, I had you down for a hard nut. Are you telling me you're scared to go any further?"

"Um, No. I don't see any point of going any further."

I shook my head at him once again. Then continued to make my way down the passageway. "What's this?" I said as I kicked a wooden box lying in front of me. I knelt and opened the box. Years of dust must have blown out. It took us by surprise, and we stumbled over each other and fell to the ground, watching this circle of dust make its way to the far end of the narrow corridor and disappear.

"Did you see that, Michael?" I asked alarmingly, as I turned my head to see his face.

"Yes, I did, boss. It is all a bit creepy, boss; I want out of here, it's scaring me."

I stood up and peered into the old box. Inside was an old doll's body with no head, covered in dust and cobwebs; I patted the dust off, revealing a frayed and torn dress. Then there was a bang which sounded like a door slamming shut, but no wind blew through the narrow corridor.

"I am out of here, now!" said Michael.

"You scared, Michael?"

"No! It's just getting late."

"Come on then, just make sure they take this internal wall down when the builders come in?"

"Of course, boss. Can we go now?"

"We need to wait for the keys. He's on his way back." When we exited the corridor, I still had the old headless doll in my hands; I put two and two together and grabbed the doll's head with golden hair. I thought a good clean-up and a new dress would be a lovely gift for Zilah.

We waited a few minutes, and the agent turned up with the shed keys.

"Oy, how well did you know the previous tenants?" I asked before he drove off.

"Not long at all, Mr Bell; they just wanted me to sell it for them, gave me a telephone number and address to contact them once I had sold."

"Thank you. Come on, Michael, let's go."

Three weeks passed, and Mum's house on Miller Way looked great, although it took longer than Michael's suggested two to three weeks.

But the inside of the house had been gutted, and new interior walls put up. The kitchen was extensive, with a proper sink and beautiful cupboards in pale blue with chrome handles that were sleek in design. Open to a large reception room, tall windows gave light from the outside overlooking the green park, boasting oak trees and ferns and a willow tree draping over the soft green grass. The reception room had velvety gold paper of authentic French damask, layered, rich shades. Cornices in each corner and a significant rose in the middle of the ceiling. The sofa was chocolate brown and made from velvet. An incredible staircase swirled up to the first floor, with a droplight pendant chandelier hanging down the centre. The light shone from opposite ends of the second floor, draping the windows in navy blue cotton. Mum's room was unreal, a four-poster bed adorned in red drapes and dressing tables of art deco style, with oval mirrors and a chaise lounge under the window. The next room was the bathroom, again vast in size, tiled in a chic grey, with a freestanding rolling bath encased at one end by a white cabinet that housed a dozen white cotton towels.

I went to the garden to see how it was coming along; the old two-seated swing in the corner was gone. Instead, the garden's border was a kaleidoscope of coloured geraniums, wild pansies and big rose bushes standing tall in the front overlooking the public pathway; "Michael? What has happened to the old swing that was in that corner?"

"Probably thrown out, boss; why?"

"Oh, nothing, just wondered. Can you tell the team what an excellent job they've done, and if the team can finish the house next week, there will be a big bonus in their pockets?"

"They'll love that, boss."

Edward then rang and asked to meet me at the pub. When I arrived, he was getting out of his car with a ginger-haired lady who was quite petite.

"Hey, bro, who's this lovely lady then?"

"This is Linda; we've been seeing each other for a few months now."

"It's very nice to make your acquaintance," I said as I kissed her hand.

"It's nice to meet you too; your brother has told me so much about you."

"All bad, I hope." I grinned at her. She smiled at my humour. Come on then, let's have a drink?" We walked into the pub where I had not been for a drink in quite a while. "There's my favourite proprietor, come on gorgeous, I will have my usual, and what would you like, Linda?"

"May I have a Martini and lemonade?"

"Of course, and bro?"

"I'll have a pint of lager, please, Tony."

I then noticed Barbara sitting in the corner, looking a little lonely. "Do you want a drink, Barbara?"

"Thank you! That would be nice, my usual, please."

I took her drink over to her and asked if she was okay. "If you need anything, Barbara, just shout, won't you." She smiled and then asked how Heather and Zilah were. I said, "Zilah's my adorable angel; he blessed me upstairs, and Heather, God bless her. She is starting to shuffle around. She can't wait to give birth to our second. It's due anytime." I then went back to the bar.

"How's the house coming along, Tony?" asked Edward.

"Almost there; it's looking brilliant, little bro." I then turned to Linda and asked her how she and my brother met. I was also curious about what she did for a living.

"Well, I am a supervisor in a grain warehouse. And we met at Barnacles."

"Barnacles...? What were you both doing in there? I thought it was a kids club?"

"I said Tony can be quite a windup merchant, Linda, don't take any notice of him. Replied Edward.

"Oh, come on, bro, it's only a joke."

"So, Edward says you're the man around here, so what exactly do you do?"

"I work within the community, making sure things are as they are supposed to be," I replied.

"Does that mean you are on the council?"

I looked at Edward, laughed, and said, "Something like that."

We both went to the toilets. "So, bro, is Linda the reason you wanted to see me?"

"No, we are getting increasingly more police cars coming into the parks. Because of the carpark tickets, ninety-nine per cent of drivers are sorted, but the odd driver coming into the parks is causing some concern."

"Right, I get that, bro, but if they don't buy in, do whatever is necessary. And bro, that means whatever's necessary." Then came the bombshell, which took me out of my comfort zone.

"I'm thinking of marrying Linda."

I spit out my drink, startled by his revelation. I looked at him, mortified. "What! You can't be serious, bro?"

In honesty, I didn't think she seemed right for him. I thought I had better insight into his wants, but he seemed sure this was right. Of course, I hoped it was because he lacked confidence, which is crazy. We were in a business where confidence was necessary. But he was my little brother, and he knew whatever happened in his life, I would always be there to pick up the pieces if they'd broke.

A couple of weeks passed, and Mum's house was completed. Mum, Edward, and Alan had moved in. Mum said she heard strange noises on some evenings while watching television. I quizzed her about the sounds she heard, but Mum was reluctant to say exactly what. Mum did say Robert and Bernie had been invited over to the house for dinner tomorrow night, along with Edward and his new love, Linda. Alan was out with some mates. Heather and I were having a quiet meal together. The business was, as usual, being taken care of by Michael. Bodyguards heavily fortified Mum's and our houses. But while Heather and I were quietly having a drink, and I whispered sweet sentiments in her ears, calling her my lovable sweetheart! I heard some gunshot sounds coming from outside. I got up and hurried to the front door, where Devon, one of my bodyguards, told me to get back inside. There was a commotion; shots were being fired in and out of the front of the house. I heard glass fall from a window as a shot pierced through the pane.

"How many?" I shouted to Devon.

"Two, three, boss. I am not sure?"

I could see where the shots were coming from. "They're behind that car." I pointed to a blue car parked right in front of my gates. I pulled my pistol out of its holster, aimed it at the car, and then opened fire on it. I must have shot one of them as the shots stopped from the vehicle's rear end. Whilst this was happening, Joe jumped over the hedge, which adjoined the house next door, and came upon the other guys firing shots at Devon and me. Joe shot one in the chest and another in the arm, and the guys dropped the weapons.

"Boss? I have them," shouted Joe.

I raced over to the car. "These are the Scottish guys supposedly looking for burglary opportunities." I could hear the police sirens in the background getting louder and louder. "Quick! Get them in the car and get away from here, quickly."

We put all three of them in the car, and Devon and Joe raced from the street.

Moments later, the police turned up; blue lights flashed everywhere; I stood tall at my front gate with my gun back in the holster.

This pig then got out of one of the cars and approached me,

"Evening, sir. We have had a report saying somebody had heard gunshots being fired nearby. Have you heard anything, sir?"

"It wasn't so much what I heard but more of what I saw, officer."

"What do you mean, sir?" asked the police officer.

"Well, I came out of my house for a quick cigarette after dinner, you know, my wife is expecting our child very soon, and I dare not smoke in the house. I saw three kids running down the street towards Parker Way, but they were letting bangers off; you know, those things you get for firework nights. And believe me; it made my poor missus jump out of her skin. Even I thought World War III had started." So, I stood smoking my cigarette, waiting to see what the officer would ask next. I did an excellent job. It was dark, and the lighting in the street was abysmal.

"Well, thank you, sir, for your co-operation. You say towards Parker Way?"

"Yep, Parker Way." I dropped the cigarette to the floor and said, "Well, Constable, I need to get back into my missus; she'll be wondering where I've got to."

"Please don't let me stop you, sir; you have a good night now, and all the best for the baby when it comes along." With that, he turned and went back to the car. I went behind my gates and watched as they drove toward Parker Way, thinking, *that was a close shave.*

I returned to Heather and told her she would need to stay with Mum for a few days.

I called Devon and told them to take the guys to the warehouse in Compton and that I would be there soon.

"I am scared, Tony; what were they after?"

"I don't know, but I'll find out tonight and deal with it accordingly. You must pack a bag for tomorrow to go to Mum's." I rang Michael to pick me up and sort out what I needed.

Heather went upstairs to the bedroom to pack a bag for her and Zilah to go to Mum. She was straining to load a bag while holding her tummy and wincing in pain. The baby should've been here by now; it was due weeks ago. Then, finally, Michael turned up, and we swiftly set off to my warehouse in Compton.

"I can't believe we finally found the Scottish bastards," said Michael.

"Well, that's not true. The bastards found me, and if I'd not had protection, I fear I may not have been sitting here now."

I finally arrived at the warehouse, where I did all my dirty work. I couldn't wait to get my hands on this Scottish bastard who attacked my home, putting Heather and my daughter Zilah in grave danger.

"We tried to talk to him, boss, but he was saying nothing," said Joe.

I could not wait to get my jacket off and roll up my sleeves. I was enraged and would not accept anything but the person's name who put my family at risk. The bastard sat tied to the chair, blood flowing down his arm from Joe's gunshot.

"Boss, let me, do it?" asked Michael.

My phone went off in my pocket; I just let it ring. "No, Michael, I need to get a quick answer before someone else tries to kill my family and me." I pulled my blade from my back pocket, quickly shoved it up the Scottish bastard's nose, and ripped out the septum. He screamed like a pig. I grinned at him and said, "You'll give me the name of the person who sent you to kill me." I waved the knife in his face. "If you don't, I'll take you apart piece by piece, starting with your tongue, and then I'll take an ear, an eye, and then the other ear. While you can see with one eye, I'll show you exactly what a tongue and ears and an eye look like in my hand; only then will I take your other eye, and then I'll start with your hands and feet. Who sent you?" My phone went off repeatedly, so I turned it off.

"I don't know," he squealed. "It was just a man in a suit. He paid us a hundred each to kill you."

I looked at Michael and then at Joe and Devon and nodded. "I'm sorry, I don't believe you. And your friends can't talk to me because they're already dead. But Joe, can you pass me those pliers on the shelf behind you?" Joe handed them to me, and I raised them to the bastard's face. "Open his mouth, Michael." As Michael stepped up to open the bastard's mouth, the bastard squealed, "No! No! I will tell you."

My emotions were running high, and I didn't know if I wanted to know who it was. I wanted to take this bastard apart piece by piece, my family were my world, and nothing could ever change that. "Who was it?" I asked.

"Jimmy... Jimmy Macdonald."

"Who the fuck is he?" I asked.

"He runs Glasgow and Aberdeen. He is a drug king in Scotland who wants your city and will not stop until he gets it. He knows you killed the Hendrick brothers; they also worked for him."

So that's where all the information came from. I paused for a few moments.

"I have told you everything. You have got what you wanted now to set me free."

I turned to Michael and told him, "I didn't want a turf war with Jimmy; he was somebody I knew nothing about. However, we must find a way to broker a deal; we can't wait for something to happen."

"But boss, how do we get to him?" asked Michael. I turned to the red-haired bastard and asked, "Where can I find this, Jimmy?"

"He can be found in Tillydrone, Aberdeen. It is his neighbourhood."

I took Michael outside whilst I had a cigarette. I contemplated my next move. "What do you think, Michael?"

"Boss, I don't want any Scottish bastards knocking on my door, so if you ask me what I think, I will find a way to work with this asshole."

"Jimmy Macdonald? You can tell he is a Scottish fucker," I said as I flicked my cigarette butt into the canal. "What if he fucks us over, Michael? It sounds like he has a bigger operation than us?"

"Well, boss, you can always kill him?"

"Umm, do I send this bastard back as a peace offering and try and deal with this asshole? Or do I kill him and march north and try to kill this, Jimmy Macdonald?"

"Whatever your decision, boss. I am right by your side, as will all the lads be. You know that."

I put my hand on Michaels's shoulder and said, "No one had ever had a truer friend than you. Give me five minutes alone; I will make my decision."

Those five minutes seemed like an eternity; my head swelled with thoughts of my next move. Is that right? Or would it be devastation? Families could be put in real danger or would peace hold, and we all work together?

I decided and walked back into the warehouse, "You say Jimmy Macdonald and his neighbourhood is in Tillydrone, Aberdeen?"

"Yes, Yes," the Scottish bastard replied.

I moved behind him flicked my knife and took his ear off with my blade. He squealed as I continued to cut pieces of his body from him, the other ear, his nose, and his tongue. Finally, I took his Scottish balls and watched while he bled to death.

"Well, that was a bit unexpected, boss. So, war it is then," said Michael.

"Michael, Joe, get rid of the bodies; you know where to, Michael. Then back to my house."

"Whatever you say, boss."

"Devon? Please take me back home, I need a drink, and we have some cleaning up. I'm sure you want one too." So, we made our way home, by which time I'd told Devon the bloodstains needed to be cleared and the glass and the bullet shells would require picking up as if nothing had happened. The car would then have to be burned out.

When we returned, I poured myself a large cognac. "What do you want to drink, Devon?"

"Boss, can I just have an ale?"

"Of course, my man, I'll pour it out of my pump behind the bar." I gave Devon the glass of ale and took a swig of my cognac. "I'm just going upstairs to get changed," I put my finger on my lips to gesture we need to be quiet. "The missus will be sleeping," I whispered. I walked quietly into the bedroom to find Heather was not there, I hurried to Zilah's room, and she was gone too. I didn't know what to do. My stomach was churning, and I felt nauseous. I started shaking uncontrollably and sweating profusely. "Heather?" I shouted. But there was no answer. Then Devon shouted up and asked if everything was okay.

I feared the worst I grabbed my phone and saw I had missed calls from Heather. I punched her number into the phone again there was no answer. I was losing it. I didn't know what to think or do. Then I rang Mum to find out if she had heard from Heather.

Bernie picked up the phone and said, "Heather was taken into hospital in labour three hours ago, and Mum has gone in with her." I put the phone down and then threw up in the bedroom. All my emotions let go together; I'd never been so happy; everything was okay. "Devon, can you drop me at the hospital? The missus is in labour." Devon looked as relieved as I, and we wasted no time getting to the hospital. He dropped me off, and I told him to tell Michael I will speak later, and he will be a godparent.

"Will do, boss. And congratulations to you both."

"Cheers." I then ran to the maternity ward, where my beautiful wife looked like she had been possessed by the

Devil, soaked in sweat from top to bottom, on all fours, panting like a dog.

"Where were you?" she yelped.

"I just had to deal with the business; you know what I mean?" I couldn't say anything else as Mum was there. I eventually got Mum a taxi and sent her home as Heather might have been in a lot of pain, but she was only four centimetres dilated, so the baby was not due for a few hours.

"I called you three times, but you didn't answer!"

"I'm so sorry, sweetheart. But I had to deal with it. Michael is sorting it out now." Heather glared at me with such intensity I had to sit up and look at her properly to make sure the Devil hadn't possessed her. "I'm here now, sweetheart, and I'm not going anywhere." I held her hand for two hours while the contractions continued. The midwife popped in every ten minutes to check on Heather. On one of the occasions, she even brought me a cup of tea and a biscuit. Of course, I was delighted, but cognac would have been better.

Heather's contractions became more frequent and more painful as the hours passed. Finally, it was Tuesday the 12th of March, a date I would never forget. Once again, she started to look like she had been possessed. Gripping my hand with such intensity, I watched as my hand turned white with a lack of blood. Without thinking, I said, to my regret, "Was the pain this bad last time, you know, with Zilah?"

She gripped my hand, dug her nails into my skin and yelled, "You... bastard, you will never come near me again. Ahh!"

I said sarcastically, "If you're going to look like that, then I'm not coming near you." Words I would never speak again. Her hands dug in even further. My inner thoughts were begging her to let my hands go. Then another contraction.

"Push... Push..." cried the midwife, "the baby's head is almost there."

"Come on, sweetheart, come on... one more push," and the baby's head was out. Heather, still panting, was asked to push again to get the rest of our baby out.

"Here we go," said the midwife. The baby was crying, and all the messy stuff was being sorted. Then they just took the baby away.

"We're just going to get her sorted, cleaned and wrapped." Said the midwife.

Heather was exhausted, as expected, but I didn't get to hold the baby as I did with Zilah. Something wasn't right, but I didn't know what. I mopped Heather's brow with a cold flannel to cool her down.

"Why have they taken her away from me? I want my baby."

"I don't know, sweetheart. They're just cleaning her up, you know, all the slimy stuff."

"They didn't do that last time; they handed Zilah straight to me?"

"I don't know. Hospitals have become more hygienic over the last year; they want less cleaning and all that stuff?"

They brought our baby back into the room a few moments later, wrapped in a white cotton blanket.

I couldn't help but cry; she was so beautiful. They handed her to Heather, and the tears flowed generously. She was our magical baby and a little sister to Zilah. "You know, sweetheart, these will crucify you when they're teenagers, especially being just sixteen months between them. Two children under two years of age, you know what they say, the terrible twos. Hahaha, I will be working." Heather did not care. She was so happy to have another child; she had all the maternal instincts anybody could have.

The doctor came in and asked questions we didn't understand, the usual doctor talk nobody understands about family life and our earlier history of different ailments. Then, finally, he looked concerned and told us he wanted to do an X-Ray on our baby.

"What are you fucking talking about? How dare you come in here while we're treasuring our magical moments to fucking tell us you want to give her an X-Ray. Radiation? All that crap! Why!" I screamed. I was so angry.

"Darling, calm down. You will frighten the baby."

"I'm sorry, sweetheart. You, doc, out with me, now!" I demanded. The doctor and I left the room and went into another room, his office or something.

"Tell me, what the fucking hell's going on?"

"Mr Bell, I'm so sorry. I can see you are terribly upset."

"I'm not fucking upset; I'm fucking angry!"

"Your baby has a problem, Mr Bell."

"What do you mean a problem?" I asked in a much calmer tone. "A problem?"

"The baby's head is much bigger than it should be. We must scan to see its cause; I am so sorry."

"You must have an idea; doc. Aren't that what you guys train years for?"

"We cannot say for certain, Mr Bell, until we do the scan, but it seems there are complications."

"She's going to be all right, isn't she?"

"We will know more after the scan; that is all we can say, Mr Bell. Can I get you a cup of tea?"

"No! But thank you for asking." I buried my face in my hands, my mind racing with thoughts. What do I tell Heather? Is this my penance for past transgressions? Then, teary-eyed, I asked the doctor to leave me alone. Slumped in the chair, I looked upward, begging God to see our magical little girl be safe and well. After a few minutes, I went back into Heather. She was still holding our little, tiny girl resting on her chest. Heather couldn't take her eyes off her. She stared across at me and noticed my swollen red eyes and that I had been crying.

"What is it, darling? What is wrong?"

I sat beside the bed, held her hand, and said, "There are complications. They don't know what it is, but she must have a scan or x-ray."

"But look? You can see there is nothing wrong with her?" Offering our tiny baby up to me.

I looked into Heather's eyes as she started to well up. "I'm sure she'll be okay, sweetheart."

The doctor returned to the room with a nurse and asked Heather for our baby, so they could find out what the problem was.

Heather initially refused to hand our daughter over, but she knew she had to. "How long will it take?" asked Heather as she handed the nurse our daughter.

"The scan won't take too long, but a specialist will look at the scans, we will better understand what's wrong. I am sure everything will be, okay?"

They both left the room, and we just cuddled each other. The next couple of hours seemed like forever. We hardly said a word, both pent up with worry but trying not to show one another our weaknesses. I paced the room the whole time, praying for our daughter to be okay. Then the doctor and the nurse walked back in without our baby.

"Where's my baby?" Heather asked in a concerted manner.

"She's sleeping in with the other babies; we thought that was best whilst we talk to both of you," said the doctor.

The doctor looked at the nurse before opening his mouth; I knew this wouldn't be good news, so I grasped Heather's hand.

"I am so sorry to say your daughter has a condition called spina bifida. It is a congenital disability of the spine. The spinal cord has severed. This means she will be paralyzed in the bottom half of her body. There would be learning difficulties as well." The doctor took a deep breath.

We couldn't hold back our tears. Our magical little daughter would never walk for the rest of her life.

"That's not all; she also has hydrocephalus, which is excess fluid on her brain."

"What does it all mean, doc?" I asked.

"Your daughter will certainly be paralyzed from the neck down. The water will certainly damage the brain. She will never walk; she may never be able to use the top half of her body. She will not be able to communicate; she may well spend most of what life she would have in the hospital."

Every moment of pause pushed daggers deeper and deeper into our hearts. We couldn't hold back the tears; the sadness was deep, and our hearts were broken. We didn't know what to do or what to say.

"I'm so sorry once again, Mr and Mrs Bell."

I struggled with a lump in my throat to utter the words, "What will happen now, Doctor?"

"She will stay with us. But you must decide whether you put her through all this for her short lifespan?"

At that moment, Heather's cries must have haunted the hospital. I struggled to hold her. The pain was crucifying us both. The nurse tried to comfort Heather, who had become hysterical. I was shaking so badly I couldn't even swallow my spit.

"You need some time to make the decision. I know this is so upsetting. We will give Heather something to help her calm down. Are you okay, Mr Bell?"

I just wanted to throw up. The doctor's words had just snapped my heart in two. The nurse gave Heather an injection to help calm her down. And shortly after, Heather had fallen asleep while my head was resting on the bed, looking up at her. I got up and walked outside for a cigarette. It was cold, grey, and quiet, like the world knew something was wrong. Eerie as nobody walked within sight. I went back inside and asked to see the doctor. He arrived shortly and took me back into his office.

"I'm trying to understand what to do, but I don't know," I said.

"It is normal, Mr Bell. But unfortunately, you have had some devastating news."

"Doctor, I have the funds to do whatever needs to make my daughter healthy."

"Unfortunately, Mr Bell, money doesn't matter."

The room was eerily silent as we both didn't utter a word. "Doc? If we keep her, in your honest opinion, what will it be like?"

"Experience with babies with spina bifida this bad has meant her disabilities are so numerous she will spend up to ninety-nine per cent of what life she has in hospital. She will not be able to do anything or understand anything."

"What would happen if we decided to let her go?" I asked. My tears rolled off my face and onto my shirt.

"She would stay in the hospital. She would naturally pick up infections whether she was here or at home. Infections can kick in within a few days, but we would make her as comfortable as possible, and you can spend twenty-four hours a day here if you wish."

"What if it was your baby, doc? What would you do, truthfully?"

"Because your daughter's condition is so bad, the likelihood of her death at an incredibly early age is advanced. I can't answer that question for you, all we can do is keep her as comfortable as possible."

I broke down again, struggling with how to tell Heather. How could we decide one way or the other? She is our blood, our magical baby, a gift from heaven. The pioneering experiments and technological advancement will improve her in a few years. There was so much to take into this naïve brain of mine. I walked to the baby unit, this tiny little wonder with beautiful eyes staring at the light as she lay on her back. I touched the glass of the incubator, desperately wanting to hold her hand to let her know I was there watching her. I left the corridor to walk back towards Heather's room. I bypassed the maternity ward. I glanced in only to see many mothers holding gifts of new life. Happy and content. I was so envious. I went into Heather's room and sat by her side whilst she still slept, agonizing over how to tell her.

I must've fallen asleep because my head was resting on the bed, and Heather, teary-eyed, stared down at me when I awoke. I grasped her hand and asked her if she was all right. Shrugging her shoulders, she started crying. I climbed onto the bed and lay beside her, wrapping my arms around her and hugging her tightly. I then tried to wipe away her tears with my fingers. Thinking it's all my fault. The brutal beatings I handed out in fights, the cutting, kidnapping, extortion, and the killings. I did it myself or authorized it. The cheating on Heather was God punishing me. I called for the nurse and asked if we could have some tea with plenty of sugar. I told Heather it might help.

I told Heather what the doctor said. Her response was shaking her head, saying, "No! I will not accept this hell we are being put through."

I didn't know how to cope with it all. It was more than I could bear.

We stayed in the hospital all day and night. I even got Heather late into the evening to see our baby. The nursing staff were so good and friendly. They did whatever we asked of them. We sat side by side on the wooden chairs beside the incubator, watching our baby all night. But Heather knew we would need the support of all the family in whatever decision we made, so we had to go home, even if it was just for twenty-four hours.

The following morning, we got a taxi back to Mum's, and I asked all the family to be there, including Heather's parents and brother, Colin.

We arrived at Mum's, and true to their words, everybody was there expecting to see the new baby, but when they didn't see either of us holding the baby, you could see their faces change, wondering what happened. Heather hurried over to her mum, bursting into tears. I went over to Mum and hugged her tightly. You couldn't hear a pin drop, just the tears on both parents' shoulders. Bernie and Linda made drinks while I pulled myself together to tell them what had happened.

"There have been some complications, and our baby daughter is still in hospital in an incubator on a specialist baby ward."

"Like what, son?" asked Mum. Heather got up and hurried upstairs, crying. Her mum followed sharply behind.

"They say she has severe spina bifida and hydrocephalus."

"But what does that mean, son?"

"She'll never walk, communicate, or understand, and her upper limbs look sure to be useless too; in other words, she will be a cabbage. And her life expectancy is noticeably short." I struggled to talk. "In general, we've to decide on letting her be like that for a brief time, or we let her go, and nature will take its course." I broke down again as I fell to the floor, praying for a beating from my father so that I knew it was all a dream. But there was nothing;

everybody said, "Oh no, I am so sorry. I needed to be with Heather. I ran upstairs and hugged her as tightly as I could. Then Heather blurted out, "Sarah, she will be called Sarah."

I nodded at her, then whispered, "Sarah." We lay there both thinking of what to do, afraid to let the other know, whilst we could hear the family engaged in conversation downstairs.

We talked and talked for the next couple of days until we could speak no more. We listened to everyone in the family, doctors, nurses, and friends. We collectively put our daughters at the forefront of everything and made our heartfelt decision. We went into the hospital to see Sarah and the doctor. When we got there, we asked how Sarah was.

"Sarah? So, you have named her, and what a beautiful name," said the nurse. "She's been a bit tetchy, but she's doing okay." Heather smiled, and we took our resident seats at Sarah's side. The doctor called us into his office sometime later and asked how we were doing.

"Okay," I replied.

"I've been told you have named your daughter Sarah?"

"Yes, Heather liked it," I said, squeezing her hand tightly.

"Have you decided what you're going to do?"

"Yes, we have. We have listened to everyone who matters, most importantly, each other. We are going to let

Sarah go." I said as my throat swelled, and tears ran down my face—whilst gripping Heather's hand.

"I know how hard this is for you, but I think you're making the right decision."

Heather and I got up and left his office to return to Sarah.

"I'm going out for a cigarette. Do you want me to bring you tea and something to eat?"

"A cup of tea, darling; I can't eat anything."

"Okay, sweetheart."

We spent the rest of the day sitting with our little magical Sarah, trying to have as many cuddles as possible.

The doctor said he was removing the sterile dressing on Sarah's back in the morning. I asked him, "Why are you doing it?"

He had a sullen look on his face and said, "It is to let nature take its course. So, Sarah is open to infection."

We knew what it meant, but we were still in shock, and a cuddle and a kiss on Heather's cheek was all I could do to comfort her.

The following morning the doctor removed the dressing. It was ghastly; it looked like half of her back was a giant water blister with flecks of red. Heather could not bear to see and turned away, putting her face into my chest.

"You know you can still put some light clothes on her, so you don't have to see," said the doctor.

The next couple of weeks were the most agonizing and cruel days we could've ever had. We spent all our time in and out of the hospital every day.

Dressing and cuddling Sarah, as we had no idea how long Sarah would be with us, we decided to get her baptized and asked if we could do it at our local church. We bought a beautiful christening dress with a bonnet and some silk booties. She looked like an angel on the day, and the priest baptized her. Mum struggled severely at the service and went home early. Once the service was finished, we took Sarah back to the hospital. When we returned to Mum's house, she wept as she told us the cancer was more aggressive. And that she was so sorry to miss some of the baptism. The strain of it all started to take its toll. We stressed over everything. It began to pull us apart when we needed to support each other through this awful time. I just wanted blood. Nobody could be hurting more than Heather and me.

I had no choice but to tell the rest of the family. She also wanted my father at home with her. I didn't understand, but Mum was dying, and I'd have done anything in the world for her.

Bernie was distraught at the grave news, and Alan said nothing. The shock was the only explanation. Edward had gone off with Linda, and my entire world had just come crashing down. How much more could I take? Michael dropped me back at Hobart Street, home of my father. I knocked, and he answered. He looked as pale as the man I knew.

I walked past him and sat down; he followed me into the lounge.

"What is it? It cannot be good if you are here."

"You need to pack a large bag and sort your dogs out if they're still here?"

"Penny, the pet dog, was knifed when somebody tried breaking into the house. Nugget is now kennelled with Jock's dogs; why?"

"I'm sorry to hear about the dog, but Mum's dying, and she wants you beside her. I wouldn't say I like it. That is the truth, but if Mum wants it, I can never stop it."

He buried his face in his hands, feeling sad, I think. I didn't care; I was doing it for Mum. "I'll be waiting outside in the car if you can make it as quick as possible."

He came out, locked the house, and then jumped into the back of the car with a large bag. Michael then took us back to Mum's.

When Dad jumped out of the car at the new house, he was stunned and amazed; he said it was beautiful. I wanted to say something, but now was not the time.

Everybody grieved in their own way, but the father in the house was adding to the despair of everyone. The only person that seemed happy to see him was Mum. But what was I supposed to say? No, you can't stay?

We all left the room and left them to it. Bernie was in a hell of a state. I could only comfort her with a cuddle and say, "Everything will be okay, sis."

I put Dad's bag into the spare room and returned to the hospital to see Heather and Sarah. Everybody said how beautiful Sarah looked in her christening outfit. I told Heather what Mum had told me, and she wrapped her arms around me, and even in her loving arms, all I could think was, why was I being crucified like this?

The following two weeks proved challenging to get around to Mum whilst he was there. Bernie had decided to move into Mum's too. Robert was okay with it. Edward moved in with Linda, and Bernie took his room. I was so thankful she made that decision. Dad was there, but Bernie spent all her time with Mum, whether shopping, cooking, or lending an ear.

It was Saturday the 13th of April, and Heather and I were at our usual seats next to Sarah when the nurse said, "Guy's, why don't you get something to eat and drink? You have had nothing all day; Sarah's asleep."

We went to the hospital canteen and had a sandwich and tea. We were there for about thirty minutes, talking about how terrible the year has been, already holding hands and wishing things were different. Then we saw our nurse approaching the canteen with a concerned look.

"What is it?" I asked.

With a tear in her eye, she said, "It is Sarah. She has passed away. I am so sorry."

We raced back to Sarah, but she was gone. The angels had taken her while we were away from her side. "No, no," I cried. Heather collapsed into my arms. We sat crying at her side for so long. Finally, they took her away, and we would see her no more until we met at the pearly gates of Heaven.

She would go into the baby garden with all the other babies in our local cemetery. The angels were sure to love and look after them until all the grieving parents would join them when the time came to take them by the hand and onward into God's paradise. On the 13th of April, she died. We had her for thirty-two days, but they would be forever in my thoughts.

In the following weeks, Heather and I put all our efforts and attention into Zilah; she needed us more than ever. Michael took over the business, and even Colin took a holiday to help Heather cope with her depression. But unfortunately, cracks were starting in our relationship. I began to get angry all the time, and I knew Heather was grieving so badly; she was not interested in love or anything; she just wanted total control of Zilah. She wouldn't let her out of her sight. She had become obsessed, and I had no choice but to get a doctor to see her.

When I told her, she went crazy. "How dare you arrange an appointment with a doctor without my consent?"

"I'm trying to help, sweetheart; you've been down on yourself recently."

"I have just lost my daughter. What do you expect?" she shouted.

"I know; I've lost her too!"

"You do not understand that it is not the same? She came from me!" she yelled as she threw an ornament at me in a wicked temper. "Get out! Get out!" she screamed. Then she slumped to the floor crying.

I went over, picked her off the floor, cuddled her, and then took her to the bedroom. "You need rest, sweetheart."

I lay her on the bed and kissed her lips. "I'll be downstairs; please try and get some sleep."

Downstairs I poured myself a cognac and tried to relax beside the fire, but as I looked deep into the flames, it felt like they were dancing at all my misfortune. So, I had another glass and tried to stop staring into the fire. Meanwhile, Colin was trying to feed Zilah at the table, which was funny; Zilah had covered him in her breakfast. He had milk all over him.

"Colin? You're supposed to feed Zilah, not play games?"

"Haven't you got somewhere you should be like your Mum's?" expressed Colin.

"Yeah, I need to see how things are going over there." So, I ran upstairs to Heather and asked, "Are you going to be all right, sweetheart?"

"Yes, I will be fine. I'll think about a shrink or the doctor."

I left the house to check up on Mum. Bernie was making drinks when I got there. "Cognac, sis."

"You're becoming an alcoholic."

"What? Because I asked for a cognac?"

"It is only nine thirty-five a.m.?"

Being sarcastic, I stated, "You're right, sis; sorry, can you make it a double then?" She looked at me with a scowl. I don't think she was impressed.

"How's Mum?"

"Staying optimistic and enjoying the demon's company."

"Better Mum than me!"

"He looks a different person and sounds different too."

"It must be all the guilt he has on his shoulders. Well, I hope he knuckles under pressure." He knew I didn't want him there, and he walked out every time I walked in to see Mum. Finally, I went upstairs into Mum's bedroom, "How are you feeling, Mum?"

"I am okay, son. How are you guys bearing up?" That was typical of Mum, always thinking about others. "Struggling a little, but that's only to be expected right?"

"Son? Thank you for letting your dad stay; I know it is against everything you believe in, but I need him here."

"It's not for me, Mum; it's for you. I'd give anything to have you well again."

"We have sat and talked about our marriage, how much he hurt and degraded me over the years, and how he treated you, kids. He is so sorry."

"Mum, I can't forgive him, and I've my own family now, and they're the most precious people in my world." I gave Mum a massive cuddle and told her if she needed anything, just let me know. I left, thinking she looked a bit worn.

I returned home to do some paperwork. I started to get behind with the business. I now needed to focus on my work; it was the only thing to keep me sane.

I entered the door, and Heather came over and kissed me, which surprised me.

"I have booked an appointment with a bereavement counsellor. It is next Monday at four o'clock. I hope that is, okay?"

"Certainly, sweetheart. I'm just going to do some paperwork, and then I'm going to take a bath."

"Okay, darling. I am going to try and cook something nice for dinner."

"Was Colin okay this morning after feeding, Zilah?"

"He was hilarious, but he got experience, and you never know; he might have to put it to practical use in the police station sometime.

"Well, that's the most likely option, as there's no sign of a woman in his life."

I rang Michael to catch up with him about the business. "How's everything going, Michael?"

"The business is fine and ticking over nicely. But I must be honest, boss, it is not me. You know I like getting my hands dirty; I need that excitement; you know what I mean?"

"We'll get together in a few days and look at the Jimmy Macdonald thing?"

"Brilliant, boss, I cannot wait."

"If you're okay running the business for just a few more days, I will let Edward have a go. See if he can bring anything different to the business?"

"I think he will be good, boss."

"Okay, Michael, we'll catch up in a few days." I put the phone down, and thought, *well? If Edward takes over the running of the business, he can start with the paperwork.* So, I ran a bath. Then, I sat back with my cognac and cigarette, looking out at the gorgeous sunshine beaming through the window. "Sweetheart," I shouted.

"I will be with you in a second, just putting the tea on." Heather came into the bathroom with her apron covered in flour. There was some in her hair and on her face.

"What is it, darling?"

"Have you been fighting with, Zilah? Only you look a bit like Colin looked this morning, trying to feed her?" I laughed.

She looked in the mirror and said, "Oh, I do look a state, don't I?"

"Come over here. I can wipe away the flour on the back of your hair."

"I have got it on the back of my hair as well. I must have touched my head while I had flour in my hands."

Heather sat on the edge of the bath turning her back to me so I could wipe the flour away from her hair. But of course, there was no flour; I just wanted to get her in the bath. So, I put my arm around her waist and pulled her into the tub. The water splashed all over the floor whilst I kissed Heather in a warm embrace.

"You bugger!"

"I know, but you still love me." It was a warm moment we'd not had for ages. It's the first time I saw her smile since we lost Sarah. One thing led to another, and we started making love under the warm water. Warm, sensual, and sexy. For those thirty minutes, we forgot everything and caressed every second of it. "Do you fancy going out for a quick drink? Just a quick one, I promise," I asked.

"What about dinner? It is in the oven. I made it especially for you, darling?"

"We could go out after dinner?"

"Okay, darling, do I need to make a massive effort? Or is it just a quick one down the pub?"

I said, "Pub or club? It's your choice. And then you can make up your mind about what to wear?"

"It might do both of us a world of good. So, let us club, yes?"

"Yeah." I got out of the bath after Heather. She was dishing up what she'd cooked; I quickly put a shirt and trousers on, splashed aftershave, and got ready to go out. Finally, the dining table was ready, and Heather laid a pie of golden crust on a platter with roasted potatoes and some vegetables and a gravy boat that smelt like aged beef, meaty and dark and then sat down opposite me.

"Do you want to cut into it, darling?"

"Oh," I said, "not sure I want to break up this thing of beauty."

"I hope you're talking about me, darling."

I smiled, winked at her, and then cut through this golden-crusted pie that oozed this rich gravy. Large chunks of beef, which melted in your mouth. "Wow! You might have missed your vocation, sweetheart. You should be working in London, in an expensive restaurant."

"You are full of crap sometimes."

"I give you a compliment, and that's your reaction?"

"It does taste good, if I have to say so myself."

We finished dinner, and Heather was getting ready to go out. So, I rang Edward and Linda to hurry over, so we could get out for that drink and back to what may seem normal.

They arrived, and Heather came down the stairs looking so beautiful. She had a midi dress that clung to her shapely body, styled in black and silver sequin stripes with a black band around her midriff and her golden curly locks hanging down over her shoulders, all propped up by sparkly silver heels. She smiled, looking at us as if she should fit on top of the world. It brought a tear to my eye. *You look gorgeous*, was all that went through my mind.

Edward and Linda were in awe. Then, Heather said, "Zilah's sleeping, so she should be out for the rest of the night? Are you okay doing this?"

"Of course," said my brother, "If anybody needed a night out, it's you two."

We got in the taxi and headed for Monroe's. "I'm not sure whether I feel dressed enough next to you, sweetheart?"

"You always look handsome and smart, my darling."

We exited the taxi when we got to the club. There was a queue about half a mile long waiting to get in. I was in a business where I knew most people, from youngsters to parents. We had some waves from the crowd, but Heather grabbed all the attention. Youngsters were asking where her dress came from and how stunning she looked. It was great, but I wanted to get inside for a drink. "Come on, sweetheart," I whispered in her ear. They're all eager to get inside the club. We're selling what they want to buy.

"Devon? Get us inside." He pushed his way through, leaving space for us to get in. "Thank you, Devon."

"No problem, boss. Enjoy the night."

"I'm just going to powder my nose, darling."

"What would you like to drink, sweetheart?"

"Champagne!"

This young barmaid came over and asked for our drinks order.

"I've not seen you here before; how long have you been here?"

"Nearly two weeks now," she responded.

"Where did you work before you started here?"

"Macauley's, but it was boring watching all these fat ladies trying to get into dresses that were too small for them; they could not even get their legs into them. Me and Petula, who also worked there, used to laugh at them."

"I thought you said the job was boring. It sounds as if you had a whale of a time."

"No, it wasn't like that all the time." Then, stunned, she looked over my shoulder and said, "Would you look at her? What is she doing in this club? She looks like an actress or a model?" She then turned her attention to me. "I'm Katy; I am sorry, I am not normally this rude. It was just her, and she is coming this way."

I turned, stood up, and pulled the chair out for Heather, "There you go, sweetheart." She sat on the chair. "Sweetheart, this is Katy, and she has only been here for a couple of weeks. But she seems very pleasant." Katy just looked dumbstruck. It was like she had frozen in time, staring at Heather. Then Zakaria came over to the table to say hello.

"Are you okay, Katy?" asked Zakaria.

She looked at Heather and said in a stuttered voice, "Do you know her? She is so beautiful."

Zakaria snapped his fingers and said, "Katy, here's your boss and his beautiful wife, Heather."

"Oh, I'm so sorry," she said in a bit of a fluster.

"Sorry? For giving a fantastic compliment to my partner? No, let me thank you." Then, I turned to Zakaria and asked if we could have her for the night; she was a breath of fresh air.

"Of course, now you look after these lovely people, Katy; they're our top VIPs."

"I'd love to. But umm, what did you want to drink?" Her hands were trembling whilst trying to take a drinks order. It was very comical.

"Bottle of champagne, please, Katy," said Heather. "What a sweet girl." As she hurried off to the bar.

"Come here, gorgeous, I need a dance." So, I took Heather's hand, and we moved to the dance floor and started to dance to 'Knock Three Times' by Tony Orlando and Dawn, which was number one for five weeks. It was like everybody left the floor for us to dance independently. Because I owned the city, I'm sure somewhere people would have talked about what we were going through. Well, that was the most logical reason. But I loved every second of it. We were wrapped in each other's arms, miles away from everyone.

Then we heard Zakaria get on the microphone, "Ladies and gentlemen, can you kindly please leave the dance floor for a few minutes."

I looked at Heather and said, "What the fuck… what's happening?"

"This is just for you, from me." Zakaria got the DJ to play 'Sealed with A Kiss' by Brian Hyland, one of our songs that meant so much. I gave him a thumbs-up, and we kissed, kissed, and kissed again throughout the whole song. It felt so good. When the song finished, the youngsters clapped, and we moved off the floor; the tempo of the music changed, and everybody was up on the floor boogeying away.

We went back to the table where Katy had made herself comfortable.

"Are you okay, Katy? Are you comfortable?" I gave her a naughty stare because I was trying to wind her up.

"Do you want me to pour your champagne? I am so sorry. I did not know what else to do. I have never been asked to look after anybody before."

"Please, pour the champagne, Katy. Have you had champagne before?"

"You are joking, aren't you? I can hardly afford a drink sometimes."

"Does Zakaria not pay you enough?"

"Oh, no, it is not like that. I must take care of my mum and my little sister. Mum cannot work, and Gilly is only nine, so everything I earn goes into food and the house.

"So, what's he paying you?" I asked.

"£18.10. Which is £1.40 more than I was getting at Macauley's, and I get to dance a bit when we close." Heather smiled graciously.

"Tom?" Who was one of the other bartenders. "Can you get me a champagne glass? Thank you."

"Certainly, Tony."

When he returned, I asked him to pour the champagne into the glass. He ran it like a true professional. "Did you see how Tom poured the champagne, Katy?"

"Yes, my pouring was all bubbles, but I thought it would spill."

"Anything else, Tony?"

"No, we're all good here. Thank you, Tom." I passed the glass to Katy, who looked nervous. "Please, have a drink with us?"

"Really? But I might get into trouble?"

"I'm technically your boss, so if I say have a drink, you can." She tasted champagne for the first time and made me and Heather laugh when she said it tickled her nose. I liked this girl a lot; she had a very family-orientated background, not too dissimilar to mine.

She sat with us all night drinking champagne; she made us laugh so much; I swear I nearly peed myself. She asked so many direct questions of Heather, where she got her clothes? And how we met? She just seemed like one of a kind.

It was midnight when I looked at my watch, so I suggested to Heather, we should call it an evening.

"Okay, darling."

"What time do you finish, Katy?"

"Umm, one o'clock," she slurred.

"Do you have transport?"

"No, I get a taxi. But oh, it was nice meeting you, both of you, of course."

"Heather, I'm going to see Zakaria and get Katy home. She can get in our taxi; I will not be more than a few moments." Zakaria agreed, and we jumped into a taxi to take Katy home safely. Halfway across the city, we pulled into her street, Peel Street, an area like the one I grew up. Rough and run down.

"Katy, are you working tomorrow night?" I asked.

"Yes, I am. Why?"

"We will see tomorrow. I will pop into the club and chat sensibly, okay?" Katy nodded and got out of the car, and we waited until her mum answered the door and let Katy in. The driver then took us home while we discussed Katy's lovely entertainment. Finally, we entered the house, where Edward greeted us with a drink.

"How's the little angel been?" I asked.

"Brilliant! We checked on her several times but have not heard a peep."

"Fantastic!"

"Well, now your home; Linda and I will get out of your way," said my brother.

"Thank you, guys," said Heather. Then they both left.

"I'm going to offer Katy a job tomorrow, sweetheart. What do you think?"

"Doing what, darling?"

"Technology out there is getting more innovative, and a computer literate could better serve the company. So, I will see how good Katy is with a computer. If she's good, I'll take her on as a personal assistant; she can oversee wages and the paperwork. What do you think?"

"Seems like a clever idea. Katy seems very switched on, and I suppose the extra wages will help the family. But first, you come here and finish what we were starting in the club?" We clenched each other in a firm embrace. "Wait a moment? We need to check in on our daughter first," I said as I grabbed Heather's hand.

"Aww, bless her," said Heather; Zilah was snuggled up with her teddy beside her with her hand on its head. She looked so adorable.

"Right, you; come here and kiss me, darling."

"I have got a better idea. Why don't we go to bed?"

"That sounds even better, darling."

I hurried into bed wearing just underwear while Heather freshened herself up. Ten minutes later, she walked into the bedroom wearing a long sexy white nightie with a pink bow on the waistline. I threw the sheet and blanket to one side of the bed and tapped the bed, gesturing for Heather to lie there. Instead, she climbed in, and I pulled the sheet and blanket over us. I then moved on to Heather and kissed her gently, which slowly intensified into a battle of tongues fighting for dominance in the mouth. I then moved the straps of her nightie off her shoulders whilst caressing her neck and shoulders with my tongue.

"Let me take this nightie off," she spoke.

I quickly removed my underwear and started to move down Heather's body, where my tongue worked vigorously on her breasts and nipples as my hand caressed her right breast. Heather sighed as she started getting aroused, her body moving gently to each touch with my tongue. Heather gently moved her fingers through my hair while moving my lips and tongue around her body, heightening her senses. She dug her fingers into my back as I moved further down her body to what I called the sweetest of life's ultimate pleasure. As I moved my tongue in and around, Heather pushed my head, gesturing to go deeper inside, deepening her senses even further. She started trembling in her excitement as I brought her to near climax. I lifted my head and crawled up the bed to straddle her breasts and gestured to take my cock into her mouth for a long and fulfilling blowjob. After some time, we moved into the missionary position, where I gently placed my moist cock inside Heather to ensure no bruising. Once inside, I gently thrust in and out whilst fondling Heather's left breast with my left hand and using my right hand on the bed to keep me balanced. And in time, we brought each other to climax. We both lay there, totally satisfied. With

beads of sweat gently running down my body, I told
Heather, "I need the bathroom." Heather looked at me,
gave me a big smile and raced out to the bathroom,
laughing,

"Not before me, darling."

I laughed back at her and called her a cheeky madam.
She turned her head towards me, her blonde hair covering
half her face, and smiled again. Eventually, we were ready
for sleep, so I turned the bedside light out. Whilst trying to
get some sleep, my brain was wired into what was
happening to my life. All the good and harmful stuff and
the sad things too. I was happy but was not sure a more
profound sense stirred in me.

Morning broke, and I had a couple of hours of sleep.
Heather noticed and remarked on how my dark eyes
appeared through lack of sleep. "I take it you didn't sleep
well; what was wrong?"

"My brain was overactive, that's all."

"Do you want some toast, darling?"

"Sounds great. Can I have some jam with that,
please?"

"You saying you won't have any free time today?"

"No, it's important I get stuck back into work.
However, if you need me, ring." With that, I kissed her,
kissed Zilah, and made my way to Mum's. I needed fresh
air, and the long walk would do me good. The sun shone,
filling the blue sky with fluffy white clouds. I quivered as
I walked up the garden path, as a sudden shiver went down
my spine. I paused for a moment. As I looked around the

garden, there was no sign of a breeze. I had a new swing put in on the old oak tree, which was swinging gently. I thought it was very peculiar but continued into Mum's house.

"Mum, you there?" I shouted as I walked into the large kitchen.

"I'm up here, son," she spoke with a shallow voice.

I went upstairs to find Mum in bed and Bernie asleep on the chair beside her.

"Is everything okay, Mum?"

"I have been a bit under the weather for a couple of days, so I stayed in bed to see if I could shift it, but I am okay." With that, Bernie woke up and yawned.

"Did you get enough sleep, sis?"

"Some, but not a lot; what are you doing here?"

"Well, I came over to see Mum. Have you been back home to Robert yet?"

"No, been here constantly with you, Mum, haven't I?"

"Yes, she has, and I have told her to go home and see Robert; they have only been married a few months."

"Sis, go home now. I will spend some time with Mum, and then I'll get Heather over to pitch in as well."

"I am all right, you two. I feel better now anyhow."

"Mum, rest, please. I will make you a cuppa, sis, go home now! I'll ring you later." Bernie left, and I returned downstairs to make Mum some poached eggs on toast for her breakfast. I heard footsteps behind me; I turned around only to see my father.

"Are you okay, son?"

I stared at him and said, "Don't call me son." He turned and walked out of the kitchen. I hated him and was not wavering in my hatred for him, just because Mum wanted him here.

I finished Mum's eggs and took them to her. "There you go, Mum, get your teeth stuck into them."

"They look lovely, son, but I am not hungry."

"You must eat, Mum; it will keep your strength up. Now Bernie has gone home, tell me what has been happening?"

"My back is killing me, and the coughing is getting worse; I also had blood in my hanky when I was coughing yesterday. In addition, I am losing weight and always feel tired."

I felt so sick to my stomach, tight knotting taking my breath away. I struggled to hold back the tears, trying to stay strong for Mum. I knew time was running out for Mum, and one day shortly, I'd have to deal with everything and everyone. "Are you taking the pills the doctor gave you to help with the pain?" I asked.

"Yes, but honestly, they do not help. The pain is increasing, and I decided not to have treatment."

"But there must be something else they can give you to help with the pain."

"Son, I want to know what's happening; I want all my senses when the time comes."

I could only accept Mum's wishes as I nodded in approval. Losing Sarah was the worst thing in my life, and now Mum is exceptionally poorly, and it's all more than I can bear. So, I called Heather and asked her to bring Zilah to see Nanny. Hoping she would bring some cheer to Mum. I just wanted to get out of the house, I called Michael to come over and pick me up. I sat with Mum until Heather arrived with Zilah; Joe had driven them over.

"Okay, sweetheart?" I grabbed Zilah and took her upstairs to see her nanny, who was delighted to see her. It did bring Mum's warm smile back to her face. Zilah, being very curious, looked under the bedspread and tried crawling around the pillows.

"She is growing so fast, son. You make sure you are always there for her, or I will look down on you and give you real grief, right?"

"Yes, Mum, I'm always going to be there." I smiled. Heather asked if I was okay.

I told her what Mum had said to me. I was concerned for her.

"She is a real fighter. Look what she has gone through; she is still here. She will fight for as long as it takes, darling."

Michael arrived and popped in to say hello to everyone.

"Come on, then, Michael; we've got work to do. Mum, I'll catch up later. Remember, keep your head up and eat! Sweetheart don't wait up. I'll get home as soon as I can." I kissed her, and we left the house.

I asked Michael outside the house, "Can you feel anything?"

"What, boss? What do you mean, can I feel anything? What am I supposed to be feeling?"

"Doesn't matter." Michael looked perplexed. But I didn't want to feel stupid after this morning's weird feeling. So, we jumped in the car and went to Compton to the warehouse. We entered and got to work on our next step, Jimmy Macdonald.

"Have you decided, boss, how we manage this?"

"I don't trust anybody apart from you and the family. We need to take him out, causing me many sleepless nights. I need ten of our best guys, but I still need the protection at the house. Michael, we know he lives in a place called, Tillydrone in Aberdeen. I don't know how big they are and how many guys he'll have around him. We must find and watch him; when we're ready, we'll hit and hit hard."

"Whenever you're ready to go, boss, we will be ready."

"Monday? The more people working, the less likely we'd get seen, and I want everybody to look at what people are wearing up there, so we fit in."

"At last, I can get my hands dirty," said Michael.

"Michael? Edward said something about a noticeboard going up in one of the lorry parks about charging for parking. Can you whip over and have a look to see what he's on about? I didn't get the chance to talk to him last night."

"Oh, yeah, what were you up to then?" asked Michael.

"More than you get up to with that gorgeous wife of yours." Michael shrugged his shoulders and went to the car park. I stayed in the warehouse working on plans to hit this Scottish bastard encroaching on my city.

Aberdeen was a big city. I had to hit Jimmy close to his home in Tillydrone. I discovered a nearby train station, so if I could coordinate the train with the hit, we'd be home and dry. I called the operator at the exchange to find train times to wherever from Tillydrone we'd find a way back from there. I spent forever on the phone, but it was worth it. There's a train pulling in on Sunday at 19.57 p.m. and one pulling out of Tillydrone to go southbound on Monday at 14.21. It was perfect. All I had to do was get the train tickets except for one car needed a few days earlier for the stakeout. But I was pleased I'd done an excellent job.

I sat down with a glass of libation and patted myself on the back. If everything goes right, my business will be intact. Which reminded me I had to visit Adalai and ensure funds were okay, he might even know the Scottish wanker?

While I was sitting and thinking about everything, I heard the warehouse door open and close. "That was quick, Michael." To my surprise it was Beryl, the reporter or columnist, that walked in. "How did you know this was my warehouse?"

"Umm, people talk when you are friendly to them. Can I come in?"

"It seems you're already in, doesn't it?" I said sarcastically.

She walked towards me, smiling, and pulling faces, holding a bottle of cognac and two glasses in her hand like a child about to get some ice cream. She wore a white woollen jacket with gold buttons down the front, a white hat with black trim, a black woollen knee-length skirt, and black-heeled shoes. And black and gold disc-shaped earrings. And a belt of gold chain.

"You look stunning! If I have to say so myself."

"Compliment indeed," she replied as she sat on the chair with one leg hanging over the over, looking very seductive. I know Heather was my partner, but I adore women who look after themselves, especially if they are drop-dead gorgeous.

"Can I say you look extremely out of place if you're working? You look as if you have hit the London high street?"

"Who said I was working?"

"So, you know where I work; anything else I can help you with?"

"Now, there's an offer a girl could hardly refuse."

"What is it you want, Beryl?"

"I have a few fascinating facts you may want to hear?"

"And…"

"Well, let's drink, and then I can tell you what I know." Beryl poured a hefty measure of cognac into each glass.

"Cheers." She offered up her glass to toast.

"So, what fascinating facts do I need to hear?"

She put her glass down, got off the chair, and straddled me.

"What do you think you're doing, Beryl? I've got lots to do."

She started to undo my tie as she gently kissed my cheek.

"No, Beryl." I pulled her hands off my tie. "What do you need to tell me?"

"Let us go for a drink. It is nice outside, and I love overlooking the canal."

I sighed and grabbed my jacket. "Where do you want to go?" I asked.

"We can always go to the Jack and Hammer. It's nice there?"

"I assume you've brought a car?"

"Yes, it's right outside."

I closed the warehouse, locked it with a huge padlock, and said, "It's what I should've done before you got in."

"I am not sure you can lock yourself in with a padlock on the outside?" she jested whilst I got in the car.

"Oh, come on, we had a good night when we last met, didn't we?"

If I had to be honest with myself, I did enjoy it. But so much has changed since then. I didn't care. I was not interested in Beryl; I wanted to know what facts she had. I was glad we were going to the Jack and Hammer. It was quite an exclusive venue; I didn't reach out to this pub; Michael dealt with the alcohol and cigarettes at this place. So, I was not well recognized, which Beryl knew.

I opened the door to the bar and let Beryl through first; being a gentleman, it was lovely inside and apart from the stale smoke of cigarettes. It was very cosy, and the menu was full of good home-cooked dishes, like steak and stout pie and pork sausage with mashed potato and the traditional ploughman's lunch. And there was a large hearth with roaring flames from the wooden logs. I heard a voice say, "Can I help you?"

"Have you a table for two, please, somewhere near your beautiful fireplace?"

The server sat us down at the table and asked if we wanted any drinks. I had my usual, and Beryl had water with sliced lemon.

"I didn't think we were going to eat?" said Beryl.

"Well, it's lunchtime, so we might as well eat. What do you fancy?" I asked whilst perusing the menu.

"I am going to have the quiche with salad."

The server returned with our drinks, and I said, "Can we have the quiche with salad for the lady, and I'll have the ploughman's, please? Thank you."

"So, while we're waiting on food, what facts do you have?"

"Your imports and exports business. I know that is what you deal in. Your contraband and alcohol distribution too. I do not know how many pubs and clubs. Tobacco to the public? The city was gripped with silent whispers almost echoing down every dirty lane."

I took a slug of my cognac to pause for thought. "Hypothetically speaking, what if you're right?"

"I did not come here to trap you, Tony. On the contrary, I like you a lot, and you are remarkably interesting."

"So, what is it you're after, Beryl? I'm not playing games."

"I am not interested in what you do or how you do it. I know you are having a tough time; I want you to know if you ever want to talk or anything else, I will always lend an ear."

I nodded and said, "Where are you getting all the information from?"

"You do not have to be the greatest detective to gather information about you, Tony. I would get chatty with people; I could not believe the number of times your name came up. You also have a brother-in-law in the force. I know someone he knows, and he talked about a brother-in-law, and his sister had to make some painful decisions about their daughter."

I didn't say much; truth be known, I was stumped; she knew so much. The look in her eyes was not of someone who was going to show me to the police, but a seductive kind of look, wanting more than I wanted to give. The server brought the food to our table, which looked amazing. Beryl started eating her quiche whilst looking seductively at me.

"The food is nice, isn't it?" she commented. "Delicious food, a warm fire, and your company, who wouldn't want this? I was so sorry to hear about your daughter."

"Thank you for your words, but I don't want to discuss it." So, we continued to eat at our quiet table and said very few words to each other. I looked at my watch as the time seemed to race by.

"Take it we are not having dessert?" said Beryl. "You are in a rush?"

"I've got so much to do and truly little time to do it in, and truthfully, lunch out with you was never in my thoughts. So, if you want dessert, then stay and have your dessert." I stood up and said, "I enjoyed your company, thank you." I put money on the table to cover the food, drinks, and extra if Beryl wanted anything else. I then walked out.

I started to go back to the warehouse to finish my plans, and then I would go to the prison to see Adalai. First, to make sure he was happy with his cut in the business and secondly if he knew anything of this Jimmy Macdonald.

I arrived at the prison and started my conversation with Adalai. Screws couldn't take their eyes off us. "Do you know a Jimmy Macdonald from Aberdeen?"

"Yes, a few years ago, he was a jumped-up street kid running a ragged outfit of misfits in his local community. Sound familiar?"

I told Adalai he was more prominent now and wanted me and my family dead.

Adalai told me he knew a few people in Scotland and that if I needed help to reach out to him.

"Thank you, Adalai; I might just do that." I left the prison and quickly rang Michael to find out what Edward's car park was about.

"Boss, the city council has sold some of the parks off to private companies who will put ticket machines in them."

"Fuck!" Something else I need to sort out. Okay, Michael, I'm making my way back to the warehouse. Can you meet me there?"

"Sure, boss."

I was mindful of how important my plan had to be. It had to be perfect. If I put a foot wrong, we might all go down. I'd be leaving Heather, my daughter, and my dying mum to their own devices. Michael was taking ages. I knew every crack on the floor in the warehouse through pacing up and down. It was six fifteen p.m., and we still had to ensure the plan was one hundred per cent. Then Michael turned up. "Where have you been, Michael? I expected you hours ago."

"Boss, there was an accident. Some poor kid was run over by a car at Sefton Park. The traffic was horrendous; it took ages to clear."

"I hope he's okay. Michael, look at the Scotland plan and tell me what you think. I've also got extra bodies in Scotland if we need them."

"So, who are we sending to do the surveillance, boss?"

"Joe and Jimmy. They can use the Cortina. Just ensure they're kitted with a second set of number plates if the car is detected when we hit."

"Well, boss, the plan looks concrete; it's going to be all about how many men he has with him?"

"Can we pull it off, Michael?" I asked as I started to question myself.

"Boss, you have bigger balls than anyone I know; everything to the fine detail is here. But first, the surveillance will be crucial. His movements and how many men around him will decide the outcome!"

I put the plan in my small black leather case and locked it away. "Come on, Michael, I need to go to Monroe's and talk to a young lady called Katy."

Michael dropped me off and returned to my house to ensure everything was okay. "Bloody hell, Devon, this place is packed," I said as I walked in the door.

"It is Saturday night, boss. So, it's always like this?"

"Can you let Zakaria know I'm in the club?"

"Yes, boss."

I walked over to the bar to track down Katy. Walking across the dance floor, squeezing through the countless ladies trying to get me to dance with them was eye-opening. But I got across safely.

"I'm looking for Katy. Is she around?" I asked at the bar.

"Yes, she should be out the back. Do you want me to get her for you?" asked Tom.

"That would be great, Tom; thank you." I looked around the dance floor at all the totty dancing away to the Beatles' 'Yellow Submarine.' There were some beautiful girls in the club.

"Hiya," I heard from behind me. I saw Katy wearing a tight black blouse and a short white skirt.

"Hey, gorgeous, time for a chat?"

"I'll just get Mary out from behind, as we are a bit busy."

"Bring yourself a drink, whatever you fancy? And if I can have a cognac, I'll find a seat." She came back with two glasses of cognac.

"I only wanted one, Katy?"

"Yes, I know, but I thought I would try one," she said, smiling.

We sat at the table, and Katy crossed her legs, revealing a bit too much; it was not intentional; I didn't think she knew sitting in that compromising position showed what it did. And as a gentleman, I did mention it discreetly. She was very thankful.

Katy took a sip of her cognac and swallowed. Then she gave me a look like, 'This drink is terrible.'

"Taste agreeable?" I asked sarcastically.

"No, it's awful," she replied, screwing her face up.

"It's a unique taste and takes some getting used to," I replied. "Right, let's talk about you, Katy, and the job and where you might see yourself in three years?"

"Well, I told you yesterday about me and home. I like to think I could have a place of my own, help my mum and little brother to live more comfortably and do an excellent job that I love doing."

"That's a set of goals anyone would be proud of. But how do you get there?" I asked. "Do you think the job you're doing now would afford you those opportunities?"

"Well, I was hoping if I do an excellent job here, I might get a supervisory position, especially if I work hard."

"Shall we get you another drink, Katy?"

"I'm sorry. Can I have a gin and lemonade, please?"

I called Mary over and asked her to bring a gin and lemonade to the table.

"Katy, have you used a computer before?"

"Yes, I can work on a computer?"

"How would you like to work for me?"

"I am already working for you here at Monroe's?" she said, squinting her face. Looking curious.

"It would be a different role. I'd like you to be my assistant. What do you think?"

"What does it all entail?"

"Computer use, papers, letters and general accounts, you'll work independently and be answerable only to me." She looked at me with a glint and seemed a bit gobsmacked.

"What have I done to deserve a job like that?"

"I love your personality and family values, and everybody deserves a chance. However, you'll see things and hear things you may not like or agree with, but the money is good. So, what do you say?"

"People talked about me all the time working in Macauley's."

"It's not that kind of talk, Katy."

"Look, you and your wife seem nice, and I would love to work with you."

"Excellent." Heather is my significant other, not my wife." I offered a toast and said, "Welcome to my team. Start next Monday?" She was deliriously happy. We sat there discussing the details of the job role when Zakaria came over. "Zakaria, I'm going to take this young lady off your hands to work directly with me. She's far too clever to be a barmaid. Is that okay?"

"Tony, whatever you ask is yours, you know that."

"Appreciate that, Zakaria. Katy, we'll talk wages on Monday, but I promise it will be much more than you earn now. But you still have a job here until then, so get back to work and get those pennies in the till. But before that, you can tell everyone on the microphone there is a free drink on Tony and Zakaria, the club owners."

Katy was excited at the prospect of working with me and let everybody in the club know, as she sounded high-pitched and giggly over the microphone. "I cannot thank you enough. Thank you so much, boss."

"I know; I'll see you Monday week and send you a driver. But if you can get me my usual before you return to work here, that would be lovely."

No sooner did Katy put my drink down, and I turned around whilst lighting up my cigarette, only to see Beryl heading towards my table.

"Are you fucking stalking me?" I asked angrily.

"No! I just came in for a dance and a few drinks, and remember you said, 'Lunchtime, you are busy today, and I quote, '<u>lots to do.</u>' So, no, I have not come here to stalk you; I want a couple of drinks. Can't a girl let her hair down without being accused of stalking?"

"I apologize, I have a lot on my mind."

"That's not an excuse for talking like you did to me."

"I've apologized, and I mean it. Can I get you a drink?"

"Vodka and coke, please."

I walked to the bar to get the drinks, only to turn and see she had made herself comfortable at my table. But I had to be careful; she knew a lot about me. I carried the drinks over and sat down at the table. Initially, it was awkward, as I had just snapped at her. But as the music became more up-tempo, the noise grew, too. I tried to compliment Beryl again for her sultry look.

"What did you have for your dessert?" I asked.

"Gooseberry pie with custard it was very sharp in its taste but was delicious. I then went shopping for this outfit. What do you think?" she said as she stood up to show it off.

It was a checker card pattern of green, black, and white, which looked fashionable. "It looks gorgeous on you, but then again, everything you wear seems to."

"So, you approve of it then?"

I smirked and then nodded.

"Dance?" she asked.

"No, I'm okay," I replied, even though I wanted to.

"Come on; it's only a dance. I have got nobody else to dance with."

I stood up, and she grabbed my hand and led me onto the dance floor.

Whilst twisting her waist left and right, she put her arms around my neck and got up close. I could smell her delicious perfume wafting up my nose, and as I touched her waistline, she drew me in and kissed me. "What do you want from me, Beryl?" I whispered in her ear.

"To have you now and again."

"What do you mean, Beryl?"

"I want to take you to bed as often as possible."

"I'm with Heather."

"I do not want to take you away from her. I want you to keep me warm sometimes."

"You want me to treat you like a whore? Why? You're stunningly beautiful, smart, and fashionable. Some men would give their right arm to give you everything you want."

"Firstly, I do not like the word whore. Lover sounds so much better, and I do not care about other men; I only have eyes for you."

"I can't do this," I said as I shook my head and walked off the dance floor to return to the table.

"I know you are attracted to me, and I do not understand the problem?"

"You're having a fucking laugh, aren't you, Beryl?"

"What's the problem?"

"The problem is, I have Heather and love her more than anything. In your mind, it's easy; in mine, I'd have to face her knowing I had just cheated on her. You have a fundamental problem, Beryl; it's called madness."

"Look at me! Look at me! Tell me you do not fancy me, and I will leave now, and you will not see me again. Look at me, and tell me the truth?"

I couldn't look at her. But I did have feelings for her, and I did want to see her again.

"You do have feelings for me, don't you? I cannot help how I feel about you; it is what it is, and if I cannot have you all to myself, I will settle for just some of you. Now kiss me so I can feel your warm lips on mine."

I'd succumbed to Beryl's seduction. I looked into her eyes and kissed her gently on the lips. She aroused me in seconds as I ran my hand up her thighs and into her panties, where I gently massaged her clitoris. All her senses were heightened, as were mine. There would not be time to go back to hers. "Come on," I grabbed her by the hand and took her upstairs to the offices; we ended up in the security office. I locked the door so no one would come in. We hastily took our clothes off in the excitement and anticipation of the moment. I pushed her to lay on the table, whipping her panties off and then pulled out my hard cock and pushed it deep inside her, thrusting as hard as I could whilst she moaned with delight, her legs over my shoulder, looking for deeper penetration whilst cupping her breasts. Her fingernails dug deep into my back as I penetrated harder until I climaxed her. We were both breathless as she lay on the table, but I said, "We have to get out of here before someone sees us."

"Now you see why I need you. I am excited whenever I am around you."

I looked at Beryl, thinking this could work. But I was not a hundred per cent sure, but I had to be on the train to Aberdeen in a few hours and needed to get home to Heather.

I got a taxi, dropped Beryl home, and said I'd see her next week. I then asked the driver to take me home.

I paid the driver and left the car only to see my bedroom light on. I knew Heather was up and waiting because the light would usually be out. So, I let myself in and went straight to our bedroom. Heather was sat up against the pillows and had been crying.

"What is it, sweetheart?" I asked. She held her arms out for a cuddle and started sobbing. I wrapped my arms around her to comfort her, knowing something was wrong. *Was it Mum?* I thought. "Sweetheart, please tell me what's wrong?"

"I'm pregnant!" she articulated and then burst into tears.

"No! You can't be!" I thought the ground was going to open and swallow me. I couldn't say anything. My head spun, and I felt sick as my stomach knotted. I pulled away from Heather, stood up and went to the bathroom without saying anything. I pounded the bathroom wall so hard it tore the skin from my knuckles. I was so angry that I punched the mirror, too, which broke into a thousand fragments that went all over the place. I sat on the toilet with my face in my hands, wondering what the fuck we do now. I could hear Heather crying, but I was too angry to return to the bedroom. So, I locked the bathroom door, so I wouldn't have to face her.

"Darling, please speak to me?" she asked as she knocked on the door repeatedly.

"Go to bed, Heather, and leave me alone." But instead, I heard her sobbing against the other side of the door.

All I could think of was all the hell we went through with Sarah. It was still too raw for me. I couldn't go through it all again. I must've fallen asleep because the next thing I heard was Zilah crying. I got up off the floor and washed the blood off my hands. I went to open the door and realized there was glass everywhere. I opened the door gently and asked Heather for a sweeping brush to sort the bathroom out. She appeared moments later with the broom, handed it to me, but never uttered a word. After sorting the bathroom and showering, I dressed, ready to go to Aberdeen.

I went into the kitchen and kissed Zilah on the head and then went over to Heather to try and kiss her, but she turned her head then said, "After last night? You must be kidding."

"We'll talk about it when I return," I replied.

"That's right, off you go again for another two days; I'm wondering whether you want to be here with us at all?"

"Now you're being stupid, sweetheart!"

"Am I? Just go and leave us be."

"Fine, I'll see you in a couple of days." And I walked out the door.

At the warehouse, everybody had come together. "Right, lads, let's arm up and get down to the train station. You all know what we must do. If you want to pull out now, then say so. No one will think any different of you." There was a moment's silence. "Right then, let's get moving. We have three changes before we get there so it will be a long day."

When we arrived at the station, I suggested they mingle amongst the other passengers, so we didn't look so conspicuous. However, Michael did sit by me.

"Have you heard from Joe yet?" asked Michael.

"Not yet; if he hasn't called by the time we get to Manchester, I'll call him." I sat there thinking about last night, everything last night. I was so scared that my hands were trembling. If I came out of this unscathed, what would I do? Another baby petrified me, and my feelings for Beryl were uncomfortably playing with my mind. *I'd be better off not surviving*, I thought. "Michael, you look a bit nervous?"

"No more than you, boss."

I tried to stay focused on the task at hand. We went over the plan once again. "Are we missing anything, Michael?"

"Boss, it's fine."

We had a short stop at Birmingham, so I took the opportunity to call Joe. "What's happening, Joe?"

"Boss, he always has three men with him. He spends most of his time in the house; we've only seen him once, and guess what, boss? He's in a wheelchair."

"Can we make the hit without the neighbours noticing?"

"The house is a hundred metres away from anywhere. There are two cars parked out the front. Both have not moved since we have been here. I do not know to whom they belong?"

"Okay, Joe, can you slash the tyres on them? If we must move quickly, we need those cars undrivable."

"We'll make it happen, boss."

"Okay, we'll be with you in a few hours."

We changed trains and headed for Scotland. Peering out the window on the train was quite relaxing; so much land was covered in grass and wheat. The landscape was beautiful, far better than at home. *This could be an excellent place for the kids to grow up,* I thought.

The train eventually arrived in Aberdeen, and we took taxis to Tillydrone in two's, so we didn't look suspicious.

Michael and I caught a Taxi to St Georges Church, Tillydrone—just a few minutes from Jimmy Macdonald's place. We started approaching Joe and Jimmy, who were staking the premises in the Cortina in Thistle Lane. We arrived and jumped into the Cortina,

"How we doing, lads?" I asked as I drew a cigarette. "Did we sort the cars, lads?"

"Yes, boss, they're going nowhere," said Jimmy.

"The house looks exposed; it wouldn't be difficult to catch sight of us approaching, so we'll wait for the others; we might have to rethink?"

"Why, boss?" asked Michael.

"We don't know how many are in there and what weapons they have. We can't get this wrong, or we'll all go down together for a long time."

Everybody had arrived within half an hour; we concealed ourselves in the lane with Joe as a lookout.

"Lads, we can't hit them in the light of day. We must wait until it gets dark. Joe, what's the access to the property like?"

"There is a door to the rear of the house, along with three glass windows. There is also a plain glassed side door which should be easy to get through. I know three guys are inside, but I don't think the cars are being used; they have not moved since we have been here. It all looks and sounds incredibly quiet, if I say so, boss."

I was a little hesitant; I couldn't be one hundred per cent sure there was only Jimmy Macdonald and two others inside. I sat in the car, racking my brains, still unsure whether this was the right way to deal with him. "We'll wait till eleven o'clock. Michael, Paul, and I will go through the front door. Joe, Jimmy, and Brian, you will hit the rear door. Roger and Ambrose, the side door. If we hit all three doors simultaneously, the chances are we'll catch them off guard. They'll be disorientated; I don't want gunfire unless it's a life-or-death scenario. But on the other hand, if only three of them exist, it should be a cakewalk. Have we got this?"

There was a spirited reaction from everyone.

"Leroy, I want you to stay with the car, especially if we must make a fast getaway."

"What does Jimmy look like, Joe?"

"He's got shoulder-length dark black hair, a scar above his right eye and a black moustache. He was sitting in a wheelchair when we clocked him, boss."

The cold darkness of night drew in, and we continued to wait nervously. Then, finally, the evening darkness had arrived, and the time was right for us to make our move. "We, ready?" I asked. Collectively, we encroached on the house of this Scottish piece of shit. Michael kicked the front door in; all I could hear was the other doors and glass breaking as it fell to the floor. Michael and I moved into what looked like the central room of the house. There was shouting from upstairs where Joe and Jimmy were, and a guy in the backroom drugged up on heroin, needle marks all down his arm. Michael grabbed the guy and put his hand around his mouth as I watched him puncture the guy franticly in his back with his knife.

I went up the stairs to find Joe and Jimmy hovering over a bed with the piece of scum. Another guy lay dead on the floor. Ambrose had slit his throat. It was so easy I couldn't believe it. The dim lighting was perfect for us. Ambrose and Roger pulled Jimmy out of bed, the piece of shit screamed, "I can't walk." Ambrose picked him up and sat him on a chair.

"Who are you? What do you want?" he squealed.

Michael came up the stairs, and I asked him to grab me a chair. Michael pulled one over for me, and I put it in front of this piece of scum and sat on it. I calmly lit a cigarette and exhaled it in his face. "You Sottish bastard, you tried to kill me."

"I don't know what you're talking about; I've done nothing wrong."

"Do you know who I am?"

"No, no, fucking idea, you cunt! You're a fucking dead man. That goes for all of you bastards!"

"Very verbal now, aren't we?" I got up real close to his face. "Hendrick brothers ring any bells?" I looked in the corner of the room, where my eye caught sight of a baseball bat. I strolled over and picked it up. I swung it as if to hit a baseball, "Oh, this feels just right," I spoke. "Ambrose, Paul, hold his arms behind him."

"What are you going to do? Please tell me what I can do?" squealed Jimmy.

"Nothing!" I swung the bat hitting him in the chest. I could hear bones cracking as he spit blood from his mouth. Again and again, I struck blows to his chest. He was almost unconscious when I told him who I was. He glared at me with his bloodshot eyes whilst choking on his blood. I said, "I'm about done here. You can go to fucking hell along with the rest of the Scottish scum you sent to kill me." I then picked up a spirit bottle and put the neck part in his mouth as deep as I could force it. I swung the baseball bat and smashed the bottle down his throat. He lingered for a few moments, his body shaking and then his breathing stopped, and I had my revenge!

"Right, lads, let's get out of here." I carried the baseball bat out, and the lads whipped off any blood-stained clothing to discard. Michael, Joe, and I returned to the Cortina, where Leroy was waiting. The rest of the lads would make their way south in their own time. We drove away from the estate, which was still dark and quiet. Nobody would have thought anything had happened. But I assume at some time, their bodies would be found. We left no fingerprints or anything else that could bring any attention to us. We made it look like a gangland hit.

When we arrived home, I visited my house to see Heather and Zilah. I was still trembling from the vile attack we caused on the Scottish scum who tried to have me killed. I walked into the house only to see Heather playing with a dough mix with Zilah. There was flour and bits of dough all over the place, including Zilah's hair and face. They were having so much fun.

"Oh, look, here's Daddy," said Heather. Zilah turned to look at me and ran towards me. I picked her up and hugged her so hard. I smiled at Heather, and she came over and wrapped her arms around me. I felt peculiar, but I had ensured Heather and Zilah were safe.

"Do you want to talk about it?" asked Heather.

"Not really, it has been sorted, and we'll never worry about that scum again. Which means we don't need the protection outside the house anymore."

"Well, I am glad you are safe. But our daughter would love some of your attention while I clean up," said Heather.

I helped Zilah build blocks with her wooden bricks, just for her to knock them down again and giggle, obviously finding it very amusing, the little monkey.

Heather had tidied up and put tea in the oven. I sat in front of the fire with a cognac and a cigarette. My hands were still trembling badly, which I couldn't control.

All I could think of was I was turning into the man I detested most on this planet. Going from petty theft to murder, getting everything, I ever wanted along the way, I couldn't control my behaviours anymore. I'd done everything terrible in this world apart from starting a war. It's time for me to get out of the business and settle down properly with Heather, Zilah, and the new child when it arrives. Somewhere up north?

The following day, I decided to go over to Mum's and see how she was baring up. She was still in bed feeling low, with Bernie keeping vigil again.

Dad had gone racing for the first time in weeks. So, I was glad he wasn't there.

I held Mum's hand as she lay prostrate on the bed, face etched in fear. She knew she was dying but didn't know when. She just grew increasingly tired every day. Finally, she smiled at me and then closed her eyes.

"How are we doing, sis? You look so tired?"

"I'm okay, I catch a knap here and there, so I'm okay."

I said, "Heather's pregnant again, and I'm not sure I can endure all that hurt again if the same thing happens?"

"They're bound to look for that kind of thing this time because of what happened with Sarah."

"Umm, I suppose so. Do you want a cuppa? I'm going to have a cognac."

"Yes, that would be nice, Tony."

I went to the kitchen to make the drinks; as I poured Bernie's tea, I caught sight of a shadow out of the corner of my eye, moving through the hallway. "Sis, is that you?" I asked, but there was no reply. I walked down the hallway, admittedly a little spooked. "Is anyone there?" Again, there was no answer. I walked into Mum's room, where Bernie was still sitting in the same position.

"Are you okay, Tony?" Bernie asked.

"You haven't heard anybody come in, have you?"

She shook her head. "No, why?"

"Nothing," I returned to the kitchen to get the drinks. As I entered the kitchen, a teaspoon fell to the floor from the work surface. I stared at it momentarily, wondering how it reached the floor. Eventually, I leaned over, picked it up, and put it into the sink. I took Bernie's drink in and asked, "Have you heard, seen, or felt anything strange in this house?"

"What are you talking about?"

"Anything, anything strange at all?"

"No! I have not," replied Bernie.

I shook my head, finished my drink, and went home to Heather.

When I got home, Edward was already there waiting for me. "Are you okay, bro?" I asked.

"No, you need to come down to Manor Park and see what the council have done?"

"I'll not be long, sweetheart. Come on then, bro, let's see what's going on?"

When we arrived at Manor Park, there were bollards across the entrance to the lorry park and a ticket machine on a wall. The council were looking for payments to park. I couldn't believe it. I knew it would happen but not as quickly as this. "Are there any machines put up at the other parks, bro?"

"No, thank fuck."

"It's only one park, bro. So, we'll push up the price of tickets to the drivers that will encourage them to stay in the parks we're working in."

"Do you want me to get over to the printers, Tony?"

"Yes! Tell them to make the tickets for £1.50 each. Remember, drivers still pay us the same but will earn a little extra from their companies. Now, can you drop me at the warehouse first?"

Once we got to the warehouse, I unlocked the door, and Edward drove off.

I sat in the office and reviewed the figures, what the parks deductions from all the businesses would cost me and if I'd have to invest more money into drugs, alcohol, and other contraband. Finally, after hours of working out the finances, I estimated the parks would cost me around ten thousand pounds a year.

But I could make it back up with more contraband shipments from France, Belgium, and Holland.

Heather rang and said, "Colin's looking for you."

"Okay, sweetheart, can you just let him know I'm at the warehouse."

"Yes, sure; what time will you be home today?"

"Six, six thirty, sweetheart."

Half an hour later, Colin entered the warehouse, "Hiya Colin, Heather said you were looking for me?"

"Yes, it's Blakely?"

"What about him?" I asked, in a concerned tone.

"The file from the killings has been put away as we cannot find anything that would help the investigation. In addition, the blood samples taken from the mirror do not bring anybody up on our records. So, you are in the clear, at least for now."

"That's great news, Colin."

Colin nodded, said, "Sure is," and left the warehouse.

I cleared up a few things and left for home. On my way back to the house, I decided to take a shortcut up through Linked Lane, as it took ten minutes off my walking time. As I walked through the lane, my sense of smell caught a putrid aroma. *What a stench?* I thought. I must have been three quarters of the way through when I saw a grain sack on the floor moving. "What the fuck?" As I bent down to see what was inside, I heard a whimper come from within. I opened the grain sack and found three puppies inside. One was alive and very skeletal, black, and tan. But sadly, the other two were dead. *Some bastard must have left them there to die. If I catch them, I'll kill them,* I thought. "Hello, little one," I said as I picked him up. The putrid smell was coming from the dead puppies, and the stench had clung to the little fellow. He was so dirty, but underneath the dirt, I knew he would look so cute; I noticed he had huge paws for such a tiny body. "Come on, fella." I cradled him in my arms. "We'll get you some food, a bath, and warmth by my fire."

I entered the house with this skinny little thing in my arms. Heather caught sight of us whilst changing Zilah.

"Oh, my God, what have you done?" said a surprised Heather.

"I've not done anything, sweetheart. I found this little fellow in Linked Lane in a grain sack with two dead puppies."

"Can we keep him? He would be great for Zilah and me, and I have free time now I am a stay-at-home parent?"

"That's why I brought him home."

"I will take care of him," said Heather as she took him out of my arms and hurried upstairs to the bathroom to bathe him. Zilah followed Mummy and the puppy upstairs, fascinated by the dog.

"Darling? Zilah's coming up over the stairs behind you," I shouted.

Heather had finished bathing the puppy and brought him downstairs to the kitchen, where she fed him small pieces of cooked chicken and a bowl of warm milk. Once provided, the puppy wobbled into the lounge and sat by the fire. "Wow! You little fella, what a difference now you're clean and smelling of perfume." I petted his ears.

"Oh, darling, he's so cute, isn't he?" Zilah didn't know what to do or make of this creature that had somehow invaded our home. She continued to annoy the puppy by trying to grab his tail. Finally, she fell over and knocked her leg against the leg of the coffee table. The puppy jumped on her and wanted to lick her. Zilah cried, not knowing what was going on. But from that moment, the puppy would become part of the family.

I turned the television on as the national news came on. Police had discovered the bodies in the house in Tillydrone and were looking for any information that could lead them to the person or persons responsible.

"This...This was an appalling and vicious attack on three male adults. Officers who found the bodies are sickened by what they saw," said the news reporter. They assumed it was gang-related as there were so many gangs in Scotland.

My vengeance was complete. For the best part of the next six months, everything went smoothly. Apart from losing one of the lads, Joseph Ball, who died of a heart attack. I ensured the family were cared for financially. Heather had put on extra weight during this time, which was to be expected because of the pregnancy, and she was just weeks away from having our baby. But I was selfish and dishonest to her. I spent the odd night with Beryl, who became comfortable with the situation. The hospital had done multiple tests throughout the pregnancy, reassuring us the baby would be born without a defect when it entered our world. The dog? Well, we called him Duke. He was a monster of a dog. We found out he was a German Shepherd. He had grown, but he was a real softie, and Zilah adored him. The business was booming, and Katy was an asset as my assistant. The parks were causing issues, but not as bad as they might have done. Mum was very poorly, and Bernie kept vigil.

Edward and Linda debated whether to marry or live as a common-law couple. Edward didn't want to, but Linda argued over it forever. My concern was that I needed to find out if he had a total focus on the area of my business. But he said he always would have the company at the forefront of his life.

"I haven't married Heather, bro, but I love her so much, and as things stand, we don't talk about it. Why don't we go out? You me and Alan for the evening—a little brotherly love. We arranged it, and off we went to the Fox-pit club—lively entertainment with drag artists and pretty dance girls. We sat at the table with a red tablecloth and a red lampshade gracing the centre. The stage was ornate in the art deco style. The waitress wore a red Basque and suspender stockings and frilly panties as she approached the table. She must have had six-inch heels that were gold in colour. Her dark hair fell straight over her shoulders with a red feather scything through it. Edward and Alan couldn't take their eyes off her.

"Would you look at that? Please tell me you two wouldn't take her to bed?" said Edward.

"Of course, I would take her to bed, bro," I replied.

"What about your little one?" I asked.

"I am no longer a fucking little one; now, can we just get drinks?" replied Alan.

"Hey, gorgeous, can I have a large cognac, Chest? What do you want?"

"I will have a Vodka and Coke, double, please,"

"Alan, what do you want, a lemonade? I jested? He looked at me with daggers. "Seriously, what do you want?"

"I will have a pint of lager."

"Have one yourself, darling. What's your name? I don't want to call you darling all night?"

"It's Precious!" she replied. Winking at me.

"I bet you are," I said. smiling back at her.

"It is my name," she said as she giggled and went to get our drinks.

The things that started running through my mind were intense. But I was here with my younger brothers. "Hey, Bros, the drag queen is Diamond Dream. He's outstanding; he sings, does comedy and strips." A few minutes later the lights dimmed, and the curtain went up and stood there in a long emerald and gold dress down to his feet, with a huge blonde wig and a mass of makeup, was Diamond Dream. The show began with Diamond Dream singing 'Hey Jude' by the Beatles. He bellowed it out like a great singer.

Meanwhile, Precious had brought our drinks to the table. I pulled out a cigarette and lit it whilst Precious placed my drink before me; she gave me another wink and a smile.

"Thank you, Precious." I smiled back at her. *She fancies me*, I thought. Well, we all laughed until we almost cried. The show was terrific, and being out with my brothers was great. I suggested we'd play a game I made up called pick and mix. We'd pick a drink from the shelves behind the bar, which we counted was forty-one. We chose a number without looking, and then we'd select a mixer to go with it, and if you refused to drink it, you had to buy the next three rounds. We tasted so many disgusting drinks because we had to match a spirit with coke, lemonade, orange juice, water, pineapple juice or peppermint. We hammered the bar and had the piss taken from us by Diamond Dream. It was the first time I had laughed so much in such a long time. Then Alan started throwing up everywhere, so I told Edward to get him home because he was just as pissed. I watched outside the club as they crawled into a taxi, laughing like shit. It was so funny. I then went back into the club. Diamond Dream had finished singing and making jokes, and the crowd were raucous.

It was time for Diamond Dream to strip. Of course, I didn't return to watch a guy dressed as a lady strip off. I went back to order another drink and hopefully get precious's attention. I sat at the table and waited for Precious to become free from serving another table. I couldn't understand why everyone was standing to watch a guy get his kit off. My brothers and I came in for entertainment, singing and comedy, and the scantily dressed waitresses.

Precious arrived at my table smiling. "Can I have a cognac, please, and would you have a drink on me?"

"What happened to your mates?" she asked.

"They're my younger brothers, they both had too much to drink, so I made sure they got in a taxi to get home safely. Just out of curiosity, what time do you finish tonight?"

She looked at her watch and said, "In half an hour; why?"

"Just wondered if you fancy a drink at another bar?"

"Would love to," she said as she smiled and walked back to the bar.

Half an hour later, we walked out of the club and went to the Malt and Shovel, a quiet club for those who just wanted to chill and relax.

I took Precious to a table and ordered a drink at the bar. Again, I got the impression Precious was a lady. Her English was brilliant, and she ordered a glass of white wine. I returned to the table with the drinks. As I put the glasses down, I jested, "It must be nice for someone else to serve you drinks."

She smiled and said, "Thank you."

We sat for a good hour conversing and laughing about anything and everything. I then told Precious I thought she was beautiful and sexy.

"Thank you, and you are very handsome too," she replied. She then leaned in to kiss me. I found out she lived outside the city, so I asked her if she fancied a hotel.

"You are quite forward, aren't you?"

"People tell me that, but I think if two people fancy each other, what's the point of trying to hide it?"

"Why not! Do you know of one nearby?" she asked. We finished our drinks and walked out to get a taxi. I pulled a cab over, and we jumped in. "The Stanton Hotel, please."

We got cosy in the taxi and started kissing. I could feel my pulse racing as we were all over each other in the back seat. We arrived at the hotel with no luggage and asked for a room. The lady, 'possibly' in her fifties, looked us both up and down with disgust.

"Have we a problem?" I asked, "Or should we move on to another hotel?"

She turned and took a key from the key box and turned back and said, "Your room number is six, and breakfast is between nine and ten."

"Please don't worry about breakfast; we're going to have breakfast with the strippers from the nightclub." I smiled, picked up the key, and said, "We'll try not to make too much noise," I winked at the old fuddy-duddy.

We hastened to the room and enjoyed a passionate night together. I was awakened by a nightmare of seeing my Sarah swinging on the old oak tree at Mum's house. I was sweating profusely. My heart was in my stomach when I realised it was a nightmare. And Sarah wasn't here anymore. My head was so fucked up I didn't know what I was doing. I betrayed Heather again, I knew I was doing wrong, but I couldn't control myself. I blamed my father for everything, and although my mind was sometimes disturbed, I could not blame him for adultery. I climbed out of bed and left the hotel, leaving the money on the reception desk and Precious still sleeping. I gave no thought to how she would feel when she saw I had disappeared. I had to go home and explain my absence overnight to Heather. What was I to say? What excuse could I make this time? I was indeed running out of constant reasons for my bad behaviour.

Before going home, I popped into Mum's and went straight to Edward's bedroom, where he still lay in a drunken stupor. "Bro," I said as I shook his shoulders. "Bro, wake up!" Linda turned and looked at me.

"What are you doing in here?" she asked whilst yawning.

"I'm sorry to disturb you, Linda. I need a word with this drunken fool!"

"What time is it?" asked Linda.

"Linda, it's seven o'clock. Bro, wake up!" I said sternly.

"What... What do you want? Why are you in here?"

"Bro, I need a favour, a big favour?"

"What?" he replied.

"I need you to say I was with you most of the night as you were so pissed?"

"What? What have you done?" he asked.

265

"I slept with Precious. You know, the brunette from the club."

"You didn't? What were you thinking, Tony? You have such a beautiful partner."

"Bro, can you please help me?" Linda looked at me with the devil's eyes. But I knew Edward would make sure she didn't say anything.

"Okay, bro."

"Thank you." I left to go home, knowing I had an alibi for my whereabouts.

Heather was as expected when I got in, feeding our little princess. "Awe, what a night I've had. Bloody brothers can't manage to drink." Heather glared at me as if she knew I was lying. She continued to feed and talk to Zilah. I went upstairs to bathe. When I came back down, I thought I was being interrogated.

"Where did you go? How long were you there? How long does it take to make a call?" Questions after fucking questions.

"Don't you trust me?" I snarled. She shook her head and went upstairs, crying. It was fucking early, but I still poured myself a cognac.

"Da-da," said Zilah as she stared at me with all the innocence you would expect from a three-year-old. I picked her up and hugged her tightly. She was my world, yet I seemed set on destroying everything in my life. Then, I heard Heather race down the stairs and thought, *here we go again*. But instead, she burst into the lounge and threw my stained, sweaty shirt covered in a perfume that Heather would never wear.

"Tell me what that is?" she shouted in tears.

"It was a dance in the club, which was all it was! If you don't believe me, then ask my brothers." She ran out of the house to God knows where! I prayed she wasn't going to evaluate my alibi with my brothers. I didn't know what to do. I couldn't go to work because I had Zilah; I rang Edward to see if Heather had gone to Mum's, but he said she had not arrived yet. So, I asked him if he could get Linda to look after Zilah until Heather got home from wherever she was.

"We are on our way over, bro."

I told them we argued when they arrived, and she ran out.

"Is that surprising?" said Linda.

I looked at Linda and said, "It's my business."

"Well, don't get us involved in it then," she replied.

I looked at Edward and said, "Sort her out!" I then left for the warehouse. I still had work to do. I got to the warehouse where Katy suggested we sit down sometime as she had an idea.

"Not now, Katy. I have a lot on my mind."

"Okay, boss, there is no rush. Are you okay? You look washed out."

"I'm fine; it was just a long night. I took my brothers out; they got so drunk I had to send them home in a taxi. You'd have laughed as I watched them crawl into the taxi; they were pissed."

"It sounds like you all had a good night?"

"Yes, we did."

"How's that little one of yours? And where did you get her wicked name from?"

"She's fine, and her name? We had no idea what to call her, so I suggested we work from the back page of names from the baby's name book. And when Zilah came up, I just went yes! That would be perfect."

"Well, it's an unusual but beautiful name."

"Okay, Katy, have we worked wages out onto the computer?"

"Yes, boss, it took a long time, but I have done it.

"Remember, we pay them in cash. So, the finances must be covered to pay more to the team and their families. Do you understand what I am saying, Katy?" I asked.

"I think so, boss."

I then had a phone call from Edward to say Heather had returned home and that she had enquired where we were last night. So, I told her what you told me to tell her."

"Thanks, bro."

Within moments of the phone going down, I got a call from Colin. He said he was leaving the police force because he could not manage the pressure of constantly seeing Inspector Blakely, and the guilt of taking wages from the police force for dealing with crime, and yet taking wages from the racketeering, a crooked outfit!

"So, you're coming back over to the dark side?" I jested. "It's more fun and a lot better pay." On the serious side, I was concerned about the killing of the Hendrick brothers, for which they had not found any leads. But it was great to have Colin back working full-time with me.

I finished the day and went home to Heather and Zilah, only to be greeted with discontent. We hardly said a word to each other all night. I occupied my seat as expected by the fireside, drinking my way through a bottle of cognac whilst listening to the rain falling outside. Duke was trying to grab my attention while chewing through a tennis ball. Finally, I nodded off in the chair. Only to be awoken by Heather. "The baby is coming; my waters have broken," she said, wincing in pain while holding her tummy crouch-like.

"Okay, sweetheart, just sit for a minute while I ring for an ambulance." I got up off the chair, a little drunk and tired. I rang for the ambulance, and then I rang Edward to come and grab, Zilah as the baby was on the way.

The ambulance arrived and drove us to Freedom Fields, where Heather delivered our second child. Seven pounds and eleven ounces of pure gorgeousness. Light brown hair and blue eyes. Heather first said, "Is she all, right?" Looking ashen and fretting as you would expect after Sarah. But the doctor said she was perfect. Heather cradled the baby in her right arm and held my hand tightly in her other hand. That joyous moment sent us both into an ecstatic frenzy.

Heather needed some stitches and was told she needed to spend a couple of days in the hospital so they could keep an eye on her. I asked Doctor Moore, "Why?"

"Her blood pressure is lower than normal, so it's a precautionary measure."

"Has this happened before, Doctor?"

"A couple of times, but there is nothing to worry about. Your wife is in the best place. But congratulations on your new baby girl." He then just walked off, leaving me concerned. So, I returned to Heather and told her she had to rest.

"Darling? You are going to help me with the children, aren't you?"

I evaded the question by asking Heather what we should call the baby.

"I was thinking of Tara; what do you think?" she said.

"Sounds wonderful, sweetheart. I'll leave you to feed Tara. Do you need anything from home?"

"Can you bring me the book I was reading? It is on the bedside table and some fruit."

"Of course, I can. I'll be in the morning before I go to work. I'll ask Linda if she can hold onto Zilah while I'm working." I kissed Heather and Tara and left the hospital to go home and get some sleep before returning in the morning.

The following day after precious little sleep, I managed to drag myself out of bed and into a cold shower to wake me properly. Linda knocked and let herself in.

"Tony, I'm here?"

"I'll be down in a second, just grabbing Zilah." When I got downstairs, I apologized for what I had said to Linda yesterday. I left Linda with Zilah and made my way back into the hospital. The weather was awful; it was lashing down with rain and thunder rumbling in the distance. I climbed out of the cab and stepped straight into a puddle of water. "Fuck it," I said with a temper. I tried to dry my foot once I got inside the hospital without success. Heather was sat up in the bed with Tara in a crib, asleep beside her.

"How did you sleep last night?" I asked.

"Okay, Tara needed another feed at four this morning, but I did catch a couple of hours. And you, darling, how did you sleep?"

"Fine, has the doctor said anything this morning?"

"Only my blood pressure is still lower than it should be."

I went around the bed to pick up my little girl. "Don't pick her up; she's sleeping," said Heather.

But I ignored her, picked her up, and held her tight. She was warm and soft to the touch as I gently stroked her with my finger over her head and through her fabulous hair. She wriggled a little, so I put her back into the crib before she awoke. The nurse came in and took Heather's blood pressure,

"How do you feel, Heather?" she asked.

"Good, I just can't wait to get home, and I am with both my children."

"Well, that could be soon, as your blood pressure returns. I will let Doctor Moore know." The nurse smiled.

"That's good news, sweetheart." I wrapped my arms around her. Everybody was happy,

I popped over to the warehouse as I had some spare time, and Katy had an idea, and I was intrigued to find out what it was. "Morning, Katy."

"Good morning, boss. You look more l like yourself today?"

"Come sit with me and tell me about your idea. Can you pour me a cognac? You'll find a bottle and glass in the third drawer down."

Katy brought my drink over, and we discussed the idea. "Katy, please call me Tony. We will be working side by side for a long time."

"Right, Tony, going through all the paperwork, you have a substantial amount of money coming in, yet, no official business to explain where the money is coming from. If a legal representative from the government investigated this, you could be in real trouble?"

Katy was right; I was too busy thinking about making money. I didn't give it a thought if somebody asked me how I made money. How could I have been so naïve and incompetent? I started earning money through bare-knuckle fighting and betting on myself all over the County. But all the rest from the businesses? I just had Michael pay the team out of the ill-gotten gains.

"Tony? Why don't you put excess money into property? It would cover any discrepancies?"

I sat and pondered for a few moments; what a great idea. Katy was right; I could start buying property. It had to be safer than the safe in my house. "Katy? I love you."

I pecked her on the cheek. "I knew you were too clever to be a barmaid."

"Thanks, Tony. You know you could set up a business here too, to make you legitimate?"

"What could I do in here? It's a warehouse and my office?"

"Well, you need to think hard about it because even buying property shows money coming in. You need something to cover up your illegal businesses."

"Thank you, Katy. I will give it serious thought."

I rang Michael to pick me up and take me over to Mum. I knew I would struggle to keep visiting as much as I would like with the baby and work.

I went into the house that gave me the jeepers, to find Bernie sitting on the sofa with Mum, who looked so pale and tired she could hardly speak.

"Hiya, Mum, how are we feeling today?" The anguish on her face was plain to see, as she struggled to talk and could barely hold my hand. Bernie used a cotton bud to roll over Mum's lips to moisten them. I was crying inside as my mum seemed to be losing her battle for life. Michael sat with Mum whilst I took Bernie into the kitchen. "Sis, how are you doing?" She broke down before me, hugging me whilst crying on my shoulder. I tried to comfort her as best as I could. Finally, I asked her if it would be better to go home to her husband, Robert. With whom she had spent extraordinarily little time since they got married.

"No! I need to be here for Mum. I do not care about Robert."

"You know that's not true, sis. I know you're hurting, but Robert can help more than anyone.

We made our way back to Mum. "Where's the bastard?" I asked.

"Same place as usual, at the racetrack; he does not give a shit. I do not even know why he must stay here?"

"Because that's what Mum wanted, sis. That's all that matters. He will get his comeuppance one day. I promise you he'll be out of our lives forever!"

"How's Heather and the baby?"

"They're fine; you should see her, sis; she's so beautiful, as is the baby, of course." I laughed at my attempt at a joke.

"When are they going to be home? I cannot wait to see the new baby?"

"Hopefully, I'll bring Tara around tomorrow for Mum to see."

"That would be nice, bro."

"Shout for me if you need me, sis, please?" Then, on my way out of the house, I felt cold in the air in the passageway. "Sis!" I shouted.

"What is it, Tony?"

"Come here and tell me what's different?" My sister made her way to me.

"What am I supposed to think is different?"

"You can't feel anything?" I asked.

"No! I cannot."

"Doesn't matter; I'll see you tomorrow if Heather and Tara come home. Michael, fancy a drink?"

"Sounds good, boss."

We arrived at the pub and ordered drinks. "Usual, Viv and a pint of your finest for Michael."

"I haven't seen you for a while; what have you been doing with yourself?"

"This and that. And I have a new baby."

"Congratulations, is it a boy or a girl?" Viv inquired.

"A little girl named Tara." I turned around, and Barbara was standing behind me.

"Are you going to get me a drink?"

"Barbara's usual, please. There you go, Barbara." I then went and sat down with Michael.

"Michael, I need a legitimate business that I can run from the warehouse, any idea? I need to declare some tax for the inland revenue."

"What about second-hand cars? You could get ten in there?"

"You're a genius, Michael. Let's make it happen. Let's get a few cars in and somebody to start selling them."

"I will get on it as soon as we finish here, boss."

"Thanks, Michael." A few drinks later, we exited the club and jumped in the car, and Michael took me back to the warehouse. "Oh, Michael, Colin is leaving the force and working full-time for me."

"That is good news. So, I take it all that business with the Hendricks is finished?"

"No leads, Michael; they've had no choice but to file them away." Back at the warehouse, I spoke to Katy, praising her for the work she had done so quickly in the brief time she had worked for me. The business was booming, and I wanted a holiday away from it all, as the last few months have had their moments. Christmas was coming, and I wanted to treat Heather to a holiday abroad. I fancied Paris, as it was supposed to be the most romantic city in the world, and I wanted some of it. We'd leave the kids with Edward and Linda and spend quality time together. So, I went to the travel shop and booked a week in a jewel of a hotel on the chic Avenue Montaigne, close to the Eiffel Tower, along with plane tickets from Heathrow to Charles de Galle, a brochure of Paris and its famous monuments. *Heather will be so excited,* I thought.

I hurried to the hospital to give Heather the excellent news. When I arrived, she fed Tara whilst lying on the bed under her gown. "How are you feeling, sweetheart?"

"Yes, good, a little a bit sore. Munchkin is giving me some welly."

"Well, I've some good news. So, you're going to want to hear about it?" Heather tried to sit up whilst smiling, waiting for the good news.

"No… not yet! Wait till Munchkin has finished feeding." At the same time, I climbed onto the bed and lay next to Heather, watching our little piece of joy suckling. "I'm glad that's you and not me; she's sucking so hard!" Finally, Tara fell asleep on Heather's breast, so Heather put her back in the crib.

"Okay, then, tell me this good news?"

I pulled the tickets from my suit jacket pocket and showed her them.

"I do not understand. Why are you showing me this?" Heather said with a disdainful look.

"It's a holiday, sweetheart, to the most romantic city in the world. You're going to love it? Shopping for Christmas on the Champs-Élysées?"

"I am not leaving my baby with Linda or anybody else. She is only a couple of days old. What would ever make you think I would leave my newborn to go on holiday? Are you mad?"

Heather took the wind out of my sails. I thought she would be happy to have a few days away. But instead, I got angry inside as my blood started to boil.

"Darling, maybe in four or five months, but not now."

I can't say I wasn't disappointed; I built myself up to go away and have a holiday abroad, which I could only imagine whilst growing up. Heather could see I was disappointed and tried to comfort me with her soft tone and choice of words. I just wanted to get out of the hospital for a cigarette and wish I had a bottle of cognac to wash away my disappointment.

While I was puffing away on my cigarette, two nurses walked past me and said something to each other; it had to be about me because they were giggling, and one turned and smiled at me. I put my cigarette out and went back inside to Heather.

"I know you are disappointed, darling, but we can go in the summer when the baby is old enough to be on a bottle. Then, the weather will be warmer too."

"Suppose so," I said with a sullen look. "What time do you want me to pick you up tomorrow?"

"I will call you once I get the go-ahead from Doctor Moore."

I nodded and kissed her forehead. "I'll see you tomorrow." I left only to go straight to the Jack and Hammer. "Bottle of cognac, please,"

"Sorry, sir. We cannot sell it by the bottle."

"Then can I have Two!... Two! doubles." I snapped.

"Any ice or water with that?" asked the bartender.

"No! As it comes out of the bottle," I said sarcastically in a harsh tone. He put them down on the bar and grinned. I took them to a table adorned in white linen. I paused for thought as I peered out the window onto the canal, the sun glistening over its shallow waters.

"Are one of those for me?"

I knew that voice; I turned only to see Beryl waiting to sit at my table, dressed in a white chiffon blouse and a dark black pencil skirt, looking as stunning as ever. I snapped, "Before you say anything, I've just had a daughter, and Heather's still in the hospital. So, I'm sorry if I've not been around for a few weeks."

"Oh, you do sound a bit temperamental. What's wrong?"

"Nothing!"

"Should I leave and come back in again?"

"Sorry, I'm just feeling sorry for myself. I planned a Christmas break with Heather in Paris, thinking it would

278

give us time alone. But Heather doesn't want to leave the baby."

"Well, you don't have to waste them, do you? I mean, I have never been to Paris," said Beryl. "I understand her, and I wouldn't take a baby that new to a foreign country."

"Do you want a drink, Beryl?"

"Don't mind if I do. Oh, you should see my place now. I have had it redecorated. You will love the bedroom?"

"Maybe I'll pop around in a couple of days?"

"Sounds great. Looking forward to it."

We chatted away all afternoon, not realising I was becoming more intoxicated.

"Come on... Why don't you come back with me?" asked Beryl.

I tried to stand up but was so intoxicated that I fell back on the table.

"No... you don't, come on, let's get you out of here and somewhere to sleep it off."

The next time I opened my eyes, I was in Beryl's bed, half-naked. Beryl asked if I felt better, as I had been asleep for hours.

"Yes, thank you. So much better, but I need to be going. Heather and the baby will need picking up in a few hours."

"Why don't you pick them up from here?"

"I need to ring my brother; they have Zilah." I phoned him as I watched Beryl's eyes light up, knowing she got me to stay. No sooner had the phone gone down than she undressed, jumped into bed beside me, and started kissing me passionately. A while later, I received a phone call from Bernie, and I must admit I was petrified of the worst.

I answered the phone to the haunting cries of Bernie wailing.

"Sis, I need you to calm down and tell me what's happened?"

"It is Mum, Tony. She will not wake up."

I felt sick; I trembled like never before. "Not my mum… Please, God, not my mum!" I cried out. Beryl rang a taxi for me, and I tried to stay as strong as I could for Bernie to keep her as calm as possible. "I'll be with you, sis, in about ten minutes. Who's there with you?"

"Nobody! Dad has not come home yet. Edward rang me earlier to say he was still at Linda's looking after Zilah."

"Go back in and sit with Mum. I'll be there shortly."

The taxi arrived, and we hastily drove to the house. I ran into Mum's bedroom, where Mum lay prostrate on the bed with her mouth slightly open and with pale skin. Bernie jumped up and almost crushed me in her hug as tears rolled down her face. I put my head against Mum's chest to see if I could hear a heartbeat. It was very faint, but it was there. I told Bernie to lay her head and listen for herself.

"Oh, Tony… She's still alive." We hugged again, but I knew it was only a matter of time before we'd lose the love of our lives. The sweetest and most maternal person we'd have ever known.

I rang Edward, who was at Linda's house, and then Alan, who was still drinking, to get here as fast as they could before it was too late to say goodbye. Bernie and I sat on either side of the bed, holding Mum's hands in a sea of emotion. We prayed that if she had to go to God our Father, could we please have her until everybody could say their goodbyes.

Edward was first to the house; I had to take him in hand before he saw Mum. He was always the baby in the family, even though Alan was the youngest. I couldn't help him from holding back his tears and shivering cries.

A few minutes later, Alan arrived a little intoxicated but in a real mess. Everyone wanted to be at Mum's side. The one person we couldn't get hold of was Dad. He was gambling or drinking with his cronies, but nobody knew where.

Everyone knelt beside the bed and prayed for Mum to recover so we could all say what needed saying. For example, how much we loved her through all the rotten years she spent tormented by Dad's behaviour.

A few minutes passed, and Mum sighed in her last breath. I hoped she knew the people who loved her were at her side in that final moment.

Waterfalls of tears flowed from inside the room as we all sought solace in each other. Never hear Mum laugh, cry, or smile again, or the protection of Mum's arms wrapped around you when you were down or needed comfort. But Heaven was sure to be a better place now that

Mum was there. And for me? I knew she would take care of my tiny Sarah.

I left the others to it and rang the Emergency services. I didn't know what else to do. They said they would send a doctor and a coroner around. I rang the hospital to try and speak to Heather, but they must have been busy. nobody would pick up the phone. So, I returned to the room and told the guys I needed to be at the hospital. And that someone was on their way to see Mum. I was numb; I could hardly combine two words or two steps. This second kick in the teeth was more than I could bear. I needed Heather so much more than anybody else in the world.

I arrived at the hospital and made my way to her room. I entered the room, but Heather was asleep, I gently tapped her on the shoulder, and she turned around to see me in a traumatised state.

"Oh, my God, what is it?" she asked.

Stuttering the words, "It's Mum… She's gone, she's gone." I crumbled in Heather's arms, feeling like a little lost boy with nowhere to go. We spent the rest of the night holding each other. I cried and cried until I could cry no more. Then sadness turned to anger and rage and even hatred. We left the hospital, and I took Heather over to Linda's with the baby, where Linda and Zilah waited. I had a quick cuddle with Zilah and then went to my house.

I saw Edward and Alan outside as I came up the drive. I cuddled them both and went into the house. Bernie came out of Mum's room and closed the door behind her. She had been crying all night.

"They haven't taken Mum yet."

"I'm sorry, sis; I rang the services and assumed they would have taken Mum away through the night."

"They're due around nine forty-five."

"Okay, sis, why don't you go home to Rob? I'll take care of everything here?"

Bernie burst into tears again and said she was not leaving Mum.

"Okay, sis, whatever you want? I'm just going in to see Mum one last time."

"No! You cannot go in there, please do not?"

"Why? What are you not telling me?"

"Please don't go in there, Tony."

Something was not right; Bernie did everything to stop me from going in to see Mum. I thought something weird had happened to Mum after she had died. But how wrong could I be? I opened the door only to see my father sitting next to Mum on the chair beside the bed. I saw red. I was hurting; I couldn't control myself. He stood up, and I hurried across the floor to lash out as hard as possible. I punched and punched and punched again; all my anger vented on this piece of shit. I kicked again into his stomach as he lay on the bloody floor. Finally, Edward and Alan burst through the door to pull me off him, petrified I would kill him.

"Get out of here, you bastard!" I bellowed at the top of my voice. He stood up with his blood-spattered face and reluctantly left the house without saying a word. The screams from Bernie, Edward and Alan echoed inside my head as I collapsed to the floor with bleeding knuckles where the skin was torn, where I had battered him.

Edward said, "A black van has pulled up outside to take Mum away."

I got off the floor and held Mum's cold hand one last time. Then they took her away. Bernie was so distraught that the doctor had to administer a drug to help her sleep for a while. After that, I called Robert, Heather, and Linda to come to the house. So, we could be close this evening. It was seven o'clock and the afternoon had taken its toll.

Drinks flowed; the only person not drinking was Heather. We still had two children in the place. But the rest of us got drunk; I suppose to numb the pain we were all feeling.

Michael took the business for the next few weeks while the family still dealt with Mum's passing. I had to organize the funeral and attend to other matters.

Bernie had taken Mum's passing extremely hard, to the extent the doctors were filling her with anti-depressants and sleeping drugs.

Robert seemed lost in a world he didn't think existed. He tried to put up with so much. Now my sister was on the brink of a nervous breakdown. Rob struggled severely to keep the marriage alive. But my sister didn't care; her life was Mum, and nothing or anyone could stop the spiralling downfall she was going through.

Christmas came and went in the blink of an eye. There was no celebration, just despair.

Tara felt like the gift of exchanging one life for another, it seemed like everybody agreed, and all the attention turned to her.

I lost my way, and my drinking increased; I couldn't stop it no matter how hard I tried. Everyone tried to get me to talk, but I couldn't. I had to be strong even though I was hitting the bottle hard. Did nobody understand me? My family meant everything, yet I seemed bent on destroying everything I have and love.

Heather tried so hard to keep me in tune with the world. But I'd lay or sit and watch the sun and moon every day, drink in one hand and cigarette in the other.

Michael and Colin kept the business alive while I spent all my time in a stupor.

Then one night, Heather had enough and started screaming at me, "Don't you ever point that at me!" Whilst I held a bottle in one hand, and a pistol in the other.

"Leave me alone," I screamed back. But Heather continued to chant foul language at me, which didn't seem to let up. Finally, I staggered and struck Heather's face with my hand. I left the house with Heather still crying.

I found myself in Butchers Corner, where the art of bare-knuckle fighting was a common sport. This is because I knew the place so well. It was where I made my money whilst growing up and fighting to the top.

I watched as two guys tried to kill each other over a few quid.

"I'll take on the winner," I shouted, slurring my words, and falling over a boulder I didn't see. I was baying for blood. "It's me! Do you know who I am?" I stated. Of course, they knew who I was; I owned the city. There was a pause in the fighting. They looked at each other to see who would take responsibility for me while I was in this drunken stupor.

"Yeah, you're all shit! I'll even put one arm behind my back." I then fell to the floor unconscious. I woke to the sound of Beryl's voice. I was still half-cooked on drugs and alcohol.

"How did I get here?"

"A friend of mine watched as you fell to the ground, down Butchers Corner, so she rang me at once. So, I came down and brought you back here. I do not think your wife would have appreciated me dropping you home."

"I have to get home."

"What you need is plenty of water and a cold shower?"

"You understand me more than anyone, and you know that, right?" I sobbed.

"Pity I am not your wife then, isn't it?"

"Oh, come here; I have a bad head; it needs soothing."

"Carrying a gun around and being pissed out of your head, I am surprised that is not all you have. You could have been killed?"

"No one can kill me, Beryl. Even though they have tried."

Beryl grabbed a glass of water and said, "Drink this; it will make you feel better."

"Come here! I'll show you what'll make me feel better." Hesitating, Beryl succumbed to my charm, and we ended up making love numerous times, and when we finished, I said, "I've still got those tickets for Paris. I'm sure I can book us in somewhere quickly."

"You want to take me? What will Heather say?"

"She thinks the tickets are gone as we never went when we should've."

"But it is for a week, you cannot go into hiding for that long?" said Beryl.

"I've been hiding all my life; one week is nothing, and you forget she kicked me out."

Beryl lay on top of me and said, "Book it? I will be there." Her eyes lit up like the stars that light the night sky. She was excited at the prospect of us spending a whole week together. The truth was I wanted it too.

I made the arrangements for the first week in February. I knew it would be cold and hoped we might see some snow. I had to get Michael and Colin to take care of business now. They were bound to have questions, so I would produce an answer when the time came. It would give me time to think.

I went back to the house for a change of clothing. Heather answered the door; it looked like she had been crying all night. She turned away from me and left the door open I went straight upstairs for a shower, a shave, and another set of clothes. I came out of the shower with a towel wrapped around my waist. Heather had Tara in her arms and then asked,

287

"Where were you last night?"

"Butcher's Corner," I replied.

"You must be insane to go to that place. I thought the worst last night. You had a gun and waved it around in front of your daughter and me. I was terrified."

"I'm so sorry; I was drunk and out of my mind over Mum."

"That's not an excuse; I was petrified!" She then broke down in tears.

"I've said sorry. I don't know what else you want from me?"

She shook her head as the tears continued to roll down her face, "You… you just don't get it do you?"

"What do you want me to say?" I shouted.

"I need to get away for a while; I need some space," replied Heather.

"You don't have to go anywhere? I'll give you a couple of weeks' space. I need to pack a suitcase, and then I'll be out of your hair for as long as you need." This allowed me to go away without answering questions. I packed a case and gave the girls a big kiss and cuddle and tried to kiss Heather on the lips, but she only offered up her cheek, which I kissed and then started to leave the house when that odd coldness in the air struck again. I paused for a moment as my body temperature dropped. I put the case on the floor and rubbed my arms to warm up. *So strange*, I thought. I picked up the case and left the house, waiting for a taxi to take me to Beryl's.

I called Michael and told him I'd be away for a couple of weeks to let things work themselves out.

Beryl and I landed at Charles de Galle Airport a couple days later to start our adventure. We arrived at the hotel, which looked over the river Seine—to the north stood Notre-Dame on its tiny island in the middle of the Seine. The romantic bridges I read about in the brochure were just beneath us. The Eiffel Tower lay southwest of the Seine. There was so much to see and do. We dressed and hurried out of the hotel. Beryl looked stunning in a black jacket with white trim, a black woollen skirt cut just below the knee, black and white stiletto heels, and a black fascinator. I wore my grey pinstriped three-piece suit with a royal blue and white striped tie and oxford shoes.

The weather was fair, although a little chilly, as we walked towards Notre-Dame along the Seine, admiring all the painters using different strokes as they painted scenes of the river Seine and Notre Dame. We peered over the river with its many riverboats cruising up and down. "Oh, look, darling. They do a riverboat cruise which includes lunch?"

"Well, let's go down those steps over there and see if we can book one?" I replied.

We were lucky as one of the riverboats was leaving in fifteen minutes and included lunch. I just had time for a cigarette. I finished it, and while waiting in the queue, Beryl put her arms around me and passionately kissed me.

I felt a little awkward as everybody stared at us. But then I thought, *this was France. Isn't it famed for its passion and love?*

We boarded the riverboat and sat at a chic little table with a menu I couldn't read. It was in French. "Can you understand what this lot says, darling?"

"No! I do not have a clue."

I pulled out a little booklet I picked up at the airport; it translated English into French, However, trying to find each word took forever. So, finally, I called the waiter over and asked him if he spoke English.

"Non!"

So, I pointed at the menu and asked for whatever it was. Of course, I didn't have a fucking clue. It could've been a roast dog, for all I knew. However, I did manage to find the word for red wine. "Vino, vino?" I asked.

"Oui, Monsieur."

I nodded, and he walked off.

"I wonder what we will eat," said Beryl with a snigger.

"I don't know; what do they eat in France?"

"It will be the same as English food, just spelt differently?"

The waiter returned, showed me the vino bottle, and poured it for us. "Cheers." I offered up my glass to Beryl. Clink, and down went the vino. We discussed what we might do in Paris while looking across the Seine. It was like a different world to back home. The waiter arrived with our food. "Oh, my God? 'Qu'est-ce que c'est?'" I asked, after looking up the words for 'What's this?'

"It looks like grainy corn beef. And French bread," said Beryl.

I tasted what was a spate of pork and chicken livers, followed by mackerel in wine, it tasted like shit. But we were to blame for not knowing the language! However, the vino was okay, and the cruise relaxed. We disembarked at the Notre-Dame Cathedral. It was bustling, and we had to queue for a while. Once we entered the cathedral, we were almost blinded by the kaleidoscope of glass-coloured windows with religious paintings. It was truly magnificent. After two hours of reading about everything and saying a prayer for Mum and Sarah by lighting candles, we exited the cathedral, heads bursting with knowledge. We took a cab to Place de la Concorde to see the famous three thousand three-hundred-year-old Egyptian obelisk.

"Can you believe that's three thousand three hundred years old?" said Beryl.

"That's what it says? Look over there; that is one of the famous fountains," I replied.

We walked hand in hand through the park until we got to a coffee bar, which sat right in the middle of the park, ideal for your walkers to take refreshments, and it sold cognac too. I was happy. "What would you like, babe?"

"Oh, I'm your babe now?"

"Sorry, darling."

"I will try a double espresso."

Now cognac? All I had to do was ask for it. "Un, double espresso Un cognac, s'il vous plait. People were laughing behind us, something I wasn't accustomed to. But at least we were trying to talk and order in their language. We sat and drank our drinks. However, I'd never have what Beryl had. Apart from it being very bitter and pungent, it came in a kid's tea set cup. I thought they were trying to rip us off because we were not coherent. But we sat and marvelled at the wonder of this place. I sat and tried to learn the basics of French for things like coffee, newspapers, and the odd meal and train station.

A few days in, I could order coffee and say hello or goodbye, thank you, and please. But that was it; it was a case of playing charades the rest of the time. Then, we often spent time in bed after getting drunk. But there were moments when I could only think about Heather and the kids; I miss them dearly. But I'll return home when Heather asks me to come home.

I was guilty of betrayal to my common-law wife and my children, and it hung around my neck like the hangman's noose waiting to tighten and send me off to our maker and accept the punishment my mother and daughter would deal to me.

Beryl asked if we could visit the Louvre, but I didn't feel well and wanted a little time alone. I told her she should not miss anything just because I felt unwell. So, she left, and I poured a drink and sat at the window overlooking the Seine, wishing Heather were here. Beryl was great fun, good in bed, and extremely attractive. She knew me well and could satisfy me in every way. But I was far from home and missing Heather and the kids.

It was close to five p.m. when I got a phone call from Robert, who had been trying to get hold of me for hours.

"Are you okay, Rob? You sound a bit stressed?"

"Tony... Bernie has been taken away and put into Freedom Fields; the doctor said she may have to go into a psychiatric ward."

"What? What do you mean taken away, Rob?"

"She has not stopped crying since your mum passed. The doctor says she's had a mental breakdown, so they took her away."

"Robert... Listen to me; I'll be with you soon. Please don't go anywhere until I get there. Do you hear me?"

"No, I will stay here," he said, crying on the phone.

Beryl had left her phone on the table. So, there wasn't any way of contacting her. But I had to get home quickly; I booked the next flight to Heathrow, leaving a note saying how sorry I was for leaving, but my family needed me.

I landed at Heathrow some hours later and then caught a cab home. On my way, I phoned Rob and told him I would be there soon. I didn't realise how bad Bernie was; I was so wrapped up in myself.

Three hours on a plane and five hours on the road left me exhausted, but I arrived at Roberts's house.

"What's been happening, Rob?"

"Bernie has been beside herself with grief. Doctors had been prescribing drugs, trying to calm her down, help her relax, and deal with her loss. But nothing is working?

Yesterday they took her to Freedom Fields for a psychiatrist to look at her. They told me they would be keeping her under observation."

"I don't know what to say, Rob. But I'll see her first thing."

"Can I offer you a drink, Tony?"

"Sure, have you got a cognac?"

"Yes, Bernie said it was your favourite drink, so we've had this bottle for a while." Robert poured both of us a cognac.

"It's the first time I've seen you drink cognac?"

"I need it. The last few months have been awful. First, I have hardly seen Bernie, and now, God bless your mum has gone; she seems more distant than ever."

"I'll be in there first thing tomorrow. I'll get some more information from the doctors. Okay, if I kip here tonight?"

"Of course, Tony."

I lay there on the sofa, cramped while trying to sleep; I'd not had a phone call from Beryl, and Heather hadn't been in touch either.

After a restless night, I made my way to the hospital. I needed to see my sister. When I arrived at the hospital, the waiting room was full of people. I went straight to the reception and asked after Bernie. I was told by the snotty-nosed nurse that I couldn't see her.

"You people brought her in against her will yesterday. I suggest you get the doctor dealing with her to get down here now!" I started to become angry, and it showed on my

294

face. The nurse called for the doctor, and he was down within moments. A short, grey-haired man wearing glasses and a white overcoat. "How can I help you, sir?"

"I want to see my sister, Bernie. I've just spent hours on a flight and even more hours in a cab from Heathrow. Now I want to see my sister, Doctor Hew," I said, looking at his name badge.

"It is irregular to let you see her while we observe her. However, I will allow this one time, if you will follow me?" We walked down the corridor and into one of the observation rooms, where I saw Bernie walking back and forth in the room with her head down. Looking outside her window, she looked like she was in a trance. Finally, she walked toward the door, turned, and continuously walked back to the wall.

I looked at the doctor and said, "Let me in."

He unlocked the door, and I walked in. He tried to walk in behind me. "No! You stay outside," and I closed the door. "Bernie! Bernie! it's me, Tony?" There was no response. I raised my voice, "Bernie! Bernie!" I got her attention. She looked pale and withdrawn; this was not my sister. Just the shadow of a sister I knew growing up together. She continued to pace up and down whilst I sat on the bed, trying to communicate with her. "Bernie… Where's Mum?" I knew I was walking on thin ice when I mentioned Mum. She looked up, and stared at me, then burst into tears. I got up off the bed to cuddle her. She collapsed in my arms into a state of unconsciousness. I picked her up and laid her down on the bed.

The doctor came in and said, "That's her first reaction since we brought her in."

"I'm going to take her home with me; I'll be able to look after her better at home. If you've any pills she needs to take, please get them packaged up?"

"You cannot just take her home. She needs help and support?"

"Yeah, you're right, doc, but home will be the best place for that; she has all the family around her. So, is there anything else?"

"That's not how our protocol works, sir. She needs specialist help."

"Screw your protocol. I'm taking Bernie home, end of story." I started to pack her bits into the bag while the doctor disappeared to get her meds. I rang Heather and told her I was bringing Bernie home until she was well again; Heather's response was to ensure the hospital had given me all the medication and appointments. I then rang Robert and told him that the circumstances of Bernie being able to come out of the hospital were to ensure she would be cared for by the family and me; and that she became my responsibility while she was out of the hospital.

"I am not happy with that; she is my wife."

"That was the condition, I told Bernie and she has accepted it. So that's the way it must be." I waited until she woke up and helped her dress so we could go home. So, with pills and an appointment to see the specialist in two weeks in hand, off home we went.

Heather opened the door to us and quickly took Bernie into the guest room, where she would stay until she recovered. Once Heather had settled Bernie in, she came down to me. I was holding Zilah; Tara was asleep.

"Where have you been for the last few nights?" Heather asked.

"Paris!" I said brazenly. "I took the opportunity as you told me to leave. I didn't want to stay with family; I had the tickets changed to coincide with being out of the family home, so off to Paris I went. It was beautiful; I wish you had been there. When I got a call from Rob, I came straight back." Of course, I was lying, but what else was I supposed to say? "If you want, I'll sleep in one of the other rooms. But I'm not leaving Bernie!"

"You are incredible! Family means the world to you, yet you waved a gun in our home with our children here?"

"I said I was sorry many times. I love you and the kids; you know that."

"Of course, I know that," she said with a wry smile.

"Then can I ask for a kiss and a cuddle?" Heather walked over to me and gave me an enthusiastic kiss. Which still tasted warm and sweet, like burst cherries.

We sat down and discussed the next steps for Bernie and what kind of support we could give her. But of course, Robert would also have a big part to play.

We sat through the night with interruptions from the kids and meds for Bernie working every detail out. We'd give Mum's house to Bernie and Robert, bringing Robert close to us, and it was a much bigger place. When we told

Robert, he was astonished. But I knew it was the right thing to do. Edward and Alan would stay there whenever they wanted to, until they had their own accommodation.

The next six months were emotional for everybody; we were all pushed to the limit rallying around and trying to support each other. Bernie had made massive progress following medication and psychiatric therapy between hospitals.

When she returned from Paris, Beryl contacted me, but I told her it was over. Heather and the kids were my utmost priority. She didn't take it very well, but she left me alone. The car business was a real hit. We now had fifty-four cars at our disposal. The extortion of lorry drivers had ended, and the council had invested in machines for parking charges. After that, we concentrated on contraband, alcohol, cigarettes, drugs, and the car business.

Zilah had started nursery school. And she was a right chatterbox. Tara was tumbling around all over the place; you always needed four pairs of eyes. I'm sure one day she will make a great escape artist.

It was time for Bernie to move into Mum's house. We always knew this would be a tricky situation. But she was much better, and it was only around the corner. Robert was eager to have her home where she belonged, but he knew he would have to tread carefully after the last few months; she was still fragile in her mind.

Heather and I agreed to take a holiday to Paris now that Tara was on the bottle, and we had the house back to ourselves. So, I stepped back from the businesses to concentrate more on the kids and Heather. However, I always knew I had to keep one eye over my shoulder, for if Beryl had ever come face to face with Heather, she would ruin my life.

It was Thursday, October 14th, 1977. I remember leaving the house to go to Compton. It was all so dark and eerie. I could hear the rattling of cans rolling along the floor in the fresh breeze and the trees and their branches haunching over as their leafy coats dropped. The lamppost light was flickering against the dark sky. I did not see a soul. It felt like I was the only person out that afternoon. I kept my head down and my shoulders up, trying to cover my ears in the collar of my long trench coat. The winds picked up and started whistling through the trees, so I hurried towards Compton, hoping a taxi would come by and take me out of this blasted chilly wind. The sky became threatening, and I could hear a rumbling off in the distance. Moments later, a lightning strike hit a tree within a few paces of where I was, and then the clap of thunder roared across the sky as if the thunder gods themselves were displeased, I took shelter in a doorway, waiting for the thunder and lightning to pass, but it hung above me for ages. I decided I had to move on to Compton.

My phone went off. I pulled it from my pocket only to see Heather calling me. And then my phone went off completely. I shook it vigorously, but the blasted thing stayed off. *Why is Heather ringing me?* I thought, talking to myself. But I was closer to Compton than home, so I'd ring her from there. Then, five minutes into my walk, I saw a car's headlights approaching me. I tried not to take any notice of it. That was until it pulled up alongside me. The window went down, and I heard a voice. "Tony?"

I looked, and it was Michael. "You're a sight for sore eyes; I've been waiting for a cab, but you can never get one when you need one."

"Boss, I had a call from Heather; she couldn't reach you. So, you need to go home."

"What is it, Michael?" I asked with a concerned tone.

"I think it's something to do with your father?"

"What do you mean, my father?"

"I do not know, boss. Heather said, 'Can you tell Tony to come home? It's about his father?'"

Michael drove me home while I pondered over what it could be. Not that I cared anyway.

I went to the front room, where my first visual sight was of Heather. "What is it, sweetheart?" Then I turned, only to see my bastard father. I nearly went for him in that split moment, but I saw Zilah on the other side of the sofa.

"Tony... Please listen to him?" pleaded Heather.

"He has nothing to say that I want to hear! Now get out of my house!" I screamed. Zilah started crying; I must have frightened her, so I hastily moved to pick her up.

"Darling... Look at me? Will you please listen to what he has to say!"

"What? Be quick about it!"

"I've got lung cancer."

"Is it terminal?"

"I have sclerosis of the liver as well. Unfortunately, there is no cure for either. I know you hate me, no more than I hate myself. I have extraordinarily little time left on this world. A couple of months at most."

I didn't know what to say. I have sworn to kill my father all these years, and he will die! I felt the fluttering of palpitations in my chest as I looked at the fear etched on his face. The memories of Mum and this infesting disease were running through my head. The torment one goes through, which only families know who've experienced this killer disease. I sat on the sofa with Zilah clenched between my arms as a tear fell down my cheek.

"I loved your mother, whatever you may think. But I should have been a better husband and father, and I know God and the angels will have their vengeance on me."

I offered him a drink only because I needed one. "I can't forgive you because of everything you have done to the family. But I'm sorry for your illness." I swallowed the drink in one go and looked to the floor. Zilah was giggling, playing with her teddy on the coffee table. I looked at how innocent and happy she looked. Thoughts of what I've done chilled me to the bone.

My father beat us and sometimes starved us through gambling and alcohol. I have done much worse. I have killed, maimed, extorted money, and dealt in drugs, which nearly killed Heather. A racketeer who bribed the police to turn their heads and even planted Colin into the police force to cover up any traces that could lead them back to me. A cheat, an adulterer, and a liar…. Who was the real bastard?

People saw me for who I was and what I did, but they didn't know the half of it. So, who am I to judge someone for committing far less than I have?

I got up and left the room to go upstairs for a shower and think things through. Trying to be guided by Mum and what she would've done in the circumstances. She loved him, no matter what!"

Heather came up and hugged me as I got out of the shower. She then stared at me as if she wanted me to sympathize with him. Instead, I said, "We've been through everything, sweetheart. Can you tell me if he stayed, we wouldn't go bonkers?"

"Maybe? We will not know unless we do it."

I went downstairs to see him. I caught him offering his hand to Zilah. "You've not been in her life, and she's nearly four?"

He pulled his hand away and said, "I'm sorry, little one."

I was compelled to say that it was his fault. "You can stay here until you die?" I then watched tears roll down his face; the man looked shattered and old. He regretted everything he'd done and knew he must pay his dues to God. I took him upstairs to one of the guest rooms, where he lay on the bed staring into the light the chandelier was emitting. I went back downstairs for another drink.

"Is he all right?" asked Heather.

"I suppose, when you know you've got three months to live, it's got to be the biggest of all shocks. If it were me, I'd curl up in a ball and wish I'd done things differently." But instead, I took Tara into my arms and said, "I pray you and your sister have a wonderful life, not like ours?"

Heather said, "I am sure you will make sure of that?"

"We may never be there for them all their lives; I just hope and pray we guide them down the right path."

"What has got into you, darling? You perceive we have had a rotten life?"

"I want the kids to have everything I never had. You never know what is around the corner until you turn it!"

"Right, come on, tea is just about done; if you can get Tara into the highchair and feed her, that would be brilliant," said Heather.

The next day I took my father back to his house to pick up some essentials. Nugget, the dog, was with Jock, one of his cronies. He asked me to sit down so he could talk to me.

"Why? I want to get out of here. There are too many bad memories here."

"Please? I need to talk to you?"

I sat down and asked, "What is it?"

He tried speaking, but his mouth had gone dry, and he needed a drink; I fetched a glass of water and watched as he gulped it down. "What is it?" I asked again.

"I want you to kill me?"

"What?" I said, stunned at his statement.

"I want you to kill me, son?"

I stood up and called him a twat. "You're off your fucking head?"

"Son, I don't want to go through this evil disease's pain and memory loss."

"You may never experience any of that, Dad?"

"I cannot live day by day, wondering if it would happen before I wake up. I would sooner get it finished."

"You can't ask people to kill you; it's unethical?" I started to shout at him. "How dare you ask me to kill you? You're a fucking coward!"

"Because you are the only one who can do it, son? I know what I am asking of you. But I fear not knowing when my time is up."

"No! No! I can't. I'm sorry, you ask too much. Come on, I want to go back to my house."

When we got back home, I told Heather what he had said. She was in disbelief. "How could he ask me to do something like that?"

"He is petrified, darling. He must be to ask you to kill him."

"I don't want to talk about it anymore." I grabbed a drink to calm myself down. And then rang Rob to see how Bernie was,

"She's okay, Tony, small steps, but she's getting better all the time."

"That's good news," I replied.

The next few weeks were tormenting, Dad wanted out of this world, and all I could think about was what Mum would do. We postponed the holiday because of his illness. And although everybody was suffering in their way, I was going through hell, and only Heather and I knew it. I returned to the church of St Peter, which I hadn't visited since the angels took Mum. Forever unforgiving as I was, I now needed help. I prayed and asked Mum for help to show me what to do while asking for God's forgiveness for not believing in him after he took Sarah and Mum to his house in the sky. I left the church none the wiser.

The next few weeks saw Dad succumb to this evil infestation of a disease that killed Mum. The house changed daily as the laughs and jokes disappeared, leaving a melancholy ambience.

My head and heart battled against each other over what I should do. The pain was much to bear. But I had decided. It was December 13th, 1977, when my dad went wherever we all went after our time in this world. I had to live with the consequences for the rest of my life for making my own choice. Right or wrong, it was my decision.

For the next few days, I struggled to deal with my emotions and whether my decision was correct. Finally, I turned to drinking and drugs in a big way, and Heather again threw me out of the house. She told me to stay away until I sorted myself out. I bedded down where I could, often at Beryl's, who wanted me so badly she'd forgive anything I'd do. She understood me. I started using heroin because I didn't want any pain anymore.

It was Friday, December 22nd, when I got a call from Michael telling me some Londoners had been down asking about me. I told Michael not to worry and put the phone down. Beryl made lots of black coffee and told me I should get to work, hoping it would relieve some pain. I got up and had a shower and a shave, and then Beryl helped me get dressed into my suit. I then had another phone call, only this time it was from the prison; one of the inmates rang to say Adalai was dead! He had been murdered in his cell. I was concerned as he was the top dog in there. My thoughts quickly turned back to the Londoners looking for me; it must have been a powerful outfit to kill Adalai in his cell. Then, my thoughts turned to, *a coincidence.*

Beryl asked, "What's wrong?"

I said, "A dear friend of mine had been killed in prison."

"I am so sorry to hear that."

I wondered if it was a kingpin of one of the London gangs. So, I picked up the phone to Michael and told him to get everybody that works for us to meet at the warehouse in Compton for a meeting.

"Is everything okay, boss?"

"I don't know, Michael. I want everybody armed with guns, not blades. Have it sorted for Monday, please?"

I walked out the door and told Beryl I would see her next week. I walked beside the canal. It was bitterly cold; even the floor was getting frosty, but I needed to clear my head. I felt awful. I tugged on a cigarette whilst sitting on a bench watching a robin pecking away at the grass looking for worms when I heard my name,

"Tony." It was Colin; he offered me a lift home. I said, "I was fine."

"Heather is distraught; she's going out of her head; you need to pop in and see her?"

"She threw me out, Colin. I will see her next week. I need you at the warehouse on Monday evening for a meeting."

"What's wrong?"

"I'll tell you on Monday, get yourself a gun; I want everybody armed from now on." Colin gave me a concerned look and drove off.

I went to Blue Jays to drink as much coffee as possible. I then spent the next few nights in the hotel where I took Precious, injecting myself with Heroin as my life seemed to be spiralling out of control. After that, I needed to think on my own. Get my head straight. Beryl was right, as usual; I needed work. I left my gun at Beryl's and returned to hers on Sunday to pick it up. I poured myself a drink, but Beryl yelled at me, so I angrily threw the glass at the wall and left her place.

Monday arrived, and I went to the warehouse to meet everyone who worked for me; I heard my brother shouting, "Wait for me, Tony."

"Hiya, little bro."

"What's the meeting all about?"

"I'll tell you when we get there. Would you look at that, little bro?" I said, "What a gorgeous lady, lovely blonde-haired and a very pretty face too, pushing that black and white pram." As she walked past me, she gave a beaming smile, I looked over my shoulder at the pram to see the baby, but I couldn't see anything, just a crochet blanket. *That's odd,* I thought. Finally, we entered the warehouse with seventy staff.

"Evening, gentleman and lady, of course," as I looked to Katy. "Michael, can you throw a few bottles of drink around? I want to make a toast. I'm sorry if there are not enough glasses; you can make do if you have a bottle. Firstly, I'd like to thank everybody for their arduous work through the rough and tough decisions I've made. Does everyone have a gun?"

"What's all that about, boss? Why do we need guns?" asked Devon.

"The reason for this is simple, I've had a close contact of mine killed in his prison cell. Now you all may think, well, it's just another geezer. But this geezer ran the prison as if it were his home. Now somebody or an organisation have got to him and killed him. Michael tells me that some Londoners have recently come down asking for me, which concerns me. If you all carry a gun, I will sleep much better. So, we need to be more vigilant whilst working. Now, cheers to everyone." I offer up my glass to toast. "Stay safe, and if anybody asks about me, I need to know quickly." Then I heard a vehicle revving louder and louder outside, and within moments a lorry crashed through the doors and straight into the crates of alcohol. In a panic, we went for our guns; I could hear the gunshots coming from all directions. Then I felt something sharp and hot in my stomach. I looked down to see blood pouring out of my gut, I fell to the floor, and my head hit the ground; I looked to Edward, who was already shot and lying beside me, holding his hand out for me to grab. My vision had clouded, but I could still see Michael and Colin, who both fell.

Then I saw a man's shadow above me, and in a Cockney accent, say, "That was for the Hendrick brothers," and everything went black.

I was in a coma for six weeks, only to wake up and remember the nightmare of that deadly night. I'd been stitched back together, not knowing what they took away from me. Edward was sitting in the chair beside the bed. He told me he had taken a bullet in his lung and was saved after an operation. Well, I was just as lucky. He said I was shot in the stomach, which pierced my kidney, but I had lost a lot of blood which sent me into a coma. I was weak, sore, and reflecting on that Cockney accent telling me it was on behalf of the Hendricks.

I grabbed Edward by his arm and asked, "What about Colin and Michael? How are they?"

"Colin was killed along with seventeen of the men. Michael is okay, but he's in prison. The London gang got away."

I threw up all over the bed. I felt the knot in my stomach tighten and the nauseous feeling whilst thinking of Colin and Heather, and that I would never see Colin again. "Katy, what about Katy?" Edward shook his head, and said nobody knows, and the tears flowed. Edward said Michael, Jimmy, Brendon, and some other lads were arrested. The others got away. There has been no mention of Katy.

"What about Heather? How is she?"

"Heather has been here daily holding your hand, waiting for you to wake up. The police have been swarming all over the hospital questioning everyone, including me, and now they're waiting to question you. Nobody has said anything; the guys and the business is okay. I've been paying wages to the families of those killed and the guys still working in the shadows."

I had no gun, so the police let me go after a few days. I just told them a London gang came in and fired shots at everyone. Everyone else was given six months in prison for carrying a lethal weapon. Quite a few got away before the police arrived. All the members of the London gang got away.

"I need to get out of here, bro. Help me up."

"There's an officer outside the door. How are we supposed to get past him?"

"I don't know, bro, you must find a way. Now help me with these bloody tubes." I pulled the wires I was attached to out of my body, and Edward helped me get dressed.

"Stay there, Tony; I'll find a way to briefly get the officer off the ward. You have been in a coma for six weeks; he will assume you're still in one."

Edward left the room, and I lay there waiting for something to happen. Minutes later, Edward came into the room and said we must move quickly. He helped me up, and we went out of the hospital, into Edward's car, and then drove off.

"What did you do, bro?"

"I told him two guys were talking about abusing a nurse called Claire in Enders Ward upstairs. So, he raced up to the ward to tell the nurse what he had heard and bob's your uncle, here we are."

"That's awesome thinking. What about the house, will there be any police there?"

"Yes, but we are not going there. Instead, Heather and the kids are waiting in a country house I purchased in the countryside, far from the city. That's where you'll recover."

I stared with a sense of pride at him. So grown up, so switched on, in such a brief time. We arrived at the country house, where I could see Heather through the window; she looked out and watched as I exited the car. She raced out of the house and into my arms, tears rolling down her face.

"I can't believe it," she cried, "you are home."

I moved swiftly into the house to see Zilah and Tara. I felt alive for the first time in a long while; I was out of hospital and with the most precious people in the world my family. "Thank you, bro." I gave Edward a huge embrace.

"Well, I need to get back to Linda. I know the police will call on me after your escape. But don't worry; I'll blag my way out."

"Can you get word to Michael and everyone else? I'll be ready in three months for our revenge. So, help me, God, I will make them pay for everything."

I spent the next three months on painkillers, alcohol, drugs, and cigarettes to the extent of being spaced out half the time. But forever reflecting on that night, I almost died. Heather had become chained to me and the house, unable to leave in fear of being caught. The police had put out a warrant for my arrest, and I was all over the papers. Our only visits were from Edward, who meticulously planned an escape from Roberts's house. Inspector Blakely was adamant I was still in the city. The police were watching several dwellings. But the only other chance they had at catching me was in London, where I intended to fuck the Cockney crime lord and his business to hell.

During the next three months, I spent hours each day working on a plan to cause havoc in the East End of London. A map of London and its tube network were all I needed to plan my getaway. But I still had to find this Cockney bastard who fucked all of us over. Waiting for Michael to get out of prison was my trump card. The intention was to send Michael to London to purchase a large quantity of LSD. I hoped this would lead to the identification of this drug lord I was so intent on taking down. Time moved slowly, and in my eagerness to get the job done, I became more anxious, so I started to take it out on Heather. The continued arguments were more than I could take. Even the kids crying started to get to me. I loved them, but I began to spend more time alone, locked

312

away in my office, secretly injecting Heroin into my body facing my fears and feeling deluded about whether I could carry this off. The Scottish thing was simple; now, I was taking on somebody much bigger.

Michael's release date was nearing, and to tell the truth, I couldn't wait for him to be released. I had a planned route set in my head to get me from Paddington station to home. I just needed to find exactly where the London outfit were dealing from until Michael came out. So, my plan was on hold. There was a knock on my office door,

"Can I come in?" asked Heather.

My eyes drifted across the room towards the door. "Of course, you can," I sighed.

"I've made dinner. Do you want to come down and join us, or do you want me to bring it up here?"

"I'll come down in a moment," I snarled. Heather slammed the door behind her as she went back downstairs. The table was silent. Heather wasn't interested in talking to me; she concentrated on Zilah, who dropped some food on the floor. I stood up and remarked, "She should be eating properly now; all you do is mollycoddle her; she won't learn anything that way." My tone was harsh, and Zilah started crying. "Bloody kids!" I then walked out of the house and lit a cigarette.

I was only there a few minutes when Heather walked out. "What's wrong with you!" she shouted. I ignored her and went back up to my office.

Heather screamed, "I can't see my parents or friends anymore because of everything you have done!"

"You knew what I did for a living," I yelled. Heather picked up a black ebonised elephant ornament and threw it at me. I raced downstairs and punched her in the face. She fled to the dining room in tears. I punched the wall in a wild temper, causing some plaster to fall off. My knuckles were bare skinned as the blood trickled down my fingers. I was shaking like never before. I don't know what came over me; I went into the kitchen to clean my hands of the blood. Heather walked in and said she couldn't do this anymore. "Do what anymore?" I asked.

"Where's the man gone I first knew? He wouldn't have treated me like you are now."

"I was nearly killed, as was my brother, by this gang from London. I want them dead!"

Heather screamed, "My brother was killed doing all your dirty work. He isn't here; I have only you and the kids."

I tried to say sorry and offered to comfort her, by offering my hands out, but she wasn't interested.

"I want my mum!"

"You know that's impossible; the police will pick you up."

"I hate you!" she screamed.

I had nothing else to say, so I went back to my office, where I fell asleep and didn't wake till the morning. I went to the bathroom to shower when I heard a car horn beep outside. I rushed to the window only to see Heather getting into a cab. I raced downstairs, but the taxi had disappeared when I got outside the front door. She left no message as to where she had gone. I hoped it was somewhere else, not at her parents' home. I called Edward to use the lads to find her and to let me know she was safe.

The days passed, and finally, I was told where she was, at an old colleague's house in Poole, Dorset. She promised her 'so-called friend' a fortune once I had overcome my treacherous visit to London. It didn't matter, I knew she was safe, and Michael was due tomorrow if he could escape his house. Naturally, the police staked out the place, hoping he would lead them to me. But of course, Michael was far too clever for the pigs.

The following morning there was a knock on the door. I opened it to Michael, the relief I felt was heavenly. The weight I'd been carrying on my shoulders just lifted. "I'm so glad to see you, my friend," I put my arms around him. "Come inside, mate." I peered around the front of the house, checking to see if anybody had followed him.

"Boss, I haven't been followed."

We went into the lounge, and I poured us both a drink. "There you go, get that down your neck." I passed Michael the glass. "How was inside, mate?"

"You know me, boss, I was lucky I was the biggest guy there, so it was a piece of shit. I did miss Nora, though, and I was relieved when I found out you survived."

"Me too, mate."

"It was a tragedy Colin died," said Michael.

"We'll get our revenge. Everyone will pay, trust me, Michael."

"So, what's the state of play, boss?"

"I need you and a couple of the lads to go to London's East End and buy a few thousand LSD pills. That's the only way we'll find the bastards that killed Colin and the other lads."

"Do we know where this bastard is in the East End?"

"I have no idea, Michael; he could be anywhere."

"I'll take a couple of the lads with me; I'll track the fuckers down."

I handed Michael ten thousand pounds from my safe. "It must be a huge buy to draw them out of their pit. Edward's been recruiting outside the city, the more bodies, the better."

"I agree, boss." Duke walked in from the kitchen. "Bloody hell, he's grown, boss."

"I remember picking him up as that scrawny little rat; now look at him. He's a beast."

Michael petted Duke, who lapped it up. "Right, boss, if that is all, I will get to London tomorrow and ask around."

"Just be careful, Michael." No sooner did Michael leave than there was another knock on the door. "Who the fuck is it now?" Speaking to myself. Opening the door, I couldn't believe my eyes. Beryl was standing in a yellow chiffon blouse and a black pencil skirt, looking stunning as usual. I pulled her inside and slammed the door shut. "How did you find me? Have you any idea how many people are looking for me? How in God's name did you find me?" Pointing my finger in her face.

"Well, that's a nice welcome."

"Heather could have been here. How dare you come to my home?"

"Nobody knows where you are apart from all your gang and me, of course."

Duke, barked, so I told him to lie down. "I can't believe this is happening to me! How? How did you find me?"

"Michael! All I had to do was wait for his release from prison and wait for him to move. I knew he would come to you; you were nearly killed. My line of business allows me to talk to anybody."

"You're stalking me, that's a dangerous game."

"I couldn't do anything, you were nearly killed, in a coma for weeks, and then you disappeared. I was hurting; I cried for weeks thinking you would die."

"Well, as you can see. I didn't. Now get out of my house." Beryl ignored me and sat on the couch, putting her yellow handbag on the coffee table.

"I know you're angry; these last few months must have been hell. I understand that, but I've gone through hell too. I have spent more time in my car than in my bed waiting to see if I would ever see you again."

"I told you it was over after Paris, I'm with Heather."

"Where is she?"

"Just out," I replied.

"Are you not going to offer me a drink? Surely that's not too much to ask?"

I poured us a drink and sat beside Beryl on the couch. My anger dissipated. And I asked how she had been. When I think about it, it must have sounded stupid.

"Worried! And longed for you. I love you. I cannot help it; I've tried hard to get you out of my head."

I leaned over and kissed her; she tasted sweet and smelt fantastic. She put her glass on the coffee table and then took mine away. She put it down on the table, and excitement ravaged my body. She clenched me tightly, and we kissed vigorously whilst taking each other's clothes off. We lay on the couch for what seemed to be an eternity making love, caressing every pore on our bodies until we were both brought to the ultimate ecstasy two people could endure.

I lay there naked and afraid of what was happening to me. My Heather left the house after I punched her because of my anxieties. I laid my hand on my beloved. I'd become no better than my father in all this darkness surrounding me. I have finally become that demon I tried to run from all my life. Finally, I sat up and took a cigarette from the packet.

"Are you okay?" asked Beryl as she sat up and put her arm around my shoulder.

I looked stony-faced and shook my head. Then, I got up and went to the bathroom to freshen up. I then went downstairs to find Beryl slipping on her skirt. "You must leave, I don't know when Heather will return."

"Don't worry, I'll leave, but I refuse to stay away."

"I don't need you to be difficult, Beryl, I need some space."

"I have given you all the space you have ever needed. Now I want more time with you! I'm sick of playing second fiddle to Heather."

"Heather is the mother of my kids, and I love her very much."

Beryl sniggered and shook her head. "You don't love her when you're fucking me. I'm fed up with being your mistress, I should get things out in the open, so Heather and I have an understanding?"

I couldn't help myself. I raised my hand and gripped it tight around Beryl's throat. "Don't you ever talk to Heather, that's a threat and not a warning!" I squeezed and squeezed her throat until she went limp. I pulled my hand away, and she dropped to the floor. I stood back for a moment, then knelt and shouted, "Beryl! Beryl!" But there was no response. What have I done? I'd killed her in my anger. I sat down and contemplated what I must do next. If somebody finds her here, I will spend the rest of my life behind bars, in Her Majesty's prison. *What was I to do?* I asked myself.

I put a bag over her face while figuring out how to get her out of the house. Finally, I called on Ambrose to get over here with a car. I looked down at the prostrate body with tears rolling down my face. My love for Beryl was genuine, even though Heather is the person I love and always will be. Ambrose arrived, and when he got into the house, he looked stunned.

"Boss? Who is she? What happened?"

"I killed her, it was an accident," I spoke.

"But boss, it looks like she has been strangled?"

"I need you to take her to an address. It's where she lives. Make it look like a break in. Leave no trace behind." Ambrose wrapped her in my orange rug and left the house. I was overcome with emotion.

Michael continued to draw blanks from the East End of London. Edward continued recruiting outside the city while keeping one eye on the business, thirty-seven additional lads he had recruited up till now. I had been waiting to hear from Heather for two weeks. I started to feel lonely and isolated from the world outside. All I did was drink, smoke and clean my pistol. I played with the bullets in my hands, forever loading and unloading the gun's cartridge. Wondering whether I should kill myself. Duke was my only solace. We'd fight on the bed whilst he gently tried to chew on my arm. The days passed, and then unexpectedly, I got a phone call from Michael.

"Boss, we have found him; he's called Freddy Hunt. He runs this part of London; his gaff is a club called The Roller Bar. I've set up a meeting for tonight to check him out."

"At last, well done, Michael. Purchase everything you can and tell him you work north of Bristol."

"Boss, why Bristol?"

"He'll not want anybody else on his turf. He's already torn into the southwest. Bristol is another part of the country. So, he won't feel threatened."

"Okay, boss."

"Michael, be careful."

"You know me, boss."

I put the phone down and started my long and agitating wait for Michael to call me back.

Meanwhile, the head of police pulled Inspector Blakely from his stakeouts on my mother's house and Michael's. So, there must have been something big happening. But it allowed me to see the family, which was better than being stuck in this house. So, I got dressed and took a train to my city. Wearing a disguise, I knocked on my mother's house door. Robert opened the door. Seeing me standing there left him stunned. "Come in, Tony."

"Thank you, Rob." I walked through the dimly lit corridor and into the front room, where Bernie was sipping coffee. "Hi, sis." She, too, looked stunned at my appearance.

"Where have you been?" she asked.

"Have you got any cognac in the house. I so desperately need a drink?"

"Of course, it's always here for your visits, Tony."

"Well, pour me a drink, and I'll tell you where I have been for the last few weeks."

My sister gave me a big cuddle, and we chatted about what, where and everything else. "Can you put me up for the night? I caught the train and have other places to go while here."

"Obviously, oh, I am so glad to see you. How are Heather and the kids? I miss seeing them."

"Heather walked out on me and has gone to stay with an old work colleague. I'm leaving her be for now, as I've some serious stuff going on."

"You two are going to be all right, aren't you?"

"Yes, sis. We'll be fine. Okay, if I get a glass of water?"

"Of course, Tony."

I went out to get my glass of water, and whilst I was filling the glass out of the corner of my eye, I saw a shadow move. Then I had a shudder go down my spine. "Sis, I know this might sound ridiculous, but have you had or heard anything strange happen in this house? I know I've asked before."

"Funny you should say that, Tony. There have been a few occasions I thought I saw a small shadow, but it is an old house."

"Well, there was that time just after your mum died. I felt a cool breeze, but none of the doors was open," said Robert.

"What? You think we have a ghost?" asked Bernie.

"A lot of strange things have happened since I bought this house. I found Zilah's doll in a corridor behind a wall. Michael and I investigated the area; it was very creepy, so Michael couldn't wait to get out of the house. When we bought the house, there was no mention of a child living here, just a couple who wanted a quick sale after they left to go to America."

"Do you think a little girl was murdered here?"

"I don't know; however, it seems very strange. Lots of things have happened in the house. A teaspoon fell on the floor from the middle of the table, eerie gentle breezes and shadows moving from time to time."

Bernie looked across at Robert with her eyes wide open. "Ooh, we have a ghost," she spoke.

We chatted a little longer and shared some fond memories of Mum. It was late in the evening when I got a call from Michael.

"Boss, we found him. A few of his men took us into The Roller Bar Club. He was seated at a table with other people around him. They searched us for guns before we could get near him. He wore an olive-green wool suit, a cerise tie, and a white shirt; he was very Gaunt looking, with a grey beard and a scar on his jaw. He handed over the case of LSD after he counted the money. He then asked where I was selling them. I told him up near the Midlands, far from his patch. He then said, 'Have I seen you before?' I told him, 'I wouldn't have thought so.'

"'Well, it was nice dealing with you; please come again,' he said in his Cockney accent; two guys followed us out the door. There's a lot of them, boss; they were carrying Tommy guns too."

"Grand job, Michael; let me know when you get back."

"Will do, boss."

I went to bed to get some shuteye, only to be awakened halfway through the night by a cold breeze. I

323

was startled by the figure of a child with blonde hair and ashen-faced staring at me. I jumped out of my skin; my heart was pounding. I leapt off the bed to turn the light on, but she had disappeared. Something was wrong; I went downstairs and poured myself a quick drink. Before I knew it, the morning was here, and Michael confirmed he'd arrived home. I told him to meet me at my mother's house and ensure he wasn't being followed.

Michael arrived at the house carrying a case full of LSD and told me everything.

I called Edward to come back with anyone who could speak Cockney or even with a London accent. While he was making his way over to the house, Michael and I started formulating a plan. Bernie poured us drinks and begged me to be careful.

My first job was getting better guns; we'd hit as hard as possible when we do hit. I wanted this piece of punk shit at my feet, begging for his life.

The Roller Bar Club would have to be our target; we didn't know London. He's got a small army around him; they're all mindful of other drug gangs. If we got this right, we would survive. It had to be the perfect plan. We threw some ideas around, but something else would fit the bill. Edward arrived at the house with a guy who had lived in London for seven years. He wasn't from the East End, but he knew how to get where we needed to and how quickly we could disappear again. His name was Elliot, and he was initially from Blackpool up north. But he knew his way around London more than we did.

"Bro, thank you for all your hard work getting these guys together."

"I want this bastard as much as you do; the cost doesn't matter."

"I think we're all in agreement to that, bro." Michael nodded in approval too.

Michael, Edward, and Elliot returned with me to my home, where we could plan without worrying about the police barging through our doors.

The next few days were tiring and almost exhaustive of planning, but we were getting there. Cognac, ale, and a few hits of cannabis and a Heroin shot for me would undoubtedly see us through.

"Bro, won't Linda be wondering where you are?"

"Yeah," said Michael, "you don't want the wrath of your lovely lady on your back. Nora knows if I'm out or away, I'm working," he jested.

"I'll give her a ring." Replied Edward.

"Yeah, you do that, bro, let her know who the boss is?" I joked. "Do you have family, Elliot?"

"No, if I did, I wouldn't be here; I'd be home with them."

I looked at Michael; I didn't know if Elliot said it with cynicism or if he was bleating out wishing he had a family.

Edward got off the phone to Linda after telling her he wouldn't be home for a few days.

"Sort it, bro?" I asked. He looked sheepish as he replied with a nod.

"I need another drink," he said.

Michael and I looked at each other, smiling. "He might need a few more," I jested.

The plan started to come together. We would set up scouts to be sure he was in *The Roller Bar* when we hit. Elliot and Michael planned the timings of traffic flow at around eleven p.m. to secure three vehicles that could get away from the area quickly. I would send Michael to get better guns from a fence I knew. Edward would assemble the best crew, which we would pay well to see this job through. I had to concentrate on one thing and one thing only: to be the first through the door and ensure my aim was accurate and deadly.

"The plan looks good, boss. When?" asked Michael.

"Sunday!" I replied. "That gives us three days to get organised, we all agreed?"

The nod of approval came from all. "Let's have a drink." I poured us all a cognac and offered our glasses to toast the plan.

The following morning a bit worse from last night's libation, Michael, Edward, Elliot, and I left the house to sort things out from the plan.

I sat on my own, cigarette in one hand and another drink in the other. I tried not to be negative, but if the worse came to the worse, I had to put my business for the well-being of my family. So, I took pen to paper and started to write my last words to my forever love, Heather, and my kids. I was competent and clever, but this letter was more than I could bear.

My Darling Heather,

I can't write or say what I mean. But if you are reading this, I am already gone to be with Sarah and Mum in God's hallowed Kingdom. But I wanted you forever when I set eyes on you. Your beauty is your heart, which is always full of joy and wonder: a beautiful friend and the most incredible mother. But most of all, you were my wife, friend, soulmate, and world. You could make me smile even on the darkest of nights.

Hand in hand, we would walk beside the canal with feelings of wonder and forever happiness. I would not have had that with anyone else. I grew alongside you; without you, I would still have been this child who couldn't grow up and become who I am today. Even through those dark times after the loss of Sarah and then Mum and Dad, you held me together when everyone else wanted more from me. You gave me strength in everything I did, and I will love you forever, in this life and the next.

Thank you xxxxx

PS

Don't ever let the kids forget me. I've made provisions for you and the kids, so you will always know how you live today.

I dropped the pen onto the table with a tear in my eye, hoping and praying Heather would never read it. But I was walking into a lion's den with a gun I hoped would protect me. I knew this was the riskiest thing I had ever done. You might call it insanity? I just wanted revenge.

Sunday drew near, and everything was going according to the plan. Michael had the necessary guns, and I handpicked the guys I wanted on the job. In less than twenty-four hours, we would know our fate.

Sunday morning came; fate or not, Heather rang to see if I would answer. I picked up the phone and heard her soft, gentle voice ask if it was me. "Yes, darling, it's me."

"I'm sorry." She spoke.

"I'm the one who's sorry; I will never forgive myself for hitting you. I've been crucified ever since. I love you, always will, and you'll be forever in my heart." I replied.

"What do you mean? Will I be forever in your heart? What's wrong? You're scaring me."

"I have a job today, and I don't know whether I can come home again."

"No! No! You do not pull that bullshit on me. I'm on my way home."

"I won't be here; stay with your friend for a couple more days; I will ring you when I get back." The phone went dead. I poured another drink and pulled myself together. The next few hours seemed like an eternity, and then the cars rolled up outside.

I put my suit jacket on and walked out of the house. I locked up and looked at the old place just before entering the car. I couldn't have ever dreamed I would own such a beautiful place as this, one of many houses I owned. Then, a wry smile at the gaff, and I got into the car.

"Let's do this, Michael."

The five-hour journey to London's East End was laborious. Everybody in this convoy of vehicles knew precisely what lay ahead. Finally, we pulled into a layby on the outskirts of Hackney.

I exited the car and walked to Edward's vehicle. "Are we all locked and loaded?" I asked.

A general nod of approval, and nobody uttered a word. A deadly silence filled the air. Elliot was in the third car; he showed his gun through the windscreen. I returned to the car when Michael said, "There's no turning back now."

"Let's get on with it," I said nervously. We continued until we reached our destination. The street was alive with music and chatter; people were smiling and dancing; we drove past the *Roller Bar Club*. Two big guys at the entrance were filtering the right people through the doors. There was a young girl and boy they couldn't have been any older than sixteen sat side by side, arms uncovered, bearing the marks of needle scars. We separated into nearby alleys; it was so dark. I didn't contemplate so many people being on the streets. I should've known better; this was London. Elliot had to get past the door attendants, and the only way he would do that was to pay them a wad of cash. I walked up the dark alley to give Elliot the money to buy himself into the club to confirm if the bastard we came up for was inside or not. I watched from a distance to see if it worked, and Elliot was in the *Roller Bar*. All we needed now was confirmation that the scumbag was in there. A few moments later, Elliot exited the bar and moved in our direction, giving us the thumbs up. We now knew he was in there, we raced down the street. An army of gunmen coming from all directions, guns aloft. People screaming and running for their lives. Elliot punched one of the door attendants and started fighting with the other. Bodies were being knocked over by the rush of a dozen men racing towards the club with guns. I kicked the door in the heated moments. A table at the far end of the club was packed with bodies, no doubt sucking up to this gangster who did his absolute best to kill me. All I could hear was the gunfire sounding off like fireworks, deafening in the confinements of a club, and the bodies dropping to the floor. The intensity I felt, and my focus was solely on the bastard who hid beneath the table, fearing for his life. Finally, the table was clear, the commotion settled, and I was hovering above this scum. Michael and Elliot grabbed him from beneath the table and sat him on a gold and red velvet chair.

"Please, please don't hurt me." He squirmed.

"Boss, get it over with; we have to go," said Michael.

I put my hand up as a gesture to wait. "You killed me inside," I spoke.

"Please, please, take everything I have," he said, continually begging for his life.

I put my gun to his head and pulled the trigger. I then watched as the pool of blood engulfed the chair.

"Boss, come on, the cars are waiting," said Michael. We moved towards the doors in haste. Sirens were coming from everywhere. Whilst exiting the club, my thoughts turned to my revenge being complete. I sighed with a tremendous amount of satisfaction. I went to get into the car when I heard a gunshot, and then I felt a sharp pain in my side; I felt myself falling to the ground in a fleeting moment. I lay on my back as I reached for the pain in my side; blood covered my hand. I looked up at the night sky. I could faintly hear Edward's voice bellowing out my name. I then saw a vision of a little girl with blond hair holding a doll in one hand and reaching out with the other for me to take. "Sarah, is that you?" I felt an irrefutable want to grab her hand. After that, everything went black, and I could hear no voice anymore.